BLINDING ECHO

TINA SAXON

Blinding Echo

ISBN Digital: 978-0-9987762-6-2
ISBN Print: 978-0-9987762-7-9

Cover design by: Hang Le
Photographer: Golden Czermak @ Furious Fotog
Model: Chase Ketron
Edited by: Ellie McLove @ My Brother's Editor
Proofreading by: Petra @ My Brother's Editor

PROLOGUE

LOVE STORIES TYPICALLY BEGIN WITH BOY MEETS GIRL. *OURS DID.* YET, our story is anything but typical.

I had always thought the heart led us to 'the one.' But, I've learned the heart doesn't have a memory. Its beat is steady until our brain triggers an emotion, making the beat so unmistakable it takes your breath away. It's blinding, life-altering and sometimes earth-shattering. The feeling of true love. We grow up with the grand illusion there is only one person made for us—our soul-mate. But what if your memories are stripped from you? Your soul-mate forgotten. The unmistakable heartbeat gone. The love that completely filled your heart, now an empty space.

That was my heart. Vacant.

He was a stranger, determined to make me fall in love with him. He made it easy. Even though I didn't know him, he felt familiar. The scars that riddled my body, illustrating my past, he made them feel invisible. Made me feel like I deserved to be cherished and loved.

He was also lying.

Doctors told me my memories were locked in my brain. Eigh-

teen years of my life was under lock and key inside my head somewhere. It was Pandora's box.

I wish I had never found the key.

Our love story began with boy meets girl. Now...

I love two men.

He loves two women.

CHAPTER ONE

KASE

THE SECOND SHE OPENED HER EYES I COULDN'T LOOK AWAY. GRAY FOG rolled in, blanketing the blue in her eyes, the storm was about to release and wreak havoc. Her fist cocked back and landed right smack on his cheek. I heard a crunching sound; I wasn't sure if it was his cheek or her tiny fist. Cheers erupted around us. "That's for snapping my bra," she screeched at the boy doubled over, crying. In that second, I knew I needed her in my life. We were ten, and I was already sure I would marry that sassy girl.

"HAVE I told you how much I'm going to miss you?" I trace the lines in Everly's palm with my finger.

"In the last hour? At least, fifty times," she giggles, squeezing her hand shut on my finger.

"Overkill?"

"Absolutely not. You can tell me every second of the day, and it still wouldn't be enough," she pouts. She sits up and straddles me in the bed of my truck. "It won't be forever though."

I try to hide the satisfaction of her sitting on top of me. She can't fault me for having a hard-on. I'm eighteen. It takes one kiss and I'm hard. But when she's sitting on me, holy shit, all bets are off.

"It'll feel like it." I swallow, trying to ignore the heat coming from her core. "Eight weeks is a long time."

"Don't remind me." She wrinkles her nose at me and jabs her finger into my chest. "Have you told your dad?"

Why would I do that?

"Screw him," I growl as I focus on the cloudless blue sky before finding her gaze again. "He won't even notice I'm gone."

She doesn't push the subject. It won't make a difference. My mom died five years ago. The cancer was God's way of setting her free from the devil himself. My dad. I begged her to leave him. She wouldn't, no matter how hard he hit her. I wasn't old enough or big enough to stop it. When she died, things got worse. He turned his rage on me. I took it for a couple of years. The hits, the bruises, the pain. Those exact things lit the fire inside me, making me stronger so that one day he would never touch me again. I didn't run. I fought back.

It makes me smile, thinking about the day my dad tried to hit me two years ago. He ended up in the hospital with two broken ribs and a broken arm. Nothing compared to what he'd done to my mom or me over the years. The cop looked the other way when my dad tried to bring charges against me. Everyone in town knows what type of man my dad is. A coward. God should have taken him instead.

"I'll notice that you're gone." She bends down again and kisses me softly on the lips. Her pouty lips are one of my favorite things about her. Their plump softness makes me go crazy every time they touch my skin. Wrapping my arms around her narrow waist, I pull her closer.

"I love you, Everly," I whisper before our lips fuse.

The shade of the tree offers little to no relief from the heat coming off her body. Or maybe that's just my body. Either way, it's freaking hot. Tires spinning on the dirt road drown out the buzz of the surrounding locusts. We both sit up and stare at the black Ford pickup coming at us.

"Great," Everly says, sarcastically. "Why can't Wayne understand you'd rather spend time with me right now?" I smirk. *He knows.* He's just being an ass like normal, feeling left out.

His truck slides to a stop next to mine and he sticks his head out the window. "You better make it to the water tower tonight," he says.

I open my mouth to respond, but Everly beats me to it. "*Really,* Wayne? Do you have a phone?"

"I sure do." He smiles and holds up his phone, taunting her. She rolls her eyes.

"Well, why don't you use it? You didn't have to come out here to interrupt us." Her huff is adorable. These two have fought like brother and sister since we were ten. He's my best friend, she's my girlfriend and I'm stuck in the middle.

"Dude, we'll be there," I say to diffuse the situation. The faster he leaves, the faster those lips will be back on me. He's throwing me a going away party tonight. I leave for boot camp on Monday. Eight weeks without either of them will be hard. But I'm ready for the challenge. I'm ready to leave this town.

He points at me. "You better be. I'll come hunt you down." We've been best friends since we were babies. Our moms were best friends until my dad's hot temper turned physical. Wayne's mom tried to talk her into leaving too, but instead of taking her advice, my mom shut her out of her life. She forced her way back in the day mom told everyone she had cancer. She's been like a second mom since my mom died.

He drives forward, does a quick U-turn, creating a cloud of dust and drives past us going back the same way he came. He yells, "Bye, Buttercup."

"Jerk!" Everly yells back. I laugh at how red her face gets every time Wayne calls her that. It's the nickname he made for her when we were twelve because she ate so many Reese's Peanut Butter

Cups she got sick. Now, she won't even eat peanut butter without gagging. She turns her red face toward me and lifts her brow. "Are you laughing right now?" She acts mad, but she's not. I can tell when she's mad; she clears her throat and her eyes turn gray. Right now, she's biting her bottom lip so she doesn't smile.

A squeal comes out of her mouth as I grab her and flip her on her back. The blanket underneath us gives a little cushion to the ridges of the truck bed. "I am. What're you going to do about it?" I stare into her eyes. Today, they're green. Her eyes are like a mystery door, you never know what color you will get from one day to the next. She tries to tell me it's what she's wearing, but my theory is it's more like a mood ring. Green is horny. It's what I'm telling myself right now as I squeeze her ass. And after years of staring into them, I'm usually right.

Her hands run up my back and through my hair. "I would tell you, but I don't want to think about Wayne right now."

"Me neither."

My hand crawls up her thigh, underneath the skirt she intentionally wore, and she squirms as I run my finger along the edge of her cotton underwear. Her breathing quickens, and she hums as I slide my finger under, tracing her opening. The second I feel her wetness, I groan. Something inside me ignites, and it wipes my mind of everything except one thing. *Everly Cole.*

Our hands tangle in a mad rush to unclothe each other. We're hidden away in our special spot on my grandfather's land. Wayne is the only person who knows where we go, but that's only because the asshole followed us one night to see where we always disappear.

I reach into my shorts pocket to grab a condom. Feeling nothing, I flip the shorts over and switch pockets. I curse under my breath.

"What's wrong," she asks, her voice as sweet as the sin we're about to commit.

I dig my head into her shoulder and groan as my dick shoots

out a pain knowing it's not getting any action. "I can't find the condom. It must have fallen out somewhere," I mutter.

"It's okay. I'm on the pill."

I jerk up, propping myself up with my elbows. "Since when?"

"Since last month."

"Do your parents know?" That's a stupid question. If her dad knew, I'd be six feet under right now. Jake Cole is the town's sheriff. No one messes with him. He's never been a fan of me, but he learned early on it was better to keep his enemy close because his daughter was going to date me whether or not he liked it.

"Kase. I'm eighteen now, they don't need to know everything I do."

I'm trying hard to think with the right head because right now my dick is the hardest it's ever been. "Are you sure?" I murmur, studying her face for any hesitation. When she reaches down between us and wraps her warm hand around my hard dick and guides it inside her, I know she's sure. The heat alone almost makes me lose my shit. It's never felt this good.

It's perfect.

She's perfect.

She's mine.

CHAPTER TWO

EVERLY

KASE MESSES AROUND WITH HIS FRIENDS IN THE MIDDLE OF THE CIRCLE outlined by truck beds. High school kids fill the beds, dancing to loud music, making out or drinking beer that Trey had his older brother get from a county over. This is what we do every weekend. The spot might be different, but the setup isn't. Every road in town leads to an open dirt field. Tonight, we're at the water tower. Tomorrow, might be the watering hole.

Welcome to Barrow, Texas, the small town with a population of 8,251. Susie and Mike Crow added that last one when they had a baby last week. Kase owns this town. He'll never admit it because he hates it here. Hates the memories of his mom's death and especially hates his dad.

Jerry Barrow, founder of Barrow Oil, which back in the day controlled the majority of the oil in the US, was Kase's great-grandfather. The land this town sits on and every mineral right underneath it has been passed down from generation to generation and it ends with Kase. Jerry Jr. died from a heart attack after his mom passed away and left everything to Kase. His fortune is tied up in a trust fund until he's twenty-eight with other stipulations no one knows about.

"I can't believe he's leaving," Stacy says, leaning on my shoulder. I nod and sigh. Me too.

And without me.

This wasn't the plan. I always thought we'd leave this town together and never look back. I don't hate it here like Kase, but there's so much more out in the world, but I can't leave here on my own. I'm not strong enough to leave my parents without him by my side. Being their only child, and as much as Kase has tried to make me gain independence, I'm terrified of being on my own.

Going to the doctor and getting on the pill was the first thing I've ever done by myself. I wanted to surprise him before he left. A part of me wanted him to see I'm trying to be independent. He says he loves me, but what happens when he gets out in the world and the options for women are endless? I'll be stuck here in good ole Barrow, Texas.

I remember the day he told me he wanted to be a Navy SEAL. I cried for days. He swore he was doing it for us. For our future. He hated school, even though it came easy to him, so the last thing he wanted to do when he graduated high school was go to college. He was using it as a way to leave this town. I had our life planned and him leaving for the military was not in the plan. Now, I'll be going to the community college by myself.

"Hey, beautiful. You from around here?" Kase jumps into the back of the truck, strolling over.

The last year, he's been working out every day, getting ready for the SEAL physical test. He was hot before, but now he's hot with muscles and I can't keep my hands off him.

"Nope, just visiting friends," I say, leaning back on my hands, acting disinterested.

Stacy giggles and hops off the cab. "You two are so freakin' cute," she mutters as she walks away.

"Guy friends?" he murmurs, uncrossing my legs so he can squeeze between them.

"Nope. Just a fun weekend with the girls before I leave for

college." I try to keep my tone aloof, but it's hard when he's touching me.

His fingers trail up my bare thighs, stopping right at the hem of my denim skirt. I swallow as goosebumps pebble my legs. Thoughts of us making love just a couple of hours ago, warm my insides.

"How much fun you wanting to have?" he asks in a suggestive tone, wagging his brows.

I laugh, sitting up. "I had that type of fun earlier. Now, I want to dance."

He yanks me forward, my skirt bunching up my thighs. "Lucky guy."

"He better always remember how lucky he is," I say, flashing a sly smile.

"I have a feeling he'll never forget." His lips slam against mine in a heated kiss. He kisses me until we're both gasping for air. "I love you," he whispers.

"From my nose to my toes," I reply. He belts out a laugh. The first time he told me he loved me, when we were thirteen, that's what he said.

"I love you from your nose to your toes."

It's been a joke between us because I was so upset his love stopped at my nose. He picks me up, setting me on my feet. "C'mon Evie, let me show you my dance moves." I playfully growl at the nickname. He knows I hate being called Evie, but I let it slide with him.

"Oh, I can't wait to see this. Maybe this time, you'll show me more than just the sprinkler," I joke. He slaps me on the butt as he pushes me to the middle of the circle where everyone is dancing.

"Just for that," he says, pointing to me with a devilish grin. "I'm doing this all night long."

The guys around join in. And there it is, folks.

The sprinkler.

"DON'T FORGET ABOUT ME," I hiccup through my tears. He cups my jaw, catching my tears with his thumb. People rush around us getting in the security line. My eyes are everywhere except on his. I can't look at him without going into hysterics.

"Everly, eyes on me," he softly demands. I squeeze my eyes shut and shake my head. "Please, baby." I open them, biting my quivering lip. His eyes glisten with tears. "Someone would have to rip my heart out to make me forget about you. And since boot camp isn't that bad, it's safe to say, that won't happen." I nod. "I love you, Everly Cole."

"I love you, Kase Nixon."

After a long kiss, he ends it with a kiss on my nose. "Don't you forget about me."

I huff and roll my eyes. "As if that would ever happen."

His smile touches his eyes. "I'll see you soon, baby." I take in a deep breath and nod. As he walks away, he keeps his eyes on me. I laugh when he runs into a lady. He looks at me, shrugs and mouths "I love you."

Wayne wraps his arm around my shoulder and we watch together as Kase disappears into a sea of other travelers. "Ready, Buttercup?" I slap him in the stomach and he doubles over with an exaggerated grunt. *Why did we have to bring him with us?*

I repeat to myself over and over on the drive home, he's coming back. I stare at the silver band he gave me a couple of weeks ago when he got down on one knee. The same one I hide from my parents when I'm home.

We're getting married and they can't say anything to stop me.

He's mine.

CHAPTER THREE

KASE

SPLASHES OF BROWN AND GREEN RUSH BY IN A BLUR AS I STARE OUT the window in the back of the taxi. The landscape is choking in this Texas heat. The lush greenery that was thriving just two months ago is slowly fading. I focus on the dying brush instead of the disappointment brewing in my head. Walking out past airport security, I thought I'd see the face that got me through the past couple of months. Instead, I got faces full of sympathy as they watched me look for someone who wasn't there. I wasn't worried that I didn't get a hold of her when I got a chance to call, but now this, it stings a little.

I close my eyes, running scenarios through my mind. She had the date wrong of me coming home. She's shopping with her friends, lost track of time. She got a job and couldn't leave. But I always end at the one that kills me inside; she's moved on.

"Bootcamp as bad as I've heard?" The driver asks, pulling me out of my thoughts.

I let out a sarcastic laugh. "Physically, no." I had it in my head that boot camp would make me more in shape than before I left. I think I gained fat being there. Pre-training is going to kick my ass.

I have the driver take me to my dad's house first so I can pick up my truck. When we pull up, I shake my head, looking at the overgrown yard. Weeds have taken over the lawn. Days of newspapers litter the driveway.

Home sweet home.

My duffle bag makes a thud sound against the old worn out hardwood floor. The stench—from god knows what—invades my nostrils. I bet the asshole hasn't cleaned anything since I left. The house is dark from the pulled curtains and the putrid smell gets worse as I walk into the living room. I pull my t-shirt over my nose hoping for a slight reprieve from the offending odor. Beer bottles are strewn across the coffee table with the caps littering the floor. I'm thankful I have shoes on when I step on one.

Yanking the curtains back, a couple of months of dust float in the air. I feel like I've walked into an abandoned house. There's no resemblance to the house I grew up in. The life inside of it died when my mom died. I grumble at the smell, it's so bad. "What the fuck is that?" I yell out.

I should turn around and leave. The only reason I came here was to get my truck, pack up some things and then go see Everly. I get pissed at myself for feeling guilty. He did this to himself. He's a fully capable human being able to take care of himself. It's like the angel and devil of my subconscious are having a fight. I'm on the devil's side, but it's the angel that's making me head toward the closet. The box of trash bags I bought before I left is unopened, proving the bastard didn't throw anything away. I yank a bag out, shake it open and start cleaning up.

When my fingers touch something wet on the counter under the mound of paper plates, I snap them back. I smell my finger and my stomach convulses and I cough through my gagging. My eyes water as I rush to wash off whatever the hell that was. I think I found the culprit of the stench. Tying a towel around my face, making sure to cover my nose, I dive back into cleaning.

The spilled curdled milk on the counter only made me gag a couple more times, but the house is somewhat clean now. I snatch my bag off the floor and walk down the hall to my bedroom. The shower is calling my name. I practically lived outside the last two months, yet I never felt this dirty. It's probably the damn smell of spoiled milk that won't go away.

"Well, if it ain't the prodigal son returning." My dad's gruff voice slurs as he walks in the front door. I look up from tying my shoe for a moment, briefly catching his blood-shot eyes, before looking back down and finishing. "I'm surprised you came back, boy." Sitting up, I watch him look around. He nods with his lips puckered like he just ate a lemon.

"You're welcome," I say, snidely.

He ignores me, walks to his La-Z-Boy and drops into it. "Not sure what you came back for. It's not like you have a girlfriend anymore." I stare at the back of the chair, stunned by his words. I'm trying to figure out if he's being his typical asshole self, or my worst scenario is actually true. *No. He's lying.*

I jump up, grab my keys and jog out the door. I can hear him heckling as I shut the door. Asshole. See if I ever clean your house again. You can die in your stench next time. The drive over, I nervously tap my thumbs to the beat of the song. Could she really have moved on from me? Did our love mean nothing to her? I knock the heel of my fist against my head. Stop thinking this shit. There is no way she forgot about me and moved on. *Never.*

"KASE, WAIT," Everly's dad says, holding out his hand. As soon as I drove up, he met me outside and stopped me. I stare at him wondering why he's keeping me from going inside. "She was in an accident." *What?* My body lunges forward needing to get to her before my brain can catch up to ask questions.

"Everly!" I yell as he holds me back. I repeat her name again.

"Kase." He shakes me, and I glare at him, my nostrils flaring. "She was hurt pretty bad."

"Where is she?" My voice is in full panic mode. "Tell me where she is!"

"She's inside, but —"

He might be bigger than me, but he's not as fast. I twist out of his grip and run inside, the screen door slamming behind me. "Everly, where are you?" I yell, trying my hardest not to scream it at the top of my lungs. Glancing into each room as I rush through the house, I finally find her in her bedroom. She's sitting up with a book in her hand, but her eyes are pinned on me when I enter the room. I'm halted by the look of panic. It's not until that second I wonder why she didn't come running for me when I was calling her name.

"Everly, what's wrong?" I take a step and her back stiffens, so I stop. She's scared. *Of me?* The rise and fall of my chest is the only movement in the room. I glance around and question myself if this is the guest bedroom. No, the guest bedroom is in the back of the house. That window, I've crawled through a million times. But this isn't her room. Pictures of us that are normally plastered everywhere, are all gone. The walls are bare. *What the hell is going on?*

"She lost her memory." Her dad stands behind me in the doorway, his words feel like needles pushing into my heart. I keep my eyes on her to see her reaction. "Everly, this is Kase. He's a friend."

I whip around and narrow my eyes at him. My hands fist at my side. "I'm more—"

His jaw tightens, and his eyes bore into me as he interrupts me and says, "Stop. She doesn't remember any of us." Everly's mom places her hand around his arm and gives me a sympathetic nod. She pulls on his arm and nods her head to the side, gesturing that he leaves us. He hesitates for a beat but gives in. "Don't say anything to upset her," he warns me before leaving.

She really did forget me. *Literally.*

I slowly turn around, wringing my fingers. What do I say? The love of my life is staring at me like I'm a stranger. Shit, I am a stranger in her head. Does her heart not feel anything when she sees me? I blink back the tears that threaten to escape.

"What was your name?"

I have dreamt of her voice for months, the pure, sweet angelic tone that I could never get enough of. But I could double over in pain from those words. I hold myself together so I don't upset her, but this is the hardest thing I've ever done in my life.

Choking on my name, I clear my throat and try again. "Kase."

"That's a weird name."

I chuckle and nod. Her answer takes me back, eight years ago, when she said the exact same thing. "So, you don't remember me?" I whisper.

She shakes her head. "I'm sorry, I don't. Were we good friends?"

I pull in a harsh breath and it shakes coming out. My knees weaken, my whole body wants to collapse, but I stand tall. "We were. I mean…we are."

We love each other. We're getting married. The words are seconds away from slipping from my mouth. I begin to close the gap between us. Maybe if I touch her, it'll spark her memories. She scoots to the side of the bed, stands up and holds up her hand. It's not until then, I see the newly scarred cuts on her arms.

"Please, stop," she says, tears trickling down her face. Rejection from her is so foreign, it's difficult to understand. "Can you just leave?"

"Everly, you're getting upset because you don't know why you're feeling something, but there's a reason. Let yourself feel it," I plead with her, trying to pull out what I know is still in there. Her brain might not be working right, but her heart is still beating, and I know it beats for me.

She shakes her head quickly. "No. That's just it. I don't feel anything, and I can see how much I mean to you. It's…" She pauses, taking in a quick breath. "It's killing me that everyone looks at me, expecting me to remember them and I just don't. I'm tired of people touching me, telling me stories that sound more like a book I read than a memory. The disappointment in everyone's faces when they leave... I don't know what to say to make y'all feel better," she cries.

"Kase, I think it's best you leave," Everly's mom says, coming into the room. She places her hand on my arm like she did her husband's. The gentle gesture feels like a hand of steel crushing me. I wipe the tears running down my face. I don't know what to do. I'm supposed to go back to training in a couple of days, but I don't want to leave her. She'll remember me. She has to.

I find her gaze again, but she looks away.

"I'm sorry I wasn't there for you." My heart splits open as I walk out of the room. Everly's dad is on the porch as I pass. I'm sure he's loving the fact that his daughter can't remember me. Everly's mom takes her place next to him.

I swallow back my emotions and spin around. "What happened?"

"We're not exactly sure. She drove right through a red light, running head-on into a truck. We're lucky she's alive," her mom answers.

My brows furrow. "She didn't stop. At all?"

She shakes her head. "A witness said they saw her leaning forward like she was passed out before she hit the truck, but we can't be sure."

"How long... how long until her memories return?" I stutter, pointing at her door.

"We don't know. The doctor says it could be tomorrow, it could be never."

I double over, gripping my jeans at the knees to keep me standing. It's hard to breathe. "How can she not remember me?" I whisper to myself.

"We need to tell him," I hear her mom say.

Standing, I murmur, "Tell me what?" Her dad glares at her mom. Whatever she wants him to say, he's not happy about. "Tell me what," I say louder this time, taking a step toward them. He firmly shakes his head twice at her like he's not going to tell me.

He sighs, looking back at me. "We're moving her to a facility that specializes in helping patients with amnesia."

"O...kay," I respond, wondering why he didn't want to tell me that? The quicker she can get help, the faster she'll come back to me. "Where?"

"It's in Arizona."

"Arizona? There isn't anywhere closer? Like Dallas? And why did you take down all her pictures? Don't they say to keep showing her pictures because you don't know what will trigger her memory?" I don't have a freaking clue if that's what they say, but it sounds reasonable. It's crazy to think, but it sounds like they're trying to take her away from me. The sadness inside me switches to anger.

"We didn't take them down, she did." I've never wanted to punch Everly's dad as much as I do right now. His smug face fuels the fire burning in my gut. He takes a solid step toward me, lifting a brow as if taunting me to do it. The only choice I have is to turn around and leave. He wouldn't hesitate to throw me in jail and it'd destroy my military career.

The slight satisfaction of leaving tire marks in front of his house as I speed away lasts less than a second before the reality of the situation sets in.

I've lost Everly.

CHAPTER FOUR

KASE

THE STEERING WHEEL TAKES THE BRUNT OF MY ANGER. I STARE AT THE water tower with blurred vision as tears burn my eyes. When I imagine what the scene of the car crash looked like, the anger overwhelms me. I should've been there for her. I shouldn't have left. This is all my fault.

I jerk my head to the side as the passenger door opens. "Figured I'd find you out here." Wayne hops in. He blows out a heavy breath and squeezes my shoulder. "It's good to see you."

I close my eyes and nod. "When'd it happen?"

"It's been about seven weeks."

One week after I left. Seven weeks, the love of my life has been suffering, and I didn't even know. I pound my fist into the wheel again, the horn blares back every few strikes. Stopping the assault, I drop my head. "Why didn't anyone get in touch with me?"

"I tried calling the Red Cross, and they said it had to be an immediate family member. I was hoping you'd call me at some point." No, I kept the few calls they granted me to call Everly. I must've talked to her right before it happened. The other two times I tried to call her, it went straight to voicemail. "My dad said it was better you didn't know since there wasn't anything you could have done."

I glare at him. "I could have been here for her!"

He shakes his head. "Kase, it was bad when she woke up. She wouldn't let anyone see her except the doctors. I know you would've dropped everything to come back, but it would've killed you."

I shove the door open, jump out and throw my arms out screaming, "It's killing me now! It fucking hurts, Wayne." I drop to my knees on the hard dirt, holding myself up with my hands. Pebbles dig into my already raw palms, but the only pain I feel is my heart twisting. "It hurts," I keep repeating in agony.

Wayne puts his hand on my back. "Dude, I'm so sorry." He sits down next to me while I cry, not caring I sound like a chick, bawling. This is what Everly would call an ugly cry.

Fifteen minutes is all I allow before I pull it all back. I can't change the past. Hope is what I'm left with that she'll regain her memories. Wayne and I sit on the ground against the truck in its shadow, throwing rocks at the tower.

"What are you gonna do?" He lolls his head my direction. Ain't that the question of the day?

I shrug. "I don't know. If I stay, my chance at being a SEAL is over. If I go, I'll always regret leaving her." Boot camp brought out a deep sense of pride in myself. I've never had to work hard to achieve anything because of my name. In the Navy, I'm not a millionaire's grandson or the son of a drunk. I have to work my ass off to prove that I'm great enough to become a SEAL like everyone else. I've never wanted something so bad in my life. Until today.

"What're you suppose to do next for the military?"

"I'm supposed to report back to Illinois for training in two days."

"If you go, can I get a hold of you?" I nod. I don't start SEAL training for another two months. This is the get your ass in shape before you go phase. "If her memory returns, I'll call you. There's nothing you can do from here, especially if they're sending her to a facility."

It helps to know I have Wayne here to keep me updated, but I'm still not sure. "I need time to think. It would've been an easier decision had I come home, and she was with someone else."

"Are you kidding me? Everly would've never left you by choice."

We stay there and talk about boot camp and what he's been up to. The sun dips low in the sky and I know I need to go home and make a decision. As I drive off, my mind is a flurry of pros and cons.

Fuck, I say to myself when I see my dad's car in the driveway. I make a conscious decision to run in, grab my bag, and hopefully leave before he sees me. I'd rather spend the night in my truck than stay here with him. The TV is blaring, masking any noise I make walking into the house. I slither down the dingy brown carpeted hallway, grab my bag and head for the front door.

As I reach for the gold doorknob, the bastard laughs. I twist my head around to see what he's laughing at; he's staring right at me. "Running away again, boy?" he jests, stumbling to his feet. "I guess you weren't very important to that girlfriend of yours. It didn't take her long to forget about you."

Staring at the door, I try to ignore the chill creeping up my spine. Leave. Walk out and forget he ever exists.

"Stop being a pussy, go over there and make her remember you. Be a man."

The bag slips from my trembling fingers; every muscle stiffens at his insinuation. My pulse spikes to dangerous heights as my vision turns red. I spin around, glaring at the monster, pushing the one down threatening to escape inside me.

"That's it. Feel the rage, it's inside you. Part of you," he pushes like he's enjoying the fury running through me. "Show your woman where her place is."

Something snaps inside me, and I lunge across the floor, slamming my fist into his face. Over and over. Every bruise my mom had flashes through my mind and it's my job to make sure he feels the pain she did.

I'm yanked off him, thrown to the side of the room, landing on my ass. An intense need to ravage him has me clawing on all fours to get to him, but I'm held back.

"Kase, if you don't back off, I'll pull my gun out and shoot you," a voice barks, pushing me back again.

My chest heaves and I stare down at my raw, bleeding knuckles then look at my lifeless father, his face already swollen, smeared with blood. What did I do?

Sheriff Jake Cole glares down at me. Everly's father. His hand resting on his holster. Tears sting my eyes as the reality sets in.

"Don't move," he snaps, and I nod. He leans down over my father, feeling for a pulse. When he shuts his eyes and shakes his head, I already know. I killed my father.

I cover my head with my hands, leaning in between my legs as my head spins. "He wouldn't stop," I wail. "He said I was just like him." I lift my head and stare at Jake. "I'm nothing like him." Nausea wreaks havoc on my stomach and I leap up, running to the trash can right before I lose my airport lunch.

"I'm not like him," I cry over and over.

"Kase, I'm kinda stuck here," Jake sighs. "I have to take you in."

My entire future crumbles before my eyes. I've lost Everly and now I've lost the military. I'll spend the rest of my life in jail.

Jakes stands above me, his hard eyes studying me. "Son, I'm only doing this because I know how much you meant to my daughter." I swallow, my mind racing, searching for what he'll say. He hates I was with his daughter, so I'm surprised by his words. "Nobody will miss your dad. Leave town and never come back. Not for my daughter, not for anything." His words are slow and calculated. My thoughts scramble to understand what he's saying.

"What about…" I pause, looking at my dad's lifeless body.

"I'll take care of it. Do we have a deal?"

I've already lost Everly, so leaving this town and never returning is an easy decision. But what if Everly's memory returns? I won't be able to explain myself, leaving right now will be the end of Kase and Everly. I squeeze my eyes shut. What do I do?

"Kase, you need to decide. I called backup when I got here and heard you fighting. They'll be here any minute. The offer is off the table once they walk through that door."

I scramble to my feet. "Okay." Everything moves in a slow-motion blur as I grab my bag and run out the door. I glance back at the house knowing it might be the last time I'll ever see it and then look to the sky.

"I'm sorry, Momma."

CHAPTER FIVE

KASE

10 Years Later

"Why'd you leave the Navy?"

It's a question I've been asked a lot. The lie I've told everyone else almost slips out. Except, this is Max Shaw. Former FBI Agent, known for his behavior expertise, who has built a security team of only the best. To be sitting here is an honor. He sits forward in his chair, leaning his elbows on his desk and watches me closely. I clear my throat and sit up taller. I haven't been this nervous since... hell, I can't even remember ever being this nervous. He knows the answer; he's just testing me to see if I will tell him the truth.

"It was time to do something else." His eyebrow cocks up. He bought that as much as he buys bullshit from a grocery store. I hate talking about this. It's a secret I've tried to forget since I left home almost ten years ago. "My trust becomes available this year." I look past Max, out the large window behind him to the vast open ranch. His chair squeaks as he sits back and I meet his eyes.

"So, why are you looking to work? Why not just kick back and enjoy being rich?"

"Because that's not me, sir."

Max shakes his head, dropping his head for a second. "Stop calling me sir."

"Sorry, Mr. Shaw."

"Max. Call me Max. You make me feel old. I'm only two years older than you." His chuckle makes me relax. I've heard so many stories about Max and his elite team. It shouldn't have been a surprise when I received an email responding to my application, but it was. I know I'm the best, it just reinforces my thinking when other people think so too.

"I'd like to learn from you and someday open my own security firm. There are stipulations in my trust I won't be fulfilling anytime soon, so I won't receive the entire amount of money. Plenty to get me started in my new life though."

"You'd be a great fit for our team." He holds up a folder and drops it on the desk. "Everything about you that's on paper, I already know. Anything else you'd like to add?" His intense eyes wait for an answer, or he's searching mine for one. My heart slams a hard beat against my chest and I swallow. Telling him I killed my dad isn't a good idea to bring up during an interview. "Look, we all have skeletons. I just don't want them coming back to life and knocking on my door. I know that your father went missing after you left for the Navy."

Missing? That explains why no one has questioned me. They never found his body. "My father was an abusive drunk. I wouldn't be surprised if he picked a fight with the wrong person." I shrug half-heartedly, trying to feign indifference rather than guilt. Max sits back in his chair, studying me. I keep my breathing even and slow. "When I left that town, I left him and all those jacked up memories." I lean forward in my chair. "Forever."

He nods in understanding. I'm not certain he believes me, but he's giving me the benefit of the doubt. "It's hard to say forever to a place you own."

I release a heavy sigh. "If my grandfathers could see me now, I'm sure I'd be a huge disappointment to them."

"I doubt that," Max states matter of fact. "I'm sure they fought for that land, just as you fought for the people of this land. Don't sell yourself short because you didn't become a rancher. They'd be proud."

"Not when I sell it." I've waited for the day I could break free from that place and the memories that haunt me. It can't come soon enough, but I still feel like I'm letting down my heritage.

"Considering they're dead, who cares what they'd think. It's your land to do as you please." I like Max and his no bullshit attitude. He reminds me of a couple of guys on my team. "The job is yours if you want it."

I flash a tentative smile. "That's it? No, 'I'll call you back in a few days. Thanks for coming in?'"

He smirks and shakes his head. "Nope."

"Okay." My grin widens and my energy spikes. "Hell yeah, I want it."

The possibilities of being on this team flash through my mind. Everyone in the security business knows about Max Shaw's team. And he asked me to work for him.

"How long do you need to move out here?"

"I've already got everything I own with me. So… I can start as soon as possible."

"You're as certain getting the job as I am giving it to you."

"I know a good thing when I see it and I was fairly confident." I leave out the part that I own nothing other than clothes and one box of important stuff.

"Wouldn't have offered you the job without it. Take a week to settle in. I have a friend who's a realtor." He reaches into his desk drawer and pulls out a card. I take it when he holds it out. "Her name's Pepper and she can help you find a place. Don't fuck her."

I jerk my head up from the girly business card to his hard stare.

"Yes, sir. I mean Max," I stumble. He cocks a smile at my obvious state of nervousness.

"Most of the guys live in Gilley Cove because it's only fifteen minutes away and off the beach. Pepper will be able to help you. I have a case I need to leave town for and I'm not sure when I'll be back. Stone will get you set up and answer any questions." He pushes his chair back and stands. I stand, adjusting my suit jacket. "And I don't know who told you to wear a suit, but that shit needs to stay in your closet. When I left the FBI, I swore I'd never wear a suit to work again. Unless you're getting married and force me to wear one," he grumbles the last part.

"Got it," I say, sticking the card in my wallet.

He holds out his hand, "Welcome to the team, Kase."

CHAPTER SIX

KASE

A RED-HEAD LOOKS UP AT ME FROM BEHIND HER DESK. "I'M ASSUMING you're Max's new guy?" Of course she's flaming gorgeous. I nod, flashing a quick smile. "Have a seat." She gestures for me to sit in the empty chair.

"Thanks." I wipe my hands along my jeans after I sit. My neck tightens, and I hold off from cracking it. I'm nervous as hell around this woman. When someone tells me not to do something, I use it as an opportunity to test my boundaries. This time, I'd be kissing my job goodbye and burning bridges I can't afford to burn if I want to be in this business. Everything I do could be construed wrong and she'll think I'm flirting with her. "I'm Kase Nixon."

She leans back, fidgeting with a pen and studies me. "Max gave me a heads up you were coming. Welcome to Gilley Cove."

"Thanks."

"What area do you like?" She spins her chair around to her computer but looks over her shoulder to me.

I shrug. This is the first time I've been in this town. "Stone told me the Village was good."

She snorts as her fingers press keys. "Of course he did." She searches for available properties and I feel I'm the butt end of this joke.

"So, what's the Village?"

She glances over at me attempting to hide her amusement by pulling in her lips. "I'll show you later. Are you wanting to rent, own? How many rooms?"

Only one requirement, I want a view of the ocean. It's the only place I found peace in my unstable world the past ten years. The sight of it every day might calm the nightmares. Pepper makes a few phone calls and I can tell by how her voice increases an octave, she located something. I squeeze into her Honda Civic, afraid if I breathe, I'll break it. She observes me and laughs. "Sorry. I should get a bigger car if I'm taking clients out."

I fold my shoulders together to make myself seem smaller. "Nah, it's okay. I'm good."

"Good thing we're only five minutes away."

Damn good thing. My junk is squished. I try to push down my jeans, hoping for a slight reprieve, but get none. As soon as the car is put in park, I jump out and adjust myself, not caring who's watching me.

"This place just became available. You'll appreciate the view, it's hard to find oceanfront units. Except for the Village," she snickers, walking toward the garage exit.

"C'mon, you have to tell me what the Village is." She snorts again, making me chuckle. Her cheeks redden, and she swats at my arm. Why does she have to be adorable too? We both wince at the sun's brightness as we step out onto the sidewalk.

"Don't make fun of my laugh," she says, pulling her sunglasses off her head, covering her eyes.

"I'm not. It's cute." I peek over at the red-head with her pouty red lips I'd wouldn't mind lined across my–

Don't fuck her. Max's words scroll through my head like a stock ticker on CNN. I jerk my head straight, looking ahead at the ocean view in front of us.

Through the corner of my eye, I notice her giving me a suspicious glance. "Goddamnit. Max told you to stay away from me, didn't he?"

"Not those exact words."

She huffs and wrinkles her freckled nose. "I swear, I'm going to kill him. If he doesn't stop interfering with my love life, I'll die a virgin." She throws her arms in the air and I whip my head in her direction. A virgin? No way. She has to be around my age. "Well, a born-again virgin."

"Is there such a thing?" I ask, bemused.

Her smile fades and she looks away from me. "In my case, yes." Her voice softens, and I sense there's a backstory. "Did Max tell you about me?"

"No. I assumed you and Max had a past. He was straightforward with his demand; I didn't need to question it."

She sighs. "We definitely have a past, but it's not what you think. Three years ago, Max and his team rescued me from a sex trafficking ring."

I stop walking, grabbing her upper arm. "Shit. I'm sorry, Pepper. I didn't mean–"

A small smile curves her lips. "Don't feel sorry for me," she says, sternly. "I'm in a good place. My past is where it belongs— behind me, but my future is up to me. I'm stronger and more independent than I've ever been, thanks to Max. Except the part about him being an overprotective ogre."

I understand Max now. Shit, I don't even know her and I'm ready to kick anyone's ass that messes with her. "He means well."

"I know," she says, rolling her eyes. "You're not my type, anyway."

Stepping back, I puff out my chest. "What is wrong with my type?" Women love me, and I've had no complaints. She laughs as she bruises my ego.

"You're hot, don't get me wrong." Through narrowed eyes, I wait for the inevitable but. "But, I don't prefer my guy… as ripped as you are." She squeezes my bicep. "It makes me think I need to work out more, or you'll expect me to."

"I'm not that shallow," I balk.

"And you're clean shaven and I have a hard time believing you're twenty-eight."

Nothing like a woman stomping on your ego a little more. "Anything else you'd care to throw in?" As much as I'm surprised by her outward case of truths, it's refreshing. She knows what she wants and isn't wishy-washy. "You sound like Stone."

A small moan escapes her lips and the wicked smile that flashes on her face surprises me. "Now, that man is my type." Which explains a lot. Stone and I couldn't be any more different.

I shrug. "I guess if you want skinny Grizzly Adams."

She slaps me again on the arm. "Jealous?"

"Nope. To each their own." Total lie. When a gorgeous woman tells you that you're not her type, it stings.

"Come on, let's go see your new apartment."

When we reach the elevator, I glance around for the staircase. "What floor?" She doesn't question why I prefer the stairs, she just meets me up there.

Pepper points out the amenities in the building before entering the apartment. When we walk into the living room, she continues rambling with her sales pitch. I'm sold when I admire the view. Across the street, white sand meets ocean blue.

"It looks perfect. I'll take it."

"You haven't even looked around." She stares blankly at me. I spin around a hundred and eighty degrees. I spot the kitchen, a bedroom, and the eating area. Done. When I glance back at her, she's shaking her head.

"What? You told me to take a look around. I did. It has everything I need. I'm assuming it has a bathroom, but I guess I should confirm that before I take it."

"You're such a man."

"Thanks for noticing." I flex my biceps knowing she's not a fan.

Her laugh echoes in the space. I don't care for the hardwood, but I can put rugs around. "It's perfect."

"How can you say it's" —she pauses for a beat— "never mind. Let's go sign your lease and you can schedule a time for someone to deliver your stuff."

"Stuff?"

"Furniture?" She gives me a quizzical gaze.

I yank on my shirt. Traveling light makes it easy to relocate. "All I have are my clothes."

"Men are basic beings, but this takes it to a new level."

We are basic. We need food, a place to live, and a woman. Not necessarily in that order. It's been ten years since I've had somewhere to call home. I'm happy just to have air conditioning.

"If I plopped a sleeping bag down right here, it'd be a hundred times more comfortable than where I've been living."

Understanding spreads across her face. "I forgot that you just got out of the military. Do you need to go furniture shopping?" I smile and nod. Her heels click across the wood floor to the kitchen bar where her purse is. She digs in her bottomless bag and pulls out a phone.

"Need help shopping?" she asks, glancing up from her phone. "I've found a couple of furniture stores not too far from here."

"That'd be great."

Her eyes light up like I offered her chocolate. Shit, I'd offer her all the chocolate she wanted if she'd go for me.

What feels like days later, we emerge from the furniture store. Throw me in the middle of hungry sharks and I'd enjoy it more than what we just went through.

Pepper is bouncing on her toes with a beaming smile. "I can't believe the great deals you got. Oh my gosh, I've always wanted to do that. Go on a shopping spree and buy everything new." She wraps her arm through mine and I smile at her over-enthusiastic excitement from furniture shopping.

"If only I was your type."

"Ha! If I knew you'd be my sugar daddy I might change my mind." She bats her eyes at me a couple of times and then burst out laughing. "Totally kidding. I'm not that superficial." It never crossed my mind she was.

"Let's get something to eat. I'm starving." I glance at my watch. Damn, we were in that store for three hours. Three hours I'll never get back.

"There's a burger place around the corner," she says, pointing ahead.

The suspicion of someone watching me tugs at my senses. I survey the area. There are a few people on the sidewalks but nothing alarming. When I turn to look behind me, my body freezes. Pepper jerks to a stop from holding my arm. Her words barely register, I'm paralyzed as I zone in on one person.

Everly?

Her smile breaks my trance. She's at least fifty yards away. I take a step toward the woman I'm almost positive is Everly, but Pepper stops me. "Are you okay?" she asks at my side. I glance over at her, not sure what to say. The only girl I ever loved, who forgot about me, is standing right there. *I think.* Turning my attention back, I groan out of frustration. She's walking away, winding around a corner.

A familiar ache shudders in my stomach and I take off in a sprint. Every beat of my heart tells me to go faster. As I turn the same corner she was at, I find an empty road. I bend over, grip my knees as I catch my breath. What am I doing? It wasn't her. My mind hasn't played that trick on me in years. I used to see her face on every dark haired, green, blue, gray-eyed woman. Hope never died that she'd remember me and come search for me. She never did. Did she finally regain her memories after ten years? Clicking heels come from behind and a hand lays across my back.

"What's going on Kase?"

"Did you notice that woman? The one standing here a few minutes ago?"

"I saw her when she turned the corner when I saw you dart that direction."

I stand up and run my hand through my hair, relieved I didn't imagine a woman. It's happened before. "She looked familiar."

"She must have looked more than familiar for you to take off running like you were in the Olympics. If I ran that fast, I'd be lying on the sidewalk dead. In fact, if you ever see my feet moving that quick, look at who is chasing me and shoot them."

My hand freezes in my hair and I stare at her. Is she serious? Max wouldn't have told her what I did in the military and I didn't put that on the application.

"Why are you staring at me like that? I was kidding. I don't want you to kill anyone."

Little does she know, I've killed plenty.

I lift my chin the direction we came from. I need a distraction. Since it can't be with a woman, food will have to work. She takes my hint and walks. "She reminded me of an ex," I mumble.

"All my ex's, I run away from."

"Things were left unsettled."

"You still love her?"

I sigh. "'Til I die."

"Do you think it was her?"

"No. It's just my head fucking with me."

CHAPTER SEVEN

KASE

"I DIDN'T NOTICE PROFESSIONAL DECORATOR ON YOUR RESUME," CODY jokes when I walk out of the bedroom. He's relaxing on my new couch, brushing his hand across the dark grey suede. "Maybe you should think about changing jobs. I'd hire you."

I chuckle, looking around the decorated room where everything coordinates. It looks awesome, but it wasn't my doing. "This is all Pepper." His brow lifts with an accusatory expression. "She helped me buy furniture," I respond, quickly. "There was zero enjoyment going to the furniture store with her. She's into Stone, anyway." I throw that out to prevent any confusion with my intentions. I have none.

He nods. "All I can say is, don't mention this to Stone. He's a vindictive shit." I get it, I'm the new guy. I understand more than most people the importance of a team. You don't want to be the one on the outside looking in.

"You don't say. I finally found the Village where he suggested I look." It's a vacated apartment building right by the beach, zoned to be torn down soon, but filled with transient people. Not quite what I was looking for, but it gave me a reason to spend some money. At least the people there now have blankets, pillows, and bath necessities.

Cody lives a floor down from me. He's a marine, so we've become quick buddies reminiscing about our days in the military. It's nice to have someone around who understands the difficult transition to civilian life.

His phone dings in his hand. He reads it and says, "They're meeting us there in five."

We're meeting at Ocean's, the bar across the street. Cody and I went last night for a couple of hours. It's a cool place, typical bar though. It's convenient being able to walk home after drinking.

Beachgoers pack the bar, looking to continue their partying. I'm wearing shorts and a polo and feel overdressed.

We grab two empty chairs around the table with the guys but before I can say hi, my phone vibrates in my pocket. I dig it out, noticing it's my buddy from my old team. I can barely hear him, so I tell him to hold on.

"Order me a Shiner," I say, scooting the chair backward and standing. Hudson nods. Before I make it out the front door, a woman's hand grips my arm, stopping me.

"Please tell me you're not leaving," a petite blonde purrs. She's wearing a see-thru bathing suit cover, showing off her fit body underneath it. I drink her in, my lips curl up to a smile and I place my hand against her lower back, leaning down so I'm close to her ear. She smells like coconut and salt.

Thank god for beach towns.

"Gorgeous, I'm not. I just have to take this call."

"Come find me later." She puts a straw in her mouth and sucks on her drink, her eyes never leaving mine. I draw in a ragged breath and nod. The things I could do to her.

Once outside, I groan into the phone, "Your timing is deplorable, brother." His laugh rings in my ear. We talk for a few minutes as I update him on where I've landed. I knew he wouldn't have a lot of time to talk, only enough time to check in with each other and make sure I was doing okay. I miss my team and hearing from him, regrets of leaving begin to pop up in my head. I shake the thoughts away. No, this is where I need to be for my sanity. Slipping my phone back into my pocket, I head back inside.

"Hey, come back here," the guy at the door yells after I walk in. I turn to see if he's having trouble with someone, but his eyes pin me. He nods when I point to myself, confirming he's talking to me. "I need to see your ID."

My eyes widen in surprise. "You've got to be kidding. I was already in there; I came out for a phone call." I point inside.

He shrugs, holding his hand out. "My shift just started, so if you want in, I need to see it."

I grumble, yanking the wallet out of my pocket. The last time anyone carded me was years ago. Right as I'm handing it over, Hudson comes out. He looks at the exchange and throws his head back in amusement. He slaps the guy on the shoulder.

"Tom, he's with us." He fights to keep his laughter in as I narrow my eyes at him. "I know he looks like a young buck, but I can vouch for him."

"What the hell? I don't look like I'm underage." I stand taller, like that will help convince them otherwise.

He shrugs. "You do have a baby face." Hudson can't hold it any longer. That's it. I'm growing a beard. Tom looks down at my ID and with a look of recognition I hoped wouldn't come, he says, "I've heard about you. You're that badass SEAL that saved someone." I paste a fake smile on my face and take my ID. I've saved a lot of *someones*. But people don't know about those. An American civilian was being held hostage, and they awarded me a medal for leading the rescue. One article and suddenly everyone knows me. They don't know shit. They think it's cool to be on the receiving end of such an honorable accolade. I'd rather have my brother back. His death still haunts me.

He holds his hand out, his smile reaches his eyes. "It's an honor to meet you."

I shake his hand to be respectful. "It's nice to meet you too, Tom."

"Hey Tom, our beers are getting hot," Hudson fires off, saving me from excusing myself. He's Army, he knows. What happens over there always comes back with us, but the last thing we want to do is rehash those tales with strangers.

Although, at the table, Hudson wastes no time telling the guys they carded me. Let the jokes begin. Everyone gets their dig in, I sit back and let them have their fun. It's easier to listen to this than talking about my past with strangers.

Draining the rest of my beer, our waitress shows up right on time. She stands between me and Cody. "Y'all need anything?" Her long tan legs catch my attention. I have to strain my neck to glance up at her. I should've swallowed the cool liquid in my mouth first.

My heart stops beating, causing my throat to close off mid-swallow. I lean forward choking, the liquid spewing from my mouth onto the floor and up my nose. The burn makes my eyes water. As I'm coughing the assholes around me get a kick out of it.

"You all right?" The waitress asks, patting my back. I nod, holding up a finger so she'll wait for me to stop dying, but I can't stop my coughing reflex. When I finally move past the coughing, she's already gone. My eyes dart around the bar, looking for the woman who just took my breath away.

She's standing behind the bar, a black shirt outlines her lean body, the V-neck showing off her cleavage. When her eyes catch mine, she smiles at me, then returns to making drinks. I slam my hand against Cody's chest and he grunts.

"Who is that?" I jut my chin in her direction.

"She's out of your league," he jokes.

I turn and glare at him. "What's her name?"

"That's Ellie," Stone answers. I whip my head around to the bar in disbelief.

Either the universe is playing a fucking joke, or it's kismet.

CHAPTER EIGHT

ELLIE

I DIP THE GLASS INTO THE LUKEWARM WATER AND PLACE IT NEXT TO the sink to dry. My feet are killing me. Why did I take a double today? Oh, yeah, I felt bad for skipping out on Tori yesterday when I had a last-minute study group pop up. Thank god this is my last semester.

"Did you see Max's new guy?" Tori purrs from behind me. She steps to the side of me, reaching for the vodka and makes a drink, not paying attention to the amount she's pouring. She can make drinks with her eyes closed. We both glance at the table of men that frequent our bar almost on a daily basis when they're in town. The only thing different is the man staring back at me right now. Our eyes meet for a moment before I busy myself snatching a towel to dry off the sink area.

"I think he likes you," she whispers.

Every day, I watch men flirt with women. They don't sneak peeks, they stare, waiting for their chance to catch the woman's eye. The slight smile with a tilt of the chin when they finally do. And her telling response, either opens doors or slams them shut. Single life is a wild world of body language. Sometimes I wish I had majored in psychology. It's intriguing. I've mastered the disinterested gaze, ignoring the heated looks. But this guy is different, I can't look away.

"He looks at me like he's trying to place where he knows me from," I say, leaning my hip against the counter, making myself look at Tori and not him.

"Do you think he does?" Her voice changes from flirty to concerned. Tori's the only person who knows about my past. We met when I ended up here trying to drown myself from the disaster my life was in. Her uncle owns Ocean's. She offered me a job that night and we've become great friends. I trusted her enough to tell her the truth. That's where it stops though. It's in the past. I don't talk about it, and I sure as hell try my hardest not to think about it.

"No… maybe… shit, I'm not sure. He looks a little familiar. He won't stop staring at me though. It makes me nervous."

She lays her hand over mine. "Don't be nervous. He's one of Max's guys, he's a good guy. For Max to hire someone, he would have combed through his life with a lice comb."

I snicker and itch my scalp. I didn't need that metaphor. Now, I'll be itching all freaking night. She's right though. I turn my head and sneak a glance at the mystery man. Thankfully, he's not looking back right now. He laughs at something Stone says, pulling the beer to his lips. I watch his Adam's apple bob up and down as he downs his drink. When he places it on the table, he looks in our direction. He smiles and holds his empty beer bottle up. He is gorgeous, that's for certain. His boyish looks are a stark contrast to the man I can see underneath that sweet smile and blue eyes.

"Looks like your admirer needs another beer."

I groan, grabbing another beer from the fridge. "Tell me again why I keep working here?" I reach into my back pocket, pull the warm metal bottle opener out and with one flip, the top pops off.

"Because you love me." She blows me a kiss and smacks my ass as I walk away.

"I'm sure it's the money," I say over my shoulder. She giggles because she knows it's true. The money is great here. Ocean's is the prime location, closest bar to the beach which keeps us slammed every night. I've been able to pay for college, bills, and put a little extra away each month.

"I'm assuming you want this?" I say, placing the bottle in front of him and picking up the empty one.

"Thanks." My body hums to life at the timbre of his voice. From one word. *Really, Ell*? It hasn't been that long.

"Ellie, this is Kase. Kase, Ellie," Stone says, waving his beer in between us.

Kase holds his hand out. "Nice to meet you, Ellie." His words lace with a polite southern accent. One I know too well and am usually turned off by, but not his. His sounds like a warm blanket you want wrapped around yourself on a frigid night. Except, as soon as I wrap myself in it, I'd suffocate from the heat.

I slip my hand in his. "You can call me Ell." His smile widens like he's enjoying an inside joke. I wait for the pick-up line that follows introductions from guys at the bar, but his smile stays plastered on his face. I'd rather have the pick-up line than the enamored stare. My exit is a lot easier when the guy is a douche, unlike this one, staring up at me like I hung the moon.

I clear my throat. "So, Stone, do you need anything?" I glance over at the other guys, searching for an out. Stone's gaze moves from me to Kase and back to me. He's as confused as I am.

"Nah, we're good," he says, picking up his full beer.

"Great. Call me when y'all need something." My words are barely out of my mouth before I pivot and make a beeline for the bar.

I hear Stone say behind me, "You sure you're a SEAL? I think your balls shriveled up in the cold, murky waters." The table burst out laughing. A SEAL, huh? Why does that make him that much hotter? Especially after what just happened. I stop and check on a couple of other tables.

The old-fashion jukebox retrofitted to play thousands of songs, turns on from the corner of the bar. I glance over at the big burly guy trying to dance to "I'm Too Sexy," by Right Said Fred. Why do we still have this song on the list? It's like a magnet for drunk guys. What happens next is so predictable, I could broadcast a live commentary. It never fails. Yep, there it is. Off comes the shirt. At least this guy is entertaining and not trying to rub himself on women. Hoots and hollers come from the patrons, urging him on. He starts cat-walking on our tiny dance floor. It's funny to see his sunburn outlined where his tank top was, obviously not enough liquid courage to take off the shirt at the beach today. Unlike right now as he does the worm across the floor.

"Every. Time." Tori walks up to my side and we watch the grown man make a fool of himself.

"I hope he wasn't planning on picking up a woman tonight," a sexy voice says. We both turn inward to find Kase standing behind us.

"That is for damn sure." Her eyes trail down his body and she lets out a low hum. If I wasn't standing so close, I wouldn't have been able to hear her over the music. I tap her on the hip to stop. A wicked smile grows on Kase's face. I guess the music isn't that loud.

"Need another beer?"

"After watching that" —he points to the guy pushing up on all fours, trying to stand up— "definitely. But I need the bathroom first." We admire his backside as he walks off. He stops and turns toward me, opening his arms wide. "Sorry about earlier. I needed a map to find my way back, I was lost in your eyes." He winks and turns to walk away.

Tori and I burst out laughing. "Awe, c'mon. You can do better than that, Cowboy," I call out to him. He motions like he's tipping an invisible cowboy hat right before he disappears into the men's bathroom.

"If I were you, I'd follow him into the bathroom and screw his brains out."

"Tori!" I stare at her dumbfounded. "That's just gross."

She grabs her rag from her back pocket and cleans off the table next to us. "You're so full of shit, Ell. Remember, I know about Steve."

She won't ever forget that. Just once, I let loose and the only mistake I made was telling her what I did. It also wasn't at a bar where god knows what is on the stall doors. I shiver just thinking about it. It was at an upscale restaurant where each bathroom had its own room and what looked to be clean. I push in the chairs and we both head back to the bar. "Shh. That was a one-time thing. And I knew Steve. He wasn't some hot stranger I followed into a bar bathroom."

She shrugs. "You could take him to the backroom. There's a bed. Just give me a heads up and I'll stay away. *Maybe.*"

I chuckle. "You're such a perv. You would so peek." I snap her with a towel on the ass and then run out from behind the bar. "If you want to see me naked, all you have to do is ask," I say with a smirk and blow her a kiss.

"It's that easy, huh?"

Shit.

My face burns from embarrassment. I peek over my shoulder where Kase is leaning against the bar looking smug. "No. You and your cheesy pick-up lines can ask all you want. It's not happening."

He takes a step forward; his chest grazes my back. "I don't need cheesy pick-up lines to get what I want." Goosebumps pebble my skin from the heat of his breath. I catch myself right before I lean back into his hard chest, stepping forward and with great detail, wipe the bar off. What is it about this guy that is making me lose control of my body? Leaning into him, Ell? What the hell? I jump when I feel him at my side. *Again.* Jesus, this guy doesn't give up. "I think you owe me a beer," he rasps, deep and sexy. He's intentionally doing this, getting me all hot and flustered.

"Oh, right… I'm sorry." The sexy crooked grin only proves he's getting a kick out of this. I huff and roll my eyes. "I'll grab it and bring it to you," I say, regaining my senses and walking around him. You'd think the bar was empty the way his laugh echoes in the room. Instead of walking behind the bar, I walk to the bathroom hallway to take a deep breath. "You need to stop this," I lecture myself like I'm talking to another person. Since my body seems to have taken a turn on its own, I need to remind it that now is not the time.

The night turns busy enough I don't have time to pay attention to my admirer. Our eyes catch a few times, but the constant orders being thrown at me keep me distracted.

"All right guys, last call," I say, gathering up the empty bottles. Kase gazes at me over the rim of his bottle while he drains it. I don't know why his intense stares make me fidget.

"We'll take one more round," Stone says.

Kase winks at me as I grab his empty bottle. "Be right back with those." I quickly turn so he doesn't see the flush on my face. I can't help the smile on my face when I walk away.

"Ohh," Tori taunts, pointing at my face. "You're having second thoughts about that cot back there, huh?"

"You know, I have a good bed at my place," I snicker. Her face lights up and I shake my head. "I mean, if I wanted to have a quickie."

"You know you want to."

"I'm not going to deny the thought hasn't crossed my mind, but—"

She squeals. "I knew it! You guys can't stop looking at each other."

I want to argue that it's him staring at me, but I can't explain why I keep returning his glances. I fill the tray with their beers, turning to her before I lift it. "Even if I've had a few dirty thoughts, it won't happen. I don't do one-night stands."

"Ell, I'm saying this from the bottom of my heart. You need to get laid." She shrugs as I glare at her pointedly. "And that man over there…" —she tilts her head in Kase's direction— "would be first in line to ride the Ell sex train."

I burst out laughing. "You are a freak."

Picking up the tray, I walk around her, and she tugs her arm up and down in the air. "Choo Choo."

I laugh off her incessant banter about sex. This isn't new. She's more of a free spirit with sex. Me, I need to trust the man first. And trust doesn't come easy.

"So, Cowboy," I say, putting the beer in front of him. "What brings you to Gilley Cove?" His lip curves into a lopsided smile, his dimple deepening. My heart skips a beat. That quick second that air escapes you and makes you wonder what the hell just happened. I hug the tray to hide my surprise feeling. I hadn't planned on asking him anything, it just came out. Call it curious, or it's my brain's way of telling me trust has to start somewhere.

"It was time for something new. And when Max Shaw offers, you accept."

My school project pops into my head, and how much Max has helped me with it. "That's for sure," I reply, absentmindedly. Kase's smile fades and he cocks his head to the side.

"Oh?" He sits back into his chair with his arms across his chest.

"No! I didn't mean it like that." The guys snicker and I smack Cody on the shoulder. "Is that the only thing everyone thinks about?" I ask, flustered as I walk away.

"Yes," they say in unison behind me.

The bar empties and Tori and I work quickly to clean up. We've gotten used to a few of Max's guys sticking around until we lock up when it's just us. We don't mind. *Usually.* Between two long days of school and work, I'm beat and a little sexually frustrated tonight. The reason for that is sitting at the bar, watching me closely. He's smart to keep quiet.

As we're locking the doors, I'm dreaming of my cold, inviting bed; ready to sleep until noon. There could be an earthquake right now and I doubt I'd notice in my comatose state.

A hand slips around my arm, stopping me. "Ellie." I turn and gaze into the blue eyes I haven't been able to get away from all night. "Is everything okay?"

"Yes, why?"

He drops his hand and stuffs both in his jean pockets. "I called out your name three times, but you kept walking. You're kinda killing my ego right now."

I flash him an incredulous gaze. "I'm not sure that's even possible." The other guys are talking to Tori by the back door and I smell a setup. "What's up, Cowboy?"

"I was wondering if you'd like to go out sometime?"

I wince, knowing this was coming. "Listen, you seem nice, but I'm really busy with my last semester of school and work, I just don't have time."

His perfect lips twist, and my thoughts turn dirty. What they'd feel like against my body. Tasting me. I shake the inappropriate thoughts from my mind. Holy shit, I'm getting delirious.

"You still with me?" He snaps his fingers in front of my face.

My face heats. "Sorry, I'm exhausted," I say, trying to hide my embarrassment. "I'm certain I'll be seeing you around." I manage a soft smile and then walk to my car. My apartment is only three blocks away, but walking home at two in the morning is out of the question.

"Oh, it's possible," he calls out.

I pinch my brows together and look at him, gripping the car door so I don't fall down. He smiles wide but holds a fist to his chest. "You're killing me, Ellie."

I shake my head, sliding into my car. "You'll live, Cowboy." He fills my rearview mirror when I pull out, watching me. He's not going to give up.

I'm not sure if I want him to.

CHAPTER NINE

KASE

"It's her," I say, adamantly.

"At least that explains why you were acting like a tool last night. There are millions of people in the US. Everyone has a doppelganger. She didn't recognize you when she rejected you." Stone slaps me on the chest, amusing only himself by his dig.

I stare at the wall of monitors flashing different areas we're running surveillance on. The feed's out of focus because my mind is too busy replaying last night. I'm certain it's her. I figured my subconscious was messing with me again. But when she came over to the table and spoke, her hand in mine, the scar that ran up her arm, there wasn't a question. Her eyes no longer shine with innocence, rather determination from a woman who's been through a tragedy. She's even more beautiful today than when we were teenagers.

"She has amnesia, asshole."

"You told me she saw you after the accident and I'm sure she had to have seen pictures of you after you left."

"Do you remember someone you met once, ten years ago? And I've changed. A lot."

It still hurts to say. *She doesn't remember me.*

Those four words became my motto during trainings. It pushed me to survive hell, I swore to myself that no one would ever forget me again. I was young and stupid then, but it worked. Thinking back, it's such an oxymoron because they train SEALs to be ghosts.

"So, ask her."

Running my hand across my unshaven jaw, I grunt. "I can't. I can't have her look at me like she did years ago. She changed her name, so she must not want her old identity for a reason. If I tell her I'm from her past, she might push me away again." I sense his eyes on me, so I glance over to him.

"Dude. She already pushed you away."

I flip him off. "I made her fall in love with me once, I'll do it again."

"*If* it's her. If you don't ask her, you're presuming it's Everly, and that's going to be a jacked-up situation if it's not."

"That's where I need you." I pull out a shot glass and hold it up, the light from the monitors shining through the prints.

"You didn't?"

"I sure as hell did. Run her prints for me?"

He stares at me, rolling his tongue in his cheek. "I've known Ell for years. I've known you for five seconds. Invading her personal life is not on my to-do list today."

The shot glass makes a ting noise as I slam it on the desk and push up from the chair, pacing the empty space in the dark room. "Come on, man, I need to find out if it's her. I tell myself that I'm over her, but something inside me woke up the second we locked eyes. If you won't help me, I'll find someone else." We had to collect DNA samples on terrorists to verify we had our target. I know people. This will happen whether he helps me or not.

He grumbles, "You're a pain in the ass." *More like determined.* Opening a drawer, he pulls out a latex glove and shoves his large hand inside it and picks up the glass. "Be right back."

My heart beats against my chest. Hard. A reality only dreamt about, is slapping me in the face. I could have Everly back. I curse under my breath. *Ellie.* If I slip, it won't matter if I know it's her. She'll run. The chair slides forward to a stop against the table as I grip the cushion between my fingers and drop my head.

Her dad's last words to me come back. *You ever try to find her, I'll tell her what you did.* It was bad enough the way she looked at me like I was a stranger, I couldn't let her view me as a murderer too. It's hard to forgive an unforgivable sin. I shake my head in frustration, the chair creaks, holding the weight of my body. I release a sarcastic laugh. I've gone from murdering my father to a trained assassin. My job was to protect my brothers, and I was great at it. I've never cared what people thought of me until right now.

What will she think? What will her dad do when he finds out I'm back in the picture? I push off the chair and pace again, my nerves frayed like ripped up jeans. The lights from the screens cast a glow around the room. Can I pretend she's a stranger to me? I can't lie to her forever. She might not remember me, but her parents will. The tense pounding of my heart has moved to my stomach as it knots from her being this close but so out of reach. She has the power to destroy me again.

The door swings open, light flooding the dark space as Stone walks in. I squint my eyes for a beat until they adjust. "Done. It's being run right now. I did a check first and Everly Cole nor Ellie Keyes is in the system, so this might be a dead end unless Ell ends up being someone else. In which case, I'll kick your ass because you're opening a can of worms."

I nod dismissively at him. Stone isn't a big guy. He works out, but he's at a computer most of his day and you can tell. "You could try," I joke.

He settles back in his chair with an exaggerated casualness and his hands behind his head. "I learned a long time ago, I can do more damage to someone with a computer than using my fists. I'll just take a mil from your account and be set for life." The smug smile on his face makes mine fall.

I cringe, despising the thought of everyone regarding me as the privileged rich kid, again. "Do the guys know?"

"What Max has me find on potential employees is only between us," he says with a serious tone. "Dude, I was just joking. I'd never take your money. I've read what you're capable of." He holds up his thumb and index finger, real close together. "And I'm this much afraid of you."

I chuckle, wondering if his ego is bigger than mine. He's a confident bastard knowing what I can do and not be scared. "You should be more than that. You can hide behind your computer, but I can hide anywhere, and you'd never see me coming."

"Never. I have cat-like senses."

I smile and nod slowly. He just threw out a challenge. I'm going to scare the piss out of him. He'll be begging me to stop.

"Go pack an overnight bag, we're going to New York City."

"Do we have a new case?" I glance at the screens.

"No. But you're about to meet Addison and Lexi. Aiden is away for work and Max wants us to check in on them."

I've gathered from the couple weeks working here that Aiden is one of Max's best friends. I scratch my chin at the obvious question. "Why can't you call?"

"You don't know Addison. Shit always finds its way to her, so Max has to physically check on her or have one of us do it so he can relax."

I mock salute and leave to go pack a bag. Seems like a waste of manpower having to go to a different state to check on someone who isn't in trouble, but Max is the boss.

———

THE TRIP IS quick and uneventful. I hate these types of trips. I want to see some action, not play with a kid. Although Lexi, Addison's seven-year-old daughter, is a hoot. I don't want kids, but if I did, I'd want them to be like her. I look around the stylish private plane and memories flood my mind from the shit-hole planes I'm used to being on. Whenever I headed out on a mission, my blood would be pumping with adrenaline making it hard to sit still. The return ride was a different story. You hoped you were coming back with the people you left with.

"The fingerprint results show no matches." Stone's voice brings me back to the present. *Dammit.* I lean my head against the chair. There has to be another way. "Before you ask, their DNA isn't in the database either."

I jerk straight up, making Stone jump. I grin. Cat-like senses my ass. "Can you hack into Family Tree server and retrieve DNA information they have on file?"

"Nope." My shoulders fall in defeat. He shakes his head and gives me an incredulous expression. "Dude, of course I can. Max didn't find the best hacker in the world to not be able to hack into small fish like Family Tree," he boasts. I look around for something to throw at him. "What makes you think her DNA is there?"

"When we were in high school, we did the DNA tests so we could view our heritage. Just for shits and grins." Everly was excited to get her results. I only did it because she wanted me to.

"Ten years is a long time. Not sure they'll still have it."

"Here. Give me your computer." I hold my hand out. I only had one password the day we met, so I'm hoping it still works.

"*What* are you smoking? You're not touching my computer." I drop my hand and stare at him as he caresses the top of his monitor. "No one touches my baby."

"You're fucking weird."

He shrugs. "Go to the website yourself, and type in my info."

After a few minutes of being lectured on the fact I need to change my password every six months, Stone successfully logs into my account. It's funny he's telling this to a person trained to be invisible. I erased all my social presence years ago. I forgot about this website, but we used fake names.

He spins his computer around showing me he found my

results. I punch through the air knowing if mine is still there, hers is too.

"Feel like having a beer tonight?" I say, clapping my hands together.

A few hours later and a strand of Ellie's hair in hand, I'm ready to find out if she's Everly. I had a few scenarios in my head before getting to the bar about how I would get a DNA sample, but when she walked up to our table, a strand of loose hair was hanging from her ponytail. It was as simple as that. She didn't even feel it.

Two days is all it took.

I can't stop staring down at the text I received from Stone.

Stone: It's her.

CHAPTER TEN

ELLIE

"You should say yes," Tori whispers in my ear from behind, startling me.

My cheeks heat from being caught peeking at Kase. I shake my head, loading my tray with empty bottles and follow her behind the bar. He's not too heartbroken from me saying no. "I'm sure he's moved on," I say with snark in my voice. Her lips quirk up as she finds this whole thing entertaining. My mom once told me that men do things just to get a reaction from you. If you're able to control your action, you'll always win. But I'm having a hard time controlling anything when I'm around him.

"He's doing it to make you jealous. Those girls" —she motions to the guys' table where three girls surround them— "he's talking to them, but he's not touching them. And he's sneaking glances as much as you are. You're crazy to say no to that."

If dreams are a predictor of reality, I am crazy. He's crept into them every night for the past week, leaving me craving more when I'm awake. I've been late twice this week to school because if I close my eyes for a little longer, I'll see him again. I'm tired, sexually frustrated, and irritated he has this much control over my body and I just met the man.

"You're right." She stops mid-pour, holding the vodka bottle up, waiting for me to continue. "I need to let loose. It's just shy of a year since Steve. That has to be why I'm so flustered, right? I need sex."

She snorts out a laugh. "Maybe you're flustered because you like him. Although, who am I to say no to a one-night stand. Have you seen his hands? What those strong, thick fingers—"

"Okay." I hold up my palm for her to stop talking. "First, I don't like him. I don't even know him. Second…" I stare up at the ceiling, not sure if I want to touch the last part. "You have Mr. Silver, so stop gawking at other men and their fingers." She shrugs at my laughter.

"I'm not dead," she retorts. "And you can't miss him. He's the quiet giant and not like most guys who have that much muscle. Most won't shut up about themselves or what workout they did that day."

He is definitely different. I peek over at him. Our eyes catch and he winks, a cocky smile playing on his lips. Damn it! I smile, but quickly turn my body. Tori flashes a shit-eating grin. "Shut up," I say, walking out from behind the bar again.

Even if I could follow through with a one-night stand, how would I even go about doing it? I'm not going to go up to him and slide into his lap, whispering "*I want you*" in his ear. I roll my eyes at the image. *Who does that?* Not this girl.

I pass Tori on the floor and she says, "You're welcome." Despite her happiness to help, I stare at her walking away with an exaggerated hip swing, scared at what she did. I hesitate to look, but I end up peeking over at Kase's table. Everything appears normal. Five guys that stand out in the crowd with girls eating up every word that comes out of their mouth.

"Hey Ell, can I get another," Dale, a regular, holds up his empty glass.

"You got it."

As I'm pouring his scotch, a new song comes on the jukebox. I clamp my lips together. *She did not play this.* I scan the room and when I find her, she wiggles her brows, a smug expression glowing. The song, "Save a Horse, Ride a Cowboy" by Big and Rich fills the room and I question how long she took to find a fitting song. I glance at the forgotten scotch. Liquid hits the brim of the glass, Dale gets a two for one this time. I sense Kase's eyes on me, wondering if I played this song. Do I take this orchestrated chance and run with it, or pretend it was a coincidence? Taking in a deep breath, I blow it out, lift my head, standing tall and confident, and meet his gaze. He looks at me with a bemused smile. Which, I return with a soft laugh and end our gaze with a bite of my lip.

The song continues to play for the next three minutes. Three minutes of every single nerve-ending in my body tingling with tiny electric shocks wondering if he's imagining me riding him. Which makes simple jobs, namely walking with one drink in hand, difficult.

"I'm so sorry. I wasn't watching where I was going," I say, toweling off the guy's shirt. Tori better be enjoying the show because this is her fault. I'm beyond flustered, and this damn song won't ever end. I glance up to the ceiling, does she freaking have it on repeat?

The over-stimulated air is choking me, and I've had all I can take. A drop of sweat trickles between my breasts as I walk out the back door. My body slumps against the dark grey brick building, and I take a few cleansing breaths. When the door swings open, I jump. A flurry of butterflies in the pit of my stomach erupt at the sight of Kase. My gaze sweeps up his muscular body as he saunters over.

"Tori told me you might be out here."

"Of course she did," I mutter.

His brow shoots up, and he points to the door. "I can go inside if you want me to." Instead of waiting for me to answer, he takes two steps closer moving within inches of me. "But I'd rather stay," he rasps. I can feel every line in the bricks against my back as my breathing speeds up. He leans over, the warmth of his breath tickles my ear. "Tell me you want me to stay." His smell is so intoxicating, my mouth is suddenly parched.

"Stay," I whisper.

His hands move to the brick wall on both sides of my head. "I like your song choice."

The idea of him taking me in the dark parking lot, fucking me like he did in my dreams, has heat tingling between my legs. I shift my weight from foot to foot, trying to put out that fire. This is not me. I don't understand the intense visceral reaction I have to him.

The door opens again, Tori sticks her head out. "Oh. Sorry." She winces as we both turn our heads her direction. "I was just checking on you. Carry on." She smiles, slipping inside. I lean my head against the wall, closing my eyes for a second to calm my racing pulse. The interruption brings me back to reality.

"I... I should get back to work." My words come out breathy and I bite my lip to stop myself from looking more desperate. And I thought the air inside was suffocating. He grins and does a slow nod, taking a step away from me. I want to reach for him and pull him back. "You should walk me home tonight," I murmur.

So much for not looking desperate.

His smile turns downward as his whole body stiffens. The abrupt change in his demeanor makes me stand taller. The desire in his eyes washes away, replaced with irritation. If I wasn't against the wall, I'd retreat backward.

"So, you won't go out with me, but you'll fuck me?" he snaps. "How many other men are you screwing, Ellie?"

My mouth gapes open and I'm at a loss for words as warning bells go off. Snapping it shut, I cross my arms over my chest, noticing his eyes flick to my cleavage before returning. Oh, you want this, asshole? Well, it's the closest you'll get to seeing them because the last thing I need in my life right now is a jealous psycho.

I grumble. "You know..." I pause to find the right words,

holding up my finger. Nope, there are no correct words. "Forget this ever happened." I slide passed him and stride to the door, not looking back as it slams behind me. The nerve of him. What the hell was he offering coming on to me like that. Coffee? 'I like your choice in song.' *Yeah, sounds like it.*

I slam a shot glass on the bar and fill it with tequila, ignoring Tori's quizzical expression. I wince once the hot liquid coats my throat. Most of the time, I'd have a chaser, but I welcome the burn, in the hope that it takes my mind off how much I looked like a fool.

"Um... I'm guessing there was no hot sex."

I turn and glare at her, shooting darts with my eyes. "Oh, no," I snicker. "There won't be any hot sex. He should be happy he still has a dick to have sex. But it won't be with me when he does." I pour another drink and swallow it in one gulp. A drop of liquid runs down my chin and I wipe it with the back of my hand. "That guy doesn't know what the hell he wants. He goes from hot in the pants to hot in the head in an instant." I snap my fingers and then begin to pour another drink, but Tori grabs it out of my hand, shaking her head.

"Not a good idea, Ell."

"You want to talk about ideas," I say, sarcastically, the Tequila already giving me the desired effect. Numbness. "The one you had with that song, was perfect. Next time, make sure the guy is sane before you tell him I want to ride him." My voice carries and a few guys at the bar listen. "Oh, good. I can ask you guys. If a girl, *like me*, suggested meeting after work, what would you say?" I throw my arms out.

They all mumble, "Hell yeahs."

"It's time for a break," Tori says, wrapping her arm around my waist and pulling me to the office. She yells at one of the other bartenders we'll be back. She pushes me into a chair. The adrenaline from the rejection fades, leaving me light-headed from the Tequila. I fall forward leaning on my knees, hiding my face. "What the hell happened, Ell? When I left you, you both seemed rather comfortable."

I moan. "I'm a slut." When Tori laughs out loud, I lift my head, giving her an icy glare.

"You are a far cry from a slut, sweet pea."

"Well, Kase thinks so. I mean, I threw myself at him, so he's not too far off."

"He called you a slut?" she snaps.

I sit up and exhale. "Not in those exact words, but when a guy asks you how many other guys you're screwing, it's implied."

Her eyes widen and she holds up a finger. "Be right back."

I jump off the chair, grabbing her shirt before she can leave. "Noooo. Just let it be. Please?"

"Fine. But if I accidentally pour a drink in his lap, don't be surprised." I smile and nod, knowing how hard it'll be for her to hold her tongue.

I hang out in the office for half an hour, snacking on peanuts, trying to get rid of the tipsy feeling. Tori reports that Kase never came back and the rest of Max's guys left too. I'm at least thankful for that. It makes it easier to return to work without meeting his blue eyes all night, reminding me how humiliated I am. An hour before closing, only a few people are still here, so I tell Tori I'm taking off. The new guy is still here, so she doesn't need me.

Stepping outside, I glance to the spot Kase and I were standing. I've replayed the scene in my head a hundred times tonight, wondering where it went wrong. His eyes were dark and needy, so I know he wanted me too. What changed? What did I say wrong?

Feet shuffling against the pavement and movement startle me. I scan the dark lot, chills creep up my spine. Someone jumps on me, knocking me to the ground. Hands wrap around my neck, my screams come out raspy instead of loud. I kick and hit any part of the man's body I can connect with, but each second that passes, my body gets heavier from lack of air.

One second I'm fighting for my life, the next, the guy is being yanked off me and thrown against the wall. I hear his grunts and cries, but I'm too busy gasping for air to call for help. Whoever saved me is beating the shit out of the guy behind a car. When he stands, he glances my way, and I'm frozen in place by a pair of familiar blue eyes.

Kase.

CHAPTER ELEVEN

ELLIE

My hands shake digging in my purse as I grab my keys, the only weapon I have attached to them. I take deep breaths, trying to calm the nerves vibrating throughout my body.

"Why are you pointing that at me?" he asks, staring at my hand stretched out from my body and gripping the pepper spray like it's my last lifeline. You never know, it might be. He stands a few feet away from me with his hands in the air. Surprisingly, my attacker ran to a waiting car when Kase was busy staring at me. It was his lucky day.

I squeeze my purse to my thumping heart, not daring to take my eyes off him. He's crazy if he expects me to put it away. He might be one of Max's guys, but tonight he's proven to be a little unstable.

"I just saved you."

"I'm not sure who's worse. A robber or a stalker." At least I hope it was a robber.

"Stalker?" His eyes widen as he crosses his arms. I glance around the dark parking lot he came from. "Okay, it looks bad. I wasn't hiding, I was just waiting for you to come out."

"You're not making it sound any better."

His head drops, and he stares at the asphalt, kicking a few rocks. He releases a heavy sigh and looks back up. "I was waiting out here to apologize for earlier. I saw the guy sneaking around, so I hid to see what he was up to. Had I known you were leaving early, I would've scared him off earlier."

He sounds sincere, however, my lack of judgment in the past makes me question his sincerity. Our eyes lock in a game of chicken.

A car blares its horn as it passes, scaring the hell out of me.

"Fuck!" Kase yells, folding over at the waist with his hands digging into his thighs.

The smell tickles my nose and my eyes water. "Oh no! Oh my god, Kase, I'm so sorry." My finger must've pressed the trigger when I jumped from the horn. He moans in agony while I fight with myself on what I should do. There shouldn't be a question. Regardless of what happened tonight, I need to take him inside so he can wash his eyes out, but his words from earlier hit deeper than they should have. *Get a grip, Ell and help the guy.*

I throw the spray in my purse and run to his side. "Come on, I'll take you inside."

Unlocking the back door, I usher him in. When he coughs and wheezes, I panic, he's going to die and it's my fault. "Should I call 911?"

"No. Just… need water," his voice breaks. My hand rests on his tense back as I lead him to the sink in the stockroom and he shoves his whole head under the water. I stand back and watch him. Curse words fly out of his mouth in between coughs. I grimace and wrap my arms around my waist, mortified I caused this. He strips off his shirt in one quick tug and washes his arms off.

I'm a horrible human being. I maced the guy whose insides are on fire, and I'm standing here admiring his gorgeous body. A tribal tattoo on his left shoulder, usually hidden under his shirt, is on full display. His hands, full of soap, move hastily up and down each muscular arm. I turn away, the heat building deep in my belly catches me off guard. I need to shut down my gawking. The last thing I need right now is to be caught staring. Instead, I grab some clean towels from the cabinet and place them on the sink.

"Here," I whisper. He reaches for them and dries off. "There's a cot you can sit on." He nods and walks over to the empty spot, sits and leans against the wall, still breathing heavy and coughing. "I'm so sorry. I didn't mean to spray it."

He waves his hand in the air. "It's okay. I've been through worse. I just need to let it wear off." His voice is raspy from the chemicals and his blood-shot eyes catch mine. His eyes travel up my arm to my hand and he smirks. I stop my finger mid-twirl and release the hair wrapped around it. Damn habit. Most of the time I'm not even aware I'm doing it.

"You want something to drink?" I ask awkwardly, folding and unfolding my arms around me. He stays quiet but nods his head. "Okay, be right back."

I deflate as soon as I'm out of the stockroom. Tori's eyes widen when she sees me. She rushes over and grabs my chin, lifting it so she can see my neck. "Who the hell did that? Did Kase do that?" she snaps.

I step back and shake my head then run to the mirror behind the bar to see what she's talking about. Bruises are already surfacing. Tears burn my eyes, memories forthcoming. Someone attacked me. *God, I hope it wasn't him.* It can't be. He couldn't have found me. Taking a deep inhale, I push those thoughts back.

"Ell, what happened?"

I rehash everything that happened, including accidentally macing Kase. "We're getting cameras back there. Do you want me to call the police?"

"You know I can't. I promise I won't go back there by myself again."

She nods in understanding. It's too dangerous. I can't have my name on record.

I reach into the fridge and grab a Shiner for him and an Ultra for me. Twisting the top off my beer, I take a quick swallow, propping my hip against the counter. What am I going to do about Kase?

My jealous admirer.

My stalker.

My hero.

All in one day.

The sound of coughing reminds me he's still in the stockroom. "Sorry. I needed a second," I say, handing him his beer. He chugs the entire beer in one gulp, handing the bottle right back. Okay then. His breathing has stabilized although his face and eyes are still tomato red. He rests against the wall again. "Do you want another one?" I hold up the empty beer bottle.

"Nah. I'm fine. Thanks. But we should call the cops." His tone turns sharp, his eyes pinned on my neck.

Letting out an uneasy sigh, I shake my head. "It'll be useless. There's not a security camera back there, and I didn't get a good look at the guy." My words are rushed as I try to talk my way out of that phone call. I can't have him call the cops.

His eyes narrow and I force my body from fidgeting. "I got a good look at him," he says in a challenge, lifting a brow.

"Kase," I sigh. "Please don't. I want to forget about tonight. You taught the guy a lesson. I'm sure he won't be back." My eyes plead with him.

"If he's stupid enough to come back, he's not leaving next time." There's not an ounce of threat in there. It's a promise. His boyish looks are replaced with an icy stare. I nod in silent understanding, hoping he'll let this go for now. Silence hangs between us until he finally nods once.

I grab a wooden chair and sit facing him, taking a quick drink. "Are your face and eyes still burning?" I crinkle my nose, still hating that I caused this.

"It's getting better. I still can't see far away, so unless you want to drive me home, we're hanging out here."

I tilt my head, surprised by the quick change in his voice. "Don't you live right around here? I thought you lived in the same apartments as Cody?" His smirk confirms I'm right. Only because I feel horrible, I let it slide. "So, Cowboy, tell me what happened earlier because I'm confused."

He sighs, looking down at his raw hands. I do a double take, having missed them. "Do you need ice?"

He shakes his head and rubs the back of his neck. "About earlier, I'm sorry. Something you said reminded me of someone and I was totally out of line asking you that."

"Sister, girlfriend, wife?"

He barks out a deep laugh. "I'm doing something wrong if you think you remind me of a sister." I shrug, not understanding how he sees me. Flirty, jealous, protective, angry... he's been all over the place. "She was my girlfriend," he finally answers. He's harboring some deep-seated feelings toward this girlfriend.

"Was?"

"Was. Many, many years ago."

"You have a lot of unresolved feelings if it was *many, many* years ago." He slowly nods. "What happened?"

"She forgot about me."

Ouch. I wonder if it had something to do with him being in the military.

"I have a hard time believing any woman could forget you." The words fall out of my mouth before I can stop them. My cheeks heat, I take a quick drink of beer, avoiding his sexy grin. This shouldn't come as a surprise to him considering I offered for him to come over tonight.

"Ellie, go out with me."

"Kase, I'm not sure that's a good idea after what happened." Despite his jealous outburst, there's no denying the chemistry between us. Yet, there's a foreign wedge I don't know if I can remove. And I wonder if he's ready to do it himself.

"Let me make it up to you for being an asshole."

"I wasn't lying before, I have so much going—"

"It's the least you could do," he says, interrupting me.

My mouth drops open. "Really? You're going to guilt me into going on a date with you?"

"If it works, hell yeah." He crosses his feet on the cot and folds his hands in his lap. "Is it working?"

I twist my lips thinking what could it hurt going out with him one time. He did save me and then had to endure torture.

Yes, it's working.

"One date. That's it."

CHAPTER TWELVE

ELLIE

"Why am I so nervous?" I ask, staring into the mirror, holding up a black dress that hits me at my knees and swapping it with a blue dress that shows a little more. More legs. More boobs. But it makes my eyes pop.

"I love the blue one," Tori states. I glance at her through the mirror.

"Of course you do."

She ruffles through my jewelry, ignoring me. "If it were me, I wouldn't wear panties. One glance from him and they'll melt right off, anyway." I focus on the black bra and lace panties I'm wearing. Probably a little too direct to forgo the panties, but I chose the blue dress.

I step into the dress, shimmying my body into it. Tori comes up behind me, zips it up, and then holds up a pair of silver dangle earrings against my earlobes. "Have you ever been on a real date?"

"Ha-ha," I snicker. "Yes. Just not anytime recently. I'm busy with school."

"That's what you continue to say."

"I. Am." Spinning with my hands on my hips, I glare at her. "Having a boyfriend complicates things. This is my last semester before I graduate. After that, I'll worry about a relationship. And you know about my history. I... can't yet."

She narrows her eyes at me. "So, why did you accept this date?"

"I almost killed the guy. What choice did I have?"

She shakes her head at me, not believing a word I'm saying. There's an attraction to the guy, but it doesn't mean I'm ready for a relationship. It's just a date. One. Date. My phone dings on my dresser and butterflies tickle my insides. He said he'd text me when he arrived. Tori reaches it before I do, waving it around, striding into the living room with it in her hand.

"Time to take a magic carpet ride, baby doll."

I snatch the phone, laughing. "You're a nerd." She smiles wide, plopping down on my couch. "You going into work?" I ask while making certain everything I need is in my purse.

"Of course. What else do I have to do?" She sighs dramatically. I stop fiddling with my purse and peek up through my lashes.

"Yeah, your life is so monotonous." She flashes a sly grin. It's not boring at all. She has a boyfriend that takes her out on his yacht or flies her to random exotic destinations a couple of times a month for the weekends. I'm not jealous of Ben, *or Mr. Silver as we call him,* our nickname for him because he's older than her by ten years and rich, but I am envious of what she does with him. I've lost count how many times he's asked her to marry him. She loves him, but she likes her freedom too. He'll need to strap her to a gurney to get her to the altar.

Tap tap tap. I smooth my dress, glance down to make sure my boobs aren't sticking out and ask, "Do I look okay?" I shake out my hands, my nerves jumping into overdrive. Why am I so wound up?

"Stunning, Ell. Calm down. Like you said, it's only a date."

Taking a deep breath, I blow out my anxieties and open the door. Our eyes meet, and I can feel the thrum of my pulse as my heart picks up speed. His eyes work their way down my body, leaving a trail of heat.

"Wow," he murmurs, his eyes blaze. "You look amazing."

He's only seen me in my work uniform, black shorts and a black tank, with Ocean's sprawled across my boobs. My dark hair is loose and curled, unlike the bun it's normally in. I even pulled out makeup which I normally don't make time for between work and school.

I stop at the elevator and tilt my head in confusion as he keeps walking. Once he realizes I'm not by his side, he turns around. "Where're you going?"

He flashes a boyish grin and shrugs. "I don't do elevators."

I glance at the mirrored doors and back at him. "Are you claustrophobic?" I'd be surprised if he said yes considering he was a SEAL.

His incredulous laugh confirms my thoughts that it's crazy. "No. I don't like to feel trapped in a box."

"Isn't that the definition of claustrophobia?"

He licks his bottom lip and it's sexy as hell even though he didn't mean for it to be. "It's more about the loss of control than the confined space."

I bob my head back and forth, kind of understanding. Although, not enough to make me take the stairs every day. I join him, walking down the six flights of stairs. I'm grateful we're going down instead of up. That might be embarrassing.

He holds the door to the garage open for me, the smell of his cologne greets me as I pass. I close my eyes for a moment, reveling in the scent. I'm in so much trouble if his scent is getting to me. When he stops at a motorcycle - a beautiful black Harley - I peer down at my fitted dress and heels and glance back up to meet his uncertain expression.

"We don't have—"

"I can go—"

We both say at the same moment. He chuckles and says, "We don't need to take this, I'll grab Cody's car."

"No," I say quickly. I've never been on a bike, but it's happening tonight. "I'll go change." I hold up a finger and take a couple of steps back before pivoting on my heels. "Don't go anywhere," I yell over my shoulder.

"That would be stupid of me," he yells back. I turn and smile at him, he winks in response.

Damn. Damn. Damn. I'm ready to jump into the visible flames he's putting off.

I dash into my apartment. Tori stands in my bedroom doorway as I shimmy into my skinny jeans, not yet taking off my dress. "See, I told you, a magic carpet ride."

I stop mid-zip and glare at her as realization dawns on me by what she meant. "You knew he had a motorcycle?"

With a taunt of a smile, she shrugs unapologetically.

"Really, Tori? You even told me not to wear panties."

She hums. "How hot that ride would be? Maybe I should talk Mr. Silver into getting a motorcycle."

"Oh my god. You are a nymphomaniac."

This shouldn't surprise me coming from a woman who doesn't wear a bathing suit when out on the yacht and all the places her and Mr. Silver have had sex out in the open. She's as comfortable naked as she is with clothes on, but I'm not. I'd rather the lights be turned off. The scars have always made me self-conscious.

The royal blue silk tank glides down my torso. It's still sexy and date-worthy. Boots in the summer sound as good as hot chocolate on a steaming, muggy day so I grab wedges out of my closet. At least they won't fall off my feet.

I glance at the stair exit and I smirk. Nope, not this time. I'll break my ankle trying to do the stairs right now.

Kase is sitting on his motorcycle when I return, messing with his phone. "Hey stranger, can you give me a lift?"

His thumbs stop moving, and his lips turn up as he mumbles

something to himself. When he lifts his head, he flashes a sly grin. I can't ignore the flush of heat burning deep in my core. I should have kept my dress on. *Without panties.*

"Where you headed?" His words are playful, but his eyes are full of fire. I try to ignore his heated stare, but it's always been hard for me to turn away from danger. And Kase is dangerous. I've seen how he interacts with other people. He's intense, reserved, yet doesn't back away from a fight. He's nothing like that with me, which makes me question everything about him. It also draws me in and makes me want to know who the real Kase is.

"Wherever you want to take me."

"Damn, woman. Don't tell me that." He grabs a helmet off his handlebar and lifts it over my head. I pull my hair back before he pops it down. His warm fingers graze my jaw as he snaps my chin-straps together. I shiver involuntarily and heat rushes to my cheeks. He flashes a knowing smile and bites his lip and it's damn sexy. "You have no idea what you're getting yourself into." He twists his body to grab his helmet. "Hop on," he says over his shoulder.

Feeling nervous, excited, and slightly aroused, I swing my leg over and straddle the seat. I hold on to the seat behind me, not knowing if I'm supposed to wrap my arms around him. "I tried to say no. You wouldn't let me."

"Ellie, you didn't try very hard." His laugh echoes in the quiet garage until he floods it out with the buzz of his bike. Instinctively, I wrap my arms around his waist, not caring what I'm supposed to do. The press of my body against his, the rumble of the bike between my legs and the adrenaline of being on a motorcycle has my body tingling with little volts of electricity. I'm more alive right now than I've been in years.

The wind rushes around us as we zip by the coast and the sun sets low in the sky behind us. The engine roars louder as Kase pushes it to go a little faster. My hands tighten around his waist and I can feel the shake of his laughter. I pinch him, and he retaliates by reaching around, grabbing my ass. Fear spikes through me. Keep your hands on the handles!

"Noooo!" I yell and tap him on his stomach. I release a sigh of relief when both his hands are where they're supposed to be. After about a twenty-minute ride, Kase pulls into a small beach-side restaurant. It's a cute, tiki-hut style restaurant with bright lights, beach themed decor and a patio that wraps around the entire restaurant.

Kase parks and takes off his helmet. "This okay?"

I lift off my helmet, hand it to him and shake out my hair. "Yes! I've never been here." North of Gilley Cove is new to me as I don't venture out this way. He helps me off and I rub the inside of my thighs, not used to the vibration between my legs. Well... for that long.

He slips his hand in mine, with no hesitation. He's worried if I'll like the restaurant, yet holding my hand is not up for discussion. I steal a quick glance up to him and he winks. The confident man leads me inside and I can't help the butterflies tingling in my belly.

"Reservation for Nixon," he says to the blonde hostess. Reservation? The restaurant is what I imagined it to be. Laid-back and casual. Typically, this is not the type of place that takes reservations.

"Right this way, Mr. Nixon." Kase's hand stays on my lower back as we follow her through the restaurant. I'm excited they're seating us on the patio. The sun hasn't disappeared yet, leaving a soft pink glow across the horizon. When we keep going, past the patio, I glance at Kase, confused. He nods his head forward and I follow it to a single table set up by the water. Candles flicker on the table from the soft breeze coming off the ocean.

He pulls out my seat for me and helps me scoot forward in the sand. When he whips my folded up napkin and lays it in my lap, I stare up at him in bewilderment. He rounds the table and sits, repeating the motion with his napkin. I'm caught off guard by his chivalry.

He takes a sip of his water, looking at me over the rim of the glass. "What?" he asks, lowering his glass.

"You surprise me."

He leans back in his chair, chuckling. "Why is that?"

I spread my arms out, looking out to the ocean and back to his amused smirk. "This. I never pictured you being a romantic guy."

Well, that sounded a bit judgmental and came out totally wrong. He nods twice, his fingers twisting his lower lip. "Why type of guy do you think I am?"

Domineering alpha. My cheeks heat at my first thoughts. "I don't know. Not this."

His eyebrow lifts and he leans forward on the table, reading through my bullshit. "You seem to have formed an opinion of me, Ellie."

I release an awkward laugh, glancing back up the beach, hoping a waiter is about to show up. They're never here when you need them. He waits for me to answer, a slight tick at the corner of his mouth. "You're confident, slightly arrogant, with a tough guy attitude. Sweet and romantic, not so much. Dominant and alpha, definitely."

He shrugs one shoulder. "I go after what I want." A shiver runs up my back as he locks eyes with me. "And one doesn't negate the other," he rasps.

We're interrupted by the waiter. *Finally.*

I notice I'm fanning myself with the menu as I'm placing my order. I shove it into the hands of the waiter, rolling my eyes. The heat coming from his words seeps into my skin, leaving me wanting more. It's irritating I can't control it. I kick off my sandals and dig my feet into the cool sand, seeking any relief I can find.

"You're not used to the word no, are you?"

His lips twist as he glances up to the sky, mulling it over internally. Finally, he answers, "I'm just persuasive."

"Ha! Remember, the only reason I'm here is out of guilt." I sit back, cross my arms and smile sweetly at him.

"Is that the only reason?"

I want to answer yes. I want to prove to myself that he doesn't affect me like he does. But when he cocks his eyebrow up and flashes a smile to match, my confidence wavers about what I want.

CHAPTER THIRTEEN

ELLIE

"You mentioned you were in school?" He leans back in his chair, giving me his full attention.

I nod, holding up a finger while I finish eating the piece of bread I stuffed into my mouth. I'm still hungry after the salad I had for dinner. Why did I order a freaking salad? I've never had a problem eating in front of a man. Then again, I've never been this nervous on a date either. "I am. Thankfully, I'm almost done. My major is Photo Journalism."

"You like taking pictures?"

"I like telling stories through my pictures. The school project I created has turned into a passion of mine. One I hope to continue after I graduate."

He gestures with his hands for me to continue. "Tell me more about this project."

I smile. Is he for real, or is he playing me? He seems too perfect. He's attentive, he's polite, he's sexy... he's single. Why? Was his fit of jealousy the other day his real personality? Because I'm not seeing a hint of that guy today. And it's confusing the hell out of me.

"What?" He eyes me with a quizzical look.

"Do you hate animals? Or snore really loud?"

His laugh is heady and sexy, and I feel guilty for trying to find a flaw as he entertains my doubt. "I'm certain I don't snore. The guys on my team would've let me know." He chuckles to himself and I assume he's talking about his military team because he doesn't room with any of Max's team. "Not a fan of cats, but I love dogs."

That's it! He hates cats. Then again, so do I.

"Why?" he muses.

"Why are you single?"

Why are you so interested in me? Since day one, he's been hell-bent on winning me over. He could have any woman. One who isn't broken. Tori's words float through my head, 'You deserve to be happy.' Although this may be true, it's the person I'm with that doesn't deserve to be saddled down with my past. When they find out the truth, they won't stay.

"I guess I haven't found the one, yet."

Keep searching, because you won't find her here.

He narrows his eyes as if he read my mind. I quickly look down and butter my bread, or try to. The melted butter drips off the foil paper onto my lap and I mutter a few curse words under my breath. Trying to accomplish simple tasks around him seems to be impossible.

"Need help?"

I peek up from blotting my jeans with the napkin. "Anything to get your hands between my legs, huh?" I say jokingly without thinking.

He licks his lips and shakes his head. "I meant buttering your bread."

I flush and squeeze my eyes shut wishing I could take back my words. "But I like where your head is at."

I try to laugh it off, folding the napkin in my lap. "So, how about we go back to talking about my project?" The slight tip of his head is all I need to move on. "It's about…. When women are…" I keep pausing, searching for the right words. "It's hard to explain. Rather, it's something you need to see. The project is called You are the Light."

"Something I have to see?"

"I'll show you when you drop me off." He flashes a disarming smile and I think about what I said to make him smile like that. "My project. I'll show you my project," I clarify.

"Well, I can't wait to see it." His genuine interest makes me like him a little more. "You're not from here, are you?"

I hesitate, peering past him out in the ocean. The waves gently roll up the beach. This is why I don't date. His question slams into me like a brick wall, waking me up to the reality I can't commit to someone right now.

"Ellie?"

"I'm from Texas." Despite the building anxiety, I answer. Small details won't open the floodgates from my past. I open my mouth to ask him where he's from but snap it shut. If I ask him a question, it opens the door to more questions. *More lies.*

"I could tell."

I've tried my hardest to lose my accent, but the damn thing won't go away. "I could say the same thing about you, Cowboy." His accent is a lot more prevalent than mine. He's certainly from the south.

"Yes ma'am," he says with a heavy accent that makes me laugh. "What brought you to Gilley Cove?"

"I came out here with my dad and I fell in love with it. I didn't want to leave, so I didn't."

He sits forward in his chair. "Do your parents live here too?"

"No. They still live in Texas." I sense he wants to ask more, so I change the subject. "You were in the military? Right?"

"Navy."

"Were you on a ship the whole time?"

Chuckling, he replies, "No." He's quiet for a moment, his attention pulled out to the ocean. I run my finger down the condensation of my water glass, wondering if he'll say more. It's obvious neither of us want to talk about our past. I stay quiet to let him gather his thoughts. Who am I to pressure him into talking? His gaze meets mine again and the intensity in his eyes makes me question if he had a bad experience in the military. I know all about PTSD, but I don't have firsthand knowledge of people in the military and what they deal with overseas.

"Should I call you Popeye?" I say to lighten the mood.

He belts out a laugh and shakes his head. "Cowboy is fine." His features soften, the tension fades. "Do you enjoy swimming?"

"In a pool, yes. In the ocean, not so much." Living creatures grazing my legs and not noticing if they're about to make me dinner scares the hell out of me. Nope, no thank you.

He grips his chest in mock horror. "I'm going to have to rethink our relationship," he jokes.

"I wouldn't call what we have a relationship."

He leans in a little and whispers, "Yet." His eyes drop to my mouth, and the spoken promise makes me fidget in my seat. "I'll make you love the ocean."

Shaking my head, I say, "I doubt it." He pushes his chair back and stands up, towering over the table. His wicked smile sends warning bells through me. "Wh… what are you doing?" I stutter.

I place my napkin on the table, not taking my eyes off him. The live band's music comes off the patio. Darkness surrounds us now except for the scattered tiki torches lit on the beach from here to the top. The fire from a torch behind me reflects in his eyes as he takes a step toward me. I push my chair back, knocking it back, and move to the opposite side of him. "Kase," I warn, holding up my hands. "How about we play around in the water, during the day?"

"There is plenty of light with the moon. Night swimming is the best."

Says the SEAL, I snicker to myself.

He stays rooted in his spot, studying me. "Oh shit! A whale," he exclaims, pointing out to the water.

I spin on my heels. "Where?"

Stupid, stupid, Ell.

He pounces like a tiger. I scream as I'm tossed over his shoulder, and he runs toward the water. Cheers from the restaurant float down to us. This guy could be attempting to kill me, and they are cheering him on.

"Kase, don't you dare!" I yell, slapping him on the ass as he gets closer to the dark waters. When water covers his feet, he stops. "Put me down, Cowboy." I try for stern, but being upside down, it comes out more strangled.

He leans forward so I can hop off. The cool water tickles my feet and my toes sink in the soft sand. I slap him in the chest, but I can't pull my hand back. "Jerk, you tricked me," I say, my voice losing its fight. He stares down at me as he lifts his hand to sweep my wild hair blowing in the wind behind my ear. His fingers graze my ear and work their way down the curve of my neck. I lean into his touch.

"I told you, I'll use every means necessary to get what I want."

Leaning down, his lips caress mine as he keeps the kiss soft and sweet. They linger on my lips, his fingers press into my lower back, and he's wavering on the line of losing control. I slide my hand up his chest, wrapping it around his neck, pulling him down into me, daring him to cross that line. He deepens the kiss, our tongues dance with each other and I melt in his arms. The world slips away and I wonder if he knows how all-encompassing he is. The need to back away dissolves. He feels safe in my unsafe world. I revel in the feeling knowing it won't stay.

When he breaks away from the kiss, he leans his forehead against mine. "That was worth the wait," he mumbles, embracing me in his strong arms and giving me a warm hug. The gentle embrace catches me off guard. It's not sexual, and it's not goodbye.

It's a hello hug you give someone you haven't seen in a long time.

I pull back and his eyes flash down to mine, his body tenses as he studies me. With a slight tick at the corner of my mouth, I ask, "Did I make you wait that long?"

"I've been dreaming about your lips on mine since the day I met you."

I touch my lips, still swollen from his, and spin to walk back up to our table so he can't read the emotions written all over my face. I try to hide that I want him as much as he wants me, try to hide my fears about my past, preventing me from moving forward and try to hide my heart, where it's been the last ten years, hidden behind scar tissue.

Slipping my shoes on, I stand tall, staring back up the beach. Why does he have to be so perfect? His chest hits my back, yet he doesn't reach for me. I close my eyes wondering how the moment got intense so fast. His uneven sigh has me turning around. "I didn't mean to scare you off." His confident voice wavers with panic as he searches my eyes for answers. I shouldn't have turned around. Not yet. "What are you afraid of, Ellie?"

You. Me. Everything.

I let out a soft sigh and look away from the intensity in his eyes, avoiding the question I can't answer. "I can't fall for you, Kase."

When I lift my gaze and meet his, there's understanding there to something he has no idea about. It's unnerving to think he can see into my past.

"The last thing I want is for you to fall and get hurt."

I swallow the lump in my throat, hating what he's implying. Hating myself for feeling upset over his reaction when I'm the one ruining this. "Are you saying you'd hurt me?" I whisper.

"Never. I'd be here to catch you. But I can't make you like me." My lip twitches. It's too late, I already do. After a few silent beats, he tips his head up the beach. "C'mon, I'll take you home."

I'm thankful we're on a bike so we don't have to talk. White lights blur as we pass them, the cooler night air blanketing us. The long ride helps me work through the tight ball of what-ifs knotted up inside me. I think back to the last ten years, where backing away from men came easy, none holding my attention long enough to want more. One date with Kase and I'm reevaluating everything.

Maybe, he'd accept my past.

Maybe, he wouldn't need to know about my past.

Maybe, he'd accept our future.

I groan knowing there isn't a man alive who would accept any of that—regardless of how hard I want to try. His hand covers mine, and he squeezes it. My heart tells me he's answering yes, my head is telling me not to be so naïve, it's just a sweet gesture.

Kase leans against the parked bike in the parking garage, giving me space, waiting for me to make the first move. He looks downright sinful. If I had my camera, I'd snap a shot so I could study it, search for his story in those blue eyes. I step forward in between his legs and press my lips to his. It's a soft, chaste kiss, knowing if I lean into it anymore, I won't be able to stop. I know I told him I'd show him my project, but if I invite him in, I'll be showing him more than just pictures.

"Thank you. I had a great time tonight."

His hands relax on my hips, thumbs gently stroking small targets that shoot an arrow of desire straight through me. I step out of his grasp, the air around us thickening. His arrogant smile a reminder that the man sees everything. He's just going to sit back and wait for me to come to him. I'm usually not the sheep. It scares the hell out of me that my body doesn't care if he's the shepherd or the wolf. Either way, I'll be his. How do I fight this instinctual pull? A spark of hope builds, if I give in and let him own me, will my past release its hold on me?

"I did too. If only you'd let me take you out again?"

I don't know if it's the spark inside me, growing into a flame each second our eyes lock, but it surprises me when I answer so quickly, "If you're lucky."

His eyes brighten when he laughs out loud, lifting his leg over his bike and revving it up. My entire body tingles from the vibration, watching him straddle his bike, his muscular arms flexing with each rev. "Ellie," he rasps. "I'm the luckiest man alive." My heart quickens and I'm pretty sure I'm in over my head. There's no turning back now.

I'm the sheep.

CHAPTER FOURTEEN

KASE

I STARE AT THE NUMBER FLASHING ON MY CELL PHONE. SAME NUMBER as the last three calls. You need to get a hold of me, leave a message, it's not a hard concept. I toss it back into the console and pick up the binoculars. To focus my eyes, I twist the center, adjust the magnification until I have what I'm searching for in my sight. "Bingo," I mutter to myself.

"The subject is at home," I say. Hudson and Stone acknowledge me in my earpiece. My job... warn the guys if he leaves. It seems Dr. Lawson might have a dangerous habit of prescribing narcotics to young women who don't need it. We have to prove he's working with a man we think is the leader of a sex ring here in Boston. A high-profile judge hired us because his seventeen-year-old daughter's been missing for a week. We're almost certain that's what happened to her. Although, finding her might be trickier the way these organizations work. Dr. Lawson was her psychologist. This isn't the first time his name has come up in missing cases. My finger itches to put a hole through his head reading the allegations. He's been smart hiding his indiscretions. But he's not that good. We'll find something.

The bad thing with stakeouts, having too much time to pick

apart my date with Ellie. I wish I wasn't so perceptive sometimes. I could detect the war in her eyes. The way they would flash green one second and turn ice blue the next. The way I scared her by opening my big fat mouth. I can't believe I slipped, but I made up for it when I told her I was backing away. She wants me, although she needs to learn to trust me, so I'll sit back and wait. A skill I've perfected — waiting until I have the perfect shot.

She'll land right in my arms.

"Wrapping up," Cody's voice rings in my ear. "Meet you back at station nine."

Station nine is code for Max's house. Each of the guys check in before we log off. My phone rings and I roll my eyes when it's the same number. I touch the answer button and bring the phone to my ear. "What?"

"Oh… Um… Is Kase Nixon there?" a weasel voice stutters on the other end.

"You keep calling my phone, who the hell else would answer?"

"Oh, Hi Mr. Nixon, my name is Joey Davidson with Kelson and Davidson. I'm the attorney of record on your trust account. I'm calling regarding your mineral rights. We've been contacted by an oil company and they are interested in leasing a part of those rights."

"What does that involve?" I own all the mineral rights in Barrow, but I don't understand how they work. It was part of the trust that became available this year. They contacted me on my twenty-eighth birthday and requested an account number. Money shows up each month, I don't ask questions. I detest that town and all the memories tied to it. I'd be content to sell the whole damn town. But it's not all mine. At least, not yet. And it might be awhile until that part of my trust is released.

The conversation is short. He lost me when he talked about maps and mineral acres. I make a mental note to hire a land broker. The less I think about Barrow, the better. Instead, I fantasize about Ellie and her lips, specifically on me.

I'm the last to arrive. When I step inside, I hear the guys in the kitchen, cabinets slamming and glass bottles hitting the counters. I stand by waiting to see if anyone acknowledges that I'm here. My adrenaline spikes when no one comes out. My hands grow warm from rubbing them together as I form a plan. I slip out to my bike, grabbing what I need and then search for a way to climb on top of the separate garage. I send two preemptive texts so I won't get killed. Then, I lie low and wait.

"Where the hell is Kase? The SUV he took out to Boston is here," Cody says, striding down the steps. Stone, Hudson, and Oscar follow him outside, stepping onto the grass. I lay my head down, draw in the excitement running rampant in my body. I can't miss. They'd never let me forget that. They form around my bike, glancing around the property.

I peer through the scope, finding my target. Squeeze the trigger five times.

The guys duck. "What the hell!" Stone screams, his ass lands on the ground and he stares down at his shirt. Blue paint covers his white shirt.

"Your reflexes aren't that fast." I pop up, throwing my arms out. Hudson and Cody burst out in laughter over Stone's red face.

"Son, you have a death wish," Oscar says, shaking his head while he wanders back inside the house. Oscar's the dad of the group and he's quick to lecture.

"You assholes knew about this?" Stone grumbles, standing up and dusting the dirt off his jeans. They both shake their head and shrug. "Fucking liars. You're going down, Nixon," he mutters, stomping up the steps.

"I need to get a paint gun," Hudson declares. "That was legit."

———

"WHAT THE HELL do I pay you people for?" I glance up and Max is standing by Cody, slapping him on the back.

"Boss man, it's good to see you're still alive," Cody jokes. Max swings a chair from the neighboring table to ours, straddling it. He looks at me and smiles.

"Figured I'd find you all here." I lean back and listen to the guys bullshit, realizing how lucky I am to be a part of this team. "Hear you've been messing with Stone," he says, looking at me with an approving smile. I smirk, raising my beer in mock cheers and take a drink. "It's about time someone has the balls to do it."

"Hey! I have a steel set of balls," Cody chimes in, grabbing his dick. "But I'm afraid he'll make me a woman in every computer in this universe."

"Just remember that, asshole, when you think of trying something," Stone points at him. His finger motions in my direction. "I'm thinking of how to get this asshole back." I laugh, winking at him. What's more fun than a little brotherly rivalry? I miss my SEAL team and the shit we used to do to entertain ourselves.

"Well, look what the cat drug in," Tori says, rounding the table, giving Max a hug. I get up to hit the bathroom. When I step out of the hallway, Tori stops me, handing me a napkin.

"I swear I washed them," I joke, holding my hands out. "You want to smell 'em?" I recall Everly used to always do that after coming out of the bathroom just to make sure I washed. I shake my head at the memory, how weird to associate the memory to one name and now making new memories with a different name, but same person. It's confusing.

She wrinkles up her nose and jerks back. "No. Ell called and begged me to send over food since she's too busy studying." A stupid grin stretches across my face as I reach for the napkin. She flicks it back. "Don't make me regret this Kase. I like you. *Right now.* But you screw with her, you will regret it."

I nod, happy that Ellie has a friend like her. "I promise I won't hurt her." If anyone gets hurt, it'll be me. She flicks the napkin forward and I snatch it. I glance up from the napkin, confused. "Do you serve this here?"

"Not unless I'm hiding a sushi chef in the back," she snickers. "I figured if you will take her something, it might as well be something she really likes."

An hour later with dinner in hand, I wonder when she started liking sushi. She hated it when she was a teenager. *She's different now.* I need to stop looking for similarities and focus on the woman she is today. It's been two weeks since our first date. Our schedules have been hectic, preventing a second, so I'm indebted to Tori for this. I only hope Ellie doesn't mind.

"Hey," she says, answering the door. "What are you doing here?"

I hold up the bag of sushi and her eyes widen. "Thought you might be hungry."

Her face transforms, one eyebrow lifts up. "Actually, I just ate."

I bite my lip from laughing, knowing she's lying. "Hmm. Guess I'm having sushi alone tonight." I shrug, and turn around to walk away, but she lunges forward, seizing my shirt.

"Okay, I lied. I'm starving."

I hide the amused smile on my face when I turn and mosey into her apartment. Papers are scattered across the living room floor, so I place the food on the dining table.

"So, how long have you and Tori been best buddies?"

I chuckle, leaning back in a chair with my legs spread out and my arms behind my head. "Not sure what you mean?"

"I call bullshit. You don't just show up with food…" She peeks at the writing outside the Styrofoam boxes. "My exact favorite rolls, after I called Tori telling her I was starving."

I shrug. "I might've had a little birdie tell me."

"More like a big mouth parrot, who likes to repeat things," she snickers, taking off the plastic lids. "But I appreciate it. I needed a break from studying." I watch her open the soy sauce packets, pouring them in a small cup and add wasabi to it, mixing it together and then rearrange her sushi in front of her. Her blue eyes peek up through her lashes and she softly smiles. "I feel as if you're studying me."

Always. Every move you make, I take note.

"I'm just enjoying your very methodical way of eating sushi."

When she takes her first bite, she moans. I try to ignore the sound, tapping my chopsticks on the table, making them even. As I'm dipping a piece into soy sauce, another moan comes out and I drop my sushi into the bowl. I glance at her. "You have to stop making those noises," I rasp, adjusting my shorts to make room for my semi-hard dick. Her cheeks redden, and she bites her bottom lip.

Fuck! Stop doing that too!

"I'm sorry. My stomach has been yelling at me to eat something for the past two hours. Thank you for bringing it."

"You should taste the sushi in Tokyo. It's amazing. The freshest sushi you'll ever have."

"I can imagine. Then again, it's probably better I not go, I'd hate to ruin my love for it here." She brings another bite to her mouth. When she finishes, she asks, "Have you been to a lot of places?"

I nod, thinking about the places I could never tell her. There are too many to count. "Most weren't glamorous though."

She lets out a quiet hum and twirls her hair. I wonder what she's thinking to make her nervous. "Are you doing okay? I would imagine being away from all that and dealing with…" She hesitates, winces and looks away. "You don't have to answer. I just—"

I lay my hand on hers to calm her fidgetiness. "I'm doing all right. I have my moments, but mostly, I'm good." I flash a reassuring smile. My nightmares aren't meant to be shared. They're becoming less frequent these days.

I can't help but use this moment to see if she'll share a little with me. "How did you get this?" I gently pull my thumb down her forearm, tracing the four-inch scar. She pulls her arm back, cradles it against her stomach.

"I was in an accident. Years ago." Her voice is calm, but the way her body tenses, her eyes dilate, I can tell she's nervous. She chews the inside of her cheek, debating if she'll tell me more. "Sorry." She shakes her head and looks away. "I don't like talking about it."

I inwardly cringe. *Why did I bring it up?* We're moving forward, I can't have her slide back, doubt creeping back into her head. "Hey, that's okay. Look, I've got a shitload of scars," I say, lifting my shirt and pointing at one. Her eyes widen, and she lets outs a small gasp.

"Is that a bullet wound?" She reaches across the table, her fingers glide over the glossy circle.

"One of three," I reply, focusing on the wound and not her touch, sparking life into the nerveless skin.

"Kase." She looks at me, worry etched in her expression. She's testing my self-control being so close and touching me. I want to pull those pouty lips to mine and devour them. Remind her how right we fit together. Instead, I pull her fingers off and drop my shirt.

"It came with the job."

"So, everything, I read about you is true?"

That depends on who you ask. The damn internet. Full of lies and truths, often a mixture of both, a constant brew of mishmash bullshit that people always take at face value. "I wouldn't say everything. I never wrestled a leopard in Afghanistan."

Her laugh is everything. I don't like talking about things I did. It was a job, one I don't regret, but to someone who wasn't in that situation, they might not see things the way I did.

I'm a trained killer.

The man who attacked her a few weeks ago, I could've snapped his neck in two seconds flat. I wouldn't have been able to get close to her having to deal with the aftermath of killing a man. After losing control with my dad, I swore to myself it'd never happen again.

"Does it scare you?" *Do I scare you?* "What you've read about me?"

She hums, picking at a piece of rice on her plate before finding my eyes. "No, actually the opposite, you make me feel safe."

Music to my ears.

"Scars are a reminder of our journey, of who we are today; a reminder of the days we were our strongest."

She puffs out a scoff. "I'm not so sure about that." I hate she has insecurities. She has to see how strong she is. I stop myself from reaching out to her as she picks up my empty plate and goes into the kitchen. Her fingers wrap around the counter ledge as she leans against it, staring at me. *Tell me everything,* I silently plead with her.

"When I look at my scars, all I see is pain. My life changed forever after… my accident." It changed mine too. I want her to keep talking so I keep quiet. "I don't know why I'm telling you this…" She lets out a small awkward noise, shaking her hands out. "Especially since we've only been on one date. But, I need to put it out there so if you're not okay with it, you can move on."

I want to laugh at the absurdity. I'm not going anywhere.

"I can't get pregnant," she blurts out. Not what I was expecting. She blinks back her tears, fanning herself. "Sorry, I'm a mess. I didn't mean to throw that in your lap all at once. You probably want to run far, far away."

She's reading my silence all wrong. I want to tell her it's okay because I don't want kids, but I'm almost certain that is not the thing to say. I push off my chair and stand in front of her.

Realization dawns on me I have no idea what affects the accident had on her, other than the obvious scars and memory loss. "Don't apologize, Ellie." I smile down at her and she looks away. She gasps when I pick her up at the waist and set her on the counter so she's eye level with me. "Thank you for telling me. But I… let's say it's not a determining factor for me."

"Don't you want kids?"

This is a no-win question. Will she judge me if I say no? "Hmm. I've seen the worst this world offers our future. I have a hard time wanting to bring a child into it. But that's not to say, I wouldn't love one if I had one," I quickly add.

She surprises me when she reaches out for my hand, slipping my fingers through hers. Is this what has been holding her back? *I hope so.* That was an easy fix.

"Thank you." The worry etched on her face, relaxes with her smile. "I didn't want to waste your time, if... you know..." She shrugs.

I run my fingers up her silky legs, forcing myself to stop when they hit the edge of her shorts. "Definitely not wasting my time."

I kiss her quick and hard, erasing every doubt she has of me in her head. I want to be here. Her fingers grip my hair, her ample tits rub against my chest and a small groan slips from the back of my throat out of frustration knowing I have to stop before it's too late. I pull back as quickly as I started, leaving her wanting more. Consequently, leaving me aching. The risk doesn't outweigh the reward. I want her forever, not for a quick score and I'm still not sure she's ready for the former.

"You need to finish studying and I have a meeting early in the morning."

"You're right," she says, breathlessly, hopping down. She walks me to the door, leaning against it, watching me walk out. "Thanks for tonight. I needed it."

"Anytime." I smile wide and tip my proverbial hat.

Her eyes shine with mischief. "Cowboy, I am a little disappointed about the leopard story."

I laugh out loud. "Is that right? I'll make it real before date number three."

"Three? I wouldn't call this a date. Maybe a point five."

"Point five?" I snicker as I reach for her and surprise her when I slam my mouth to hers in a heated kiss. My fingers wrap around her ponytail and I pull her into me. I kiss her until I feel her body melt into mine, her knees weaken, her moans telling me she wants more of this. I break the kiss, her heavy breaths and half hooded eyes are exactly what I want.

"Okay, you win. It's two."

That's what I thought. I'm not wasting time with halves.

I found my forever. I just need her to catch up.

"Make next Saturday night number three?"

"That depends if Tori lets me off work."

"She will. She wouldn't let her best buddy down." She shakes her head watching me walk backward toward the stairs. "What can I say, everyone loves me."

And you're on your way.

I can see it in her eyes.

CHAPTER FIFTEEN

KASE

"Hey, Max," I say, knocking on the office door. He glances up and motions for me to come in.

"Have a seat." It seems like yesterday I was sitting here interviewing with him, yet it's been almost two months. So much has transpired since then. "How are you adjusting? I heard something about you and Ell." Max likes to get straight to the point. Stone let me decide who I would tell about Everly, but I'm obligated to tell Max since I used his resources.

"It's different, but the transition is going as well. Although, being part of the team has certainly helped. Now, about Ellie... remember when you asked about skeletons in my closet?" His brow lifts and he nods slowly. I tell him everything up to that point.

"Why did she change her name?"

I shake my head and sigh. "I'm not sure. She doesn't have her old memories. It's possible, she wanted a clean slate."

"Sounds like someone else," he grumbles. He runs his hands through his hair in frustration.

"Does this have to do with the woman you traveled to California for?"

"She's not up for discussion." The way he shuts down the conversation is telling. I nod, deciding it's probably best I drop the subject.

"It's not a problem that I'm with Ellie, right?" I do worry that my work ethic will be called into question if he thinks I'm spending all my time thinking about Ellie. As much as my mind is occupied with her, I know how to turn it off.

"She's a friend of the group, but she's not our business, so as long as you can keep your head out of your ass and do your job, I'm good with it."

I give him an accusatory stare knowing his case in California is crossing that line. "Well if that isn't the pot calling the kettle."

He chuckles. "I'm seeing why you've got a target on your back with Stone."

"I live with a target on my back," I retort. It comes with the territory of being a sniper. I'm a wanted man in countries I've never been in. "Max, I shoot straight, and you respect that. I have an idea why you went to California. One look at you when someone mentions her name, it's obvious how you feel about her." He tents his fingers, staring at me, hating that I'm able to read him. I shrug a shoulder. "It's what they trained me to do. I notice every-thing. It's why you hired me. I'm the best."

"I certainly didn't hire you for your humbleness," he belts out a laugh while standing up, reaches into his desk and pulls out a set of keys. I guess he's done talking. He glances at me, fisting the keys. "Feel like jumping out of a plane?"

I shoot up out of my seat. "Fuck yeah!"

TIME TO GET ready for my date with Ellie. I'm still wired with adrenaline from my jump this afternoon, I should've hit the gym to release some of it, but I fell short of time stopping by the store on my way home. Grabbing the bag off my counter, I strut into the bathroom. She might not remember me, but maybe she'll remember my smell. I pull out the distinct green bottle of Ralph Lauren Polo. I stopped wearing this stuff when I left for the Navy, but it drove her crazy when I did. In a good way. One sniff and her eyes turned as bright as the bottle. Green with desire.

I slide into Cody's Corvette, turning over the engine so it roars to life. I'm not a car kind of guy. Give me a truck and I'm set, but this car fucking rocks.

When Ellie's door opens, my heart hammers against my chest. It's still hard to believe I found her. The best decision I made was telling her we were taking Cody's car because she's wearing a dress that shows off every luscious curve she has. Last time it was disappointing when she changed. My fingers tingle thinking about running them up her silky tan thighs. I need to take my time with her, but it's hard when every part of my body itches to touch her.

"I'm almost done." She wanders away, leaving the door open. "You can come in," she says over her shoulder.

Music drifts out from her bedroom and the scent of vanilla fills the air. I glance around her apartment noticing the flicker of a candle in her kitchen. A camera and a photo book lay on her coffee table. She's disappeared, so I sit on the couch and open the album, expecting to catch a glimpse into her life outside the bar. I'm surprised I'm not looking at pictures of her at all. Pulling the book into my lap, I flip from page to page, but not before studying each picture. There are two on each page.

"Ah, my project." I startle at her voice, stunned that I was so pulled in I didn't notice her watching me. She leans in her bedroom doorway, flashing a shy smile.

"I hope you don't mind. These are… heartbreaking, yet amazing." I see what she meant by I'd have to see it. I continue to flip the pages but stop at one. "This is Pepper." I look up at her confused and she nods. "Are these all women that Max–"

"Not all," she interrupts. "There's a woman's shelter, close to Max's place." I nod, knowing where the place is. Stone took me there and introduced me to the lady that runs the place. But I'm confused about Ellie's part. "I took those pictures two years ago for a class about narratives and documentary. After I completed the class, I couldn't stop. I was helping these women, and it was so much more than I ever imagined, deep down, I knew it was my calling. So, I continued. That's the final project."

"So, you take pictures when they first come in? And then..."

She blows out a heavy breath and looks away for a beat. "I volunteer at the shelter. When they first arrive, I talk with them, gain their trust as a friend. I explain what I'm doing, and we go from there. Some say no and that's okay, I'm still there to help them. Most of these women have been so beaten down mentally and physically by a man that they don't think they're worth anything. I take a picture of them, but then a few months later, when they have gone through counseling and we work with them to get back on their feet, I take another one to prove how beautiful and strong they really are. It's not about their clothes or their makeup. It's not superficial, it's real. The life in their eyes, the happiness in their smile, the strength in their posture. I want them to see what courage looks like. I want them to see they are the light in a world of darkness and nobody can take that away."

I'm speechless. So many things run through my head. The dependent girl I fell in love with has grown into a woman I'm in awe of. I have firsthand knowledge of the courage needed for these women, my mom didn't have it. What these women have gone through, I lived it.

"Stop looking at me like that." She blushes, glancing down.

"Like what? Like I think you're amazing, beautiful inside and out? Like the more I get to know, the more I want to know? Like *I really like you*?" I push off the couch and stride toward her, drawing her to me when I get close enough. "I'll never stop looking at you like that."

I lower my head so I can kiss her. When she scrunches her nose and pulls back, I pause. "What's wrong?"

She coughs once and clears her throat. "Nothing," she says, holding her breath. My brows furrow and I straighten, knowing there's something.

"Do you not want to kiss me?" I've never had that reaction trying to kiss someone. Not going to lie, it stings.

"Oh, no! I'm sorry," she says, taking a couple of steps *away* from me. "I want you to kiss me. Especially after everything you said." Her voice softens and her hand goes over her heart. "But, it's hard…" She pauses. It's clear she's trying to find the right words. "Geez, I ruined the moment."

"What stopped you?" I'm so confused.

"Cowboy… your cologne is kinda strong," she drawls, wincing.

I snatch my shirt, pulling it up to my nose and take a large whiff. "You don't like it?" Not the response I was shooting for.

"I don't *not* like it. I think I like your normal cologne better."

"I don't usually wear cologne."

"Oh." She bites her lip, looking damn sexy.

"Is it terrible?" I continue smelling different parts of my shirt.

"Uh… yes."

I sigh, dropping my shirt. "Do you mind if we stop off at my apartment so I can take a quick shower?"

"Not at all."

CHAPTER SIXTEEN

KASE

AFTER STEPPING INTO MY APARTMENT AND THE LINGERING CLOUD OF cologne hitting me smack in the face, all I want is fresh air. I take a sharp inhale when we step out of my building. I could blame it on the adrenaline from the jump that made me swim in the cologne rather than me being a dumbass, but it's probably a little of both. I tossed the stuff in the trash.

I slip my fingers through hers, determined to make tonight better than it started. "Where are we going?" she asks, squeezing my hand. Stone told me about a place but told me I wouldn't get in without a reservation. Son-of-a-bitch. I snap my wrist to glance at my watch, dropping my head in disappointment.

"Something wrong?"

Yes. I'm screwing this entire night up. "Well, I had something lined up, but we won't make our reservations."

"There's an Italian food restaurant a few blocks away. Since it's a gorgeous night, we can walk." She tugs my arm and gives me an encouraging smile. I'm trying too hard to impress her. Fancy dinners, cologne I wore in high school... could I be any more pussy whipped. Without even getting pussy? It's time to up my game without forgetting who I am. I'm not the same boy I used to be and she sure in the hell isn't the same girl I left behind.

I pull her into my chest, our linked hands knot behind her back. She bites her lip again and I watch as her teeth scrape along it. When it pops free, I lean down and suck on it. She opens, and I take full control.

This is who I am.

"So, I guess you're good with that," she says when we break apart, her voice breathier than it was a few seconds ago.

"Whatever makes you happy."

She pulls in a quick breath and her eyes widen, and I glance at her wondering what happened. "What's today's date?" Her excitement builds when I tell her. "I know what we're doing."

"Care to share?"

"Nope. You'll have to trust me."

"That's asking a lot from someone I don't know very well," I tease her. If she only knew, I'm handing her my heart again, full tilt, no holding back. Trust is not an issue.

"Too late. You already told me you liked me." She sticks her tongue out.

I lean down so I'm close to her ear. "I do. Now I need to get you to like me back." Despite the lack of response with words, her flushed cheeks give it away. *She likes me too.*

She pulls on my arm to walk. "What'd you do today?" The abrupt change of subject makes me smile.

"Jumped out of a plane."

She lets out an audible gasp and looks up to the sky. "That was you? I watched you from the shelter," she says, excited. "Who else went? I saw two people jump."

"Max. You should go with me sometime. You can jump tandem with me."

"Really?" She turns, her voice jumps an octave. "That'd be awesome. Wait, I'd be entrusting you with my life. Are you sure you're good enough to jump tandem?"

I think of all the crazy jumps I've done. "Ellie, I'm positive my gear weighed more than you when I used to jump. And most of those jumps were in the middle of the night, high altitude where I had to land in an unmarked drop zone, or I'd be dead."

"When you put it that way, I trust you."

My chest tightens from her words, a reminder I'm lying to her. I keep telling myself, it's not bad I'm keeping our past a secret. It's not like we hated each other and she's in bed with the enemy. We loved each other. I need to get her to love me again before I come clean.

"Do you miss it?"

"A little. For ten years, I craved adrenaline rushes, so adjusting to civilian daily life has been a little challenging." After dropping out of the plane that craving came back.

"Would you ever go back?"

And miss out on my chance to be with you?

"No. That craving can be unhealthy. Feeling invincible to the point of having superhuman powers, is a hard reality to live with day in and day out." Especially when one of your brothers, who have the same powers, dies in your arms.

"I can't imagine the things you saw."

Sighing, I respond, "I'd suggest not even trying."

We stroll in silence for the next block. This is why I hate bringing up the military. The glory of the job comes from deep within a person, the pride of fighting for our country. The details are top secret for a reason, they don't paint a pretty picture.

"Tell me how you did on your tests."

"I'm a badass and got all A's," she says with extra pep in her voice.

"Admit it. It was the sushi."

When she laughs, I glance over, her dark hair shines in the sunlight, framing her beautiful beaming face. "Are you saying I'm not a badass?" Her sass reminds me of the day we first met. It's definitely grown with her.

"No, you're a badass. You have amazing pepper spray skills."

She pokes me in my bicep. "Don't you forget it."

The restaurant is small, ten tables sit close together. Two wait-resses and a waiter move from table to table, dropping plates piled high of noodles or rolls. The waiter notices us first when we walk in. "Welcome, please, find a seat anywhere," he says in a strong Italian accent. When I look around the crowded room, I spot only one empty table.

"How about that one," I jest, pointing to it.

"That one is perfect."

Throughout dinner, I catch the owner who I thought was a waiter, frequently glance at me. So often, it's distracting me from dinner with Ellie. Finally, he wanders over and says, "I thought you looked familiar." He waves his hands around. Here we go. "And then I remember I read about you." He pulls out a rolled-up magazine from his back pocket, his tan leather skin opening it and shoving it in my face. "This is you, right?" It's a cover of Society Magazine and in bright red letters says, 'American Hero' with a picture of me wearing the medal, the weight of it heavier than the dead brother I carried back to the helicopter.

I hate everything about that picture.

I glance at Ellie and her smile touches her eyes. Even though she's excited, it does nothing to calm my resentment. I nod, expecting the validation alone will be enough. Instead, his arms flail around more, and he adds an excited noise. By then the entire restaurant is looking over.

"Can you sign it for me?" he asks, placing it in front of me with a Sharpie. I hate that people sensationalize this. There is nothing glorifying about this. "I want to add it to my famous wall." He points to a wall with at least fifty black framed pictures with auto-graphs of famous people. I don't belong on that wall.

"I'm sorry, I can't. We're here trying to have a quiet dinner." I pick up the pen and cap it, handing it back to him.

"I don't mind," Ellie says, cheerfully.

"I do." My voice is flat, and it pisses me off more when she jerks her head back in surprise. I curse under my breath. "I need a minute." The chair scrapes across the floor and I brush past the owner. "Excuse me," I snap over my shoulder and walk out the door.

My feet pound the pavement, pacing back and forth. Everyone read the damn article. Everyone knows we didn't all come back alive. But do they care what I went through to get that medal? Is there any compassion in their eyes when they meet me. Hell no. They only want a piece of fame. The exact fame I didn't ask for. I glance up from the ground when I hear the door open from the restaurant. Ellie tilts her head as she walks over.

"You okay?"

"I didn't mean to screw up dinner."

"You didn't. We were finished, anyway. I'm more worried about you." She places her hand on my bicep.

"I'm fine. I don't like how people act all star-struck when they recognize me. I'm not a movie star. I'm a SEAL. I was doing my job. The mission was successful, but I'm not a hero. If I was a hero, I would've left there with my whole team alive."

"Oh." Her voice softens with understanding. "I wish I knew what to say to make it better."

"You don't have to say anything." I pull her into me and kiss her. Her sweet taste suppresses any bitterness left in my mouth. "See, already feeling better." The anger is fading, but the guilt I can't control burns inside me. Letting this fester inside me isn't healthy. I need a better way to manage it. The ocean is calling my name. The one place I can let go of everything and refocus.

"Let me go pay so we can get out of here," I say, walking toward the door.

She yanks on my arm, stopping me. "I already paid." My smile drops and she shrugs as I stare at her. "I didn't think you'd want to go back in there." People pass us by, walking toward the park. My jaw tightens as I breathe through the anger of letting someone who wanted an autograph ruin my dinner. *Just sign the damn thing next time.* "Kase," she says, grabbing my chin so our gazes are locked. "I'm a modern woman. I'm okay with paying sometimes."

"I'm not."

"I would hope you're not a modern woman," she jokes, trying to lighten the mood.

"You know what I mean. I can promise you that won't happen again."

"Cowboy, it's not like I'm poor and you're a millionaire. I can pay sometimes."

I'm an asshole for not being transparent. The hidden truths need to stay hidden for a little longer. "Ellie," I say, firmly. "I pay. End of story."

She rolls her eyes and sighs. "Fine. Now that we've established you're stubborn and old-fashioned, let's go, or we'll miss the movie."

She grabs my hand and tugs for me to walk. "It surprises me you're just now noticing." I squeeze her hand and the sweet smile she flashes reminds me of when we were younger. Innocent. I've wondered if my obsession with her is only because of our past. If the love I had for her is blinding me. At the same time, I can't stop thinking of her. She fills my dreams, my thoughts, my wants and needs. I'm falling in love with her all over again. I'm falling in love with Ellie.

"So what movie are we seeing?" People fill the sidewalks in front of us, carrying blankets and coolers toward the beach park.

"No clue," she chuckles. "It's movie in the park night. Is that okay?" She looks at me hesitantly. Like there isn't anywhere I wouldn't follow her.

"Sounds fun," I reassure her.

For two hours, I've tried to keep my hands to myself. Keep my thoughts pure through the PG movie with hundreds of kids around us, but with each passing second, each innocent brush of her body against mine, I've been fighting a losing battle. My head aches, both of them, from trying to read into her touches. Her bare foot sliding against my calf as she sits up or her hand on my thigh, grip tightening when she laughs at something funny. They might be the simplest, purest touches but in my mind, she's leaving hints to where tonight will lead. And in my head, it leads to her lying beneath me, screaming my name.

"I loved that movie," she beams as we walk back to her apartment. "I wasn't sure how I'd like it since the original is my favorite Disney movie, but wow, it was perfect." *No, it's not. Little Mermaid is.* Her confession catches me off guard. My feet fumble a little as I stare down at her. Catching myself, I shake out of my stupor. "What, you didn't like it?"

I clear my throat. "No, it was great. Although, I pegged you for the Little Mermaid type." I regret the words as soon as they clear my lips.

She flashes a lop-sided grin, but her brows pull together. "It's a strong second place, but Beauty and the Beast is the winner in my book. Why would you think that?"

With a shrug, I relax my shoulders. "I figured you could relate to the independent woman choosing to live her life how she wants. Chasing her dreams." The bullshit rolls off my tongue like it's the truth. It's not. She loved the movie because she always wanted to be a mermaid. Which is funny now I think about it because she lives at the beach, but doesn't like to go into it?

She rolls it around in her head and nods. "I guess I can relate. But I can relate to Beauty and the Beast too," she says, softly.

I grip my heart and gasp jokingly. "Are you calling me a beast?"

Her lip barely raises to a smile as she keeps her face forward and the response pisses me off. I know what she's thinking. "No.

You are definitely not the beast." Her voice is a whisper and I'm not sure she meant to say it out loud. But she did, and she couldn't be more wrong.

She's not the beast.

I am.

CHAPTER SEVENTEEN

ELLIE

WILL THE VISIBLE LIES MARKED ON MY BODY MAKE HIM LOOK AT ME different? Will he finally taste the lies on my lips? He assumes he knows me. I didn't choose to be an independent woman; I was forced into this solitary life to survive. All my insecurities rise to the surface the closer we get to my apartment.

I've never cared about what men thought of my scars. Our time together was as forgettable as they were so there wasn't any need to harp on my flaws. But Kase isn't forgettable and I do care. Too much. The desire flashing in his eyes, burns inside me too but the war going on with my feelings has me twisted.

He has scars too. I repeat over and over to myself. Except his are admirable, mine are just a reminder of how parts of my life were ripped away from me. Sighing heavily, I push the thoughts from my head. Kase stops us outside my apartment building and stands tall in front of me. The overhead street lamp shines down, illuminating his strong facial features. His eyes flicker across my face. "If I snapped a picture what would your story be?"

I turn my attention to the red brick building and softly chuckle having heard this question a million times in my photography classes. What would my story be right now? A paralyzed woman who feels her body wake up, each nerve sparking to life. It's terrifying, yet exhilarating at the same time.

"Little Red Riding Hood?" he teases. "Or maybe Hansel and Gretel?"

I peer up at him. "Why are you picking stories where I'm about to be eaten alive?"

The wicked gleam in his eyes sends a rush of heat down my back. I swallow as he leans down and kisses the curve of my neck. "You should definitely run," he whispers against my skin. Every brush of his lips against my warm skin melts away the concerns. I want this. I want him.

If a man can't accept my flaws, our story won't be worth reading. He'd be moved to my did-not-finish pile. *It happens.*

I link our fingers, flash a sweet smile and lead him inside my building. We walk up the stairs, stealing quick glances at each other. I try not to focus on how many levels we have left, how my breathing accelerates — and not because of the anticipation — but the apparent need to walk the stairs more often. It's only six freaking flights of stairs. He fights back a smile, mocking my athletic ability.

I slap him on the arm. "Stop making fun of me," I say, winded.

His laugh echoes down the hall as he holds up his hands. "I didn't say anything."

I squeal in surprise as he swoops down and tosses me over his shoulder. "What're you doing?"

"I'd hate for you to faint from exhaustion before I get you inside."

I snort. "My door is only a few feet away. I could've managed."

"Better safe than sorry." He slaps my ass when we get to my door. "Where's the key?"

The blood rushing to my head doesn't make digging through my clutch upside down easy. "You could put me down," I huff.

"I could. But I'm not." He holds out his hand, waiting for the key.

I place the key in his hand. "You're so romantic," I snicker. It results in another swat to my ass. Heat spreads across my face and I'm thankful he can't see me. I shouldn't like it, but holy shit, desire surges through me, starting with the sting on my ass.

When he slides me down his body, he leans me against my door. I drop my clutch to the side and he drops my keys. He focuses on my mouth and runs his thumb across my bottom lip. "These lips could heal a dying man," he rasps. The way he says it, profoundly intense, I wonder what's on his mind. With a slight tilt to my head, his eyes flash to mine.

"I thought I was the one about to die in this story?" I say to lighten the sudden serious mood. He shakes his head, snapping out of his thoughts. He smirks and slowly runs his hands down my arms. When he gets to my wrists, he grips them, moving them over my head.

"Ecstasy induced death. It might be a thing."

"God, I hope," I say, sounding a little too desperate. He hums when I let my head settle back against the door and close my eyes.

"God has nothing to do with this." He seizes both my hands with one of his and snakes his other one down my waist to the hem of my snug dress. His fingertips graze my hypersensitive skin and I shiver. "Fuck, Ellie," he breathes heavily on my neck. "I'm trying so hard to take this slow." His chest heaves against my aching breasts.

"Slow is overrated," I whisper. I don't need slow or gentle. I need him. "Unzip my dress."

He lets go of my hands, and I fold them around his neck, leaning forward into him so he has plenty of room. With the speed of a racer getting out of a burning car, my dress is pooling at my feet, we're entangled in a frantic case of hungry kisses, and drowning with need. He lifts me up and carries me to my bedroom. It surprises me when I hit the soft bed we didn't run into anything since our mouths never came up for air.

It's not until he stands and the frosty air hits me while he reaches back to pull off his shirt, do I realize I'm laying almost naked, overhead lights glaring down on me like a spotlight. The vulnerability of the situation is heavy as I grab the throw blanket. He watches me as I cover my stomach, his brows pinch in confusion. I swallow, not wanting this to be a thing.

He crawls back on top of me, the soft blanket acts as a barrier between us and he kisses me until my body relaxes, just past the point of forgetting about being naked. He knows too because his hand slips the cover out from between us. I grip it when it's almost out.

"Uh-uh," he whispers, taking hold of my hand and peeling the blanket out from my fingertips. I close my eyes, steadying my breathing. I guess baring your soul isn't as easy as one thinks. "Look at me, Ellie." I chew the inside of my cheek, a storm of emotions brewing inside my heart. "You're so beautiful. You need to get out of your head." He lifts my hands again. "Keep them here," he demands. I nod but keep my eyes closed. Seeing pity or worse, a recoil reaction, would not only ruin tonight, but it'd break me.

As his lips skim the small scar on my chest, I fist the comforter underneath me knowing he's yet to see the others. Every muscle in my body tenses when he moves down. Soft kisses graze the tops of my breasts, and I can't help but smile when he groans. But it fades fast when he continues his path. The air conditioner kicks on, blowing ice cold air on my clammy face. I'm about to faint. The five-inch scar across my stomach, that doesn't have feeling, is sparking to life as Kase drags his lips across it.

"What's this mean?" He scrapes his finger up my side, over my tattoo and I shiver.

"Sii la luce che ti guida," I whisper in Italian. "It means be the light that leads you." I chance looking down to catch his expression. He nods twice while tracing the sentence with his finger, seemingly deep in thought.

"I like it. Do you speak Italian?"

"No," I grin. "But I liked how it sounded in Italian."

When he climbs back up my body and kisses me again, I'm able to release the breath I was holding.

"I'm not done," he murmurs. "I'm just getting started." The muscles that had just relaxed coil tightly around his words.

Stop thinking and just feel.

I push the insecurities, the darkness that looms right behind them out of my head. He's seen the scars and still wants more. That's enough to release the tension I'm harboring. He reaches behind my back and pops open my bra with one hand, slipping it up my arms and throws it to the side. I thread my fingers through his hair and pull him to my mouth in a hungry kiss, craving the intoxicating feeling I get when he kisses me. Where I drown in his taste and nothing else matters.

He makes good on his promise and worships my entire body with sweet kisses and soft praises. His touch seeps into my skin, tranquilizing my fractured soul. He's healing me from the outside, in. By the time he's done, my body is buzzing with desire and my mind is too fuzzy to worry about anything.

"You're the most beautiful woman I've ever seen," he whispers, nibbling my ear, my skin pebbles with goosebumps. "Your body is the fuel to my storm. The heat is so intense, I've never wanted a woman more than I do right now."

I swallow his words, and whimper as they spread heat inside me. It's been months since I've been with a man but I never remember it being like this. My nails curve along his broad shoulders, down his muscular back and his whole body shudders, his fingers dig into my hips as he lets out a low hum.

He moves from my lips down my chest and I cry out when he engulfs my breast into his hot, hungry mouth, sucking, while his fingers pinch my other nipple. He's done with the tender endearments and has proceeded straight to ravenous hunger.

My body's buzzing with the desperation to feel each other. The feel of his muscular body underneath my hands makes me feel powerful. This perfect man wants me. My eyes roll back when his tongue circles my swollen clit and I moan at the delicious shiver it causes. He holds on to my thighs as he licks and sucks, my body is on fire as I beg him to stop, and then keep going. Unintelligible words and sounds slip from my mouth as my orgasm pulses through me.

He growls when he comes up, wiping my wetness off with his hand. "You taste like candy." I laugh, doubting it's true. He leans down with a wicked gleam in his eye.

"You don't believe me? Taste," he murmurs against my lips. I open and his tongue dances with mine in a heated kiss. It consumes our air, the erotic xxx of tasting myself on his tongue robs all my inhibitions. I moan against his lips as I wrap my legs around him, his hard cock rubbing against my wet center.

He pushes up, kneeling between my spread legs as he puts on a condom. It's sexy as hell watching him grab his heavy cock in his hands. When he slides into me with ease, he grips my thighs. Hard. His nostrils flare as his control slips. He pulls back as he begins moving in and out of me. My groans get caught in my throat whenever he pushes into me full tilt, the feeling devouring my senses.

I grind my hips causing him to growl between thrusts. He picks up the pace, my thighs slapping against his pelvis and the punishing pace pulls us over together. Our bodies tense and convulse as he falls over onto me. He buries his face in my neck, kissing and sucking. I whimper when he pulses inside me, the nerves still sensitive. "Keep making that noise and round two is coming." He bites my jaw and pushes up on his elbows. I shift underneath him, lifting my hips and biting my lip knowing it drives him crazy.

A lazy grin spreads across his face. "I'd stay inside you forever if I could." He pulls out and I wince at the emptiness, surprised I already miss the feel of him inside me. Our union was perfect. A small part of me was hoping it wouldn't be, it would be my way out. But it wasn't. It was everything.

The bed dips as he lays down next to me on his side. He grabs part of the sheet and drapes it below his navel. The deep V, like a sign pointing to an erotic destination, is displayed perfectly. His whole body is a work of art. Chiseled with perfection. My eyes drag up his torso when he clears his throat. Our eyes meet and his wicked grin tells me he enjoyed my perusal. I glance up to the ceiling and blush. He's acutely aware of my body language and it's such a contrast to most guys whose main goal is how fast they can insert body part A into B. Not Kase. He memorized my body like a map, returning to my favorite places before traveling to his favorite place.

"Why are you embarrassed?" He cups my jaw with his hand, pulling me to face him.

My eyes widen. "I'm not. I'm just not used to being with a guy like you. You're so intense."

His brows crease. "Is that good or bad?"

I roll to face him and smile. "Good. It's refreshing."

"*Like a breath of spring air,*" he mocks.

"Not like that. I mean this"— I wave my hand between us— "it was different. It's hard for me to explain because I've never felt like this before." I moan, laying back, covering my eyes with my arm. "God, I hope I didn't just sound like a clingy, psycho girl, especially if you're ready to bail."

He moves my arm and I loll my head to look at him again. "I'm not ready to bail. I want you to be open about your feelings, to trust me." How is this man a trained killer? They're not supposed to have feelings or like talking about them. At least that's what I'd assume being able to take a life without a blink of an eye. Kase is an enigma—a killer with a conscience. "And I hope someday you'll trust me enough to tell me what happened." His hand moves to my sheet covered stomach. I swallow back the panic rising. "Not now," he murmurs as if he's in my head, hearing everything.

I swat at him, hiding my worry behind a smile. "Stop reading my mind. I thought it was a good thing being with a guy who's perceptive, but now I'm not so sure."

He rolls on top of me and says, "I think I need to remind you why it's so good." Moving the sheet out from between us, I immediately feel how hard he is.

Yes, I definitely need a reminder.

And a distraction from the conversation I'm not sure I'll ever be ready to have.

CHAPTER EIGHTEEN

KASE

"Things still good?" Cody tips his beer toward Ellie before taking a gulp.

I glance over as she takes orders from a group of college guys. I've found coming here isn't as fun as it used to be when I was pursuing her. Now, I have to sit back and watch her flirt for tips. It's infuriating. Once school is over, I'll make certain working here is in her past. I keep my jealousy in check. Most of the time. One touch, I grit my teeth; if she doesn't stop it, there's a shit storm raining down on someone. It's only happened once. The guy totally deserved the broken nose.

"Better than good."

"It's been, what, a couple of months now?" I nod, bringing the brim of the bottle to my mouth. "It's time to tell her."

The bottle clinks on the table as I stare at him, taking in a heavy breath. He shrugs unapologetically, knowing he speaks the truth. Ellie and I have a solid relationship but I'm scared to mess it up. It weighs on my conscience every day, but the fear of losing her wins the internal battle.

"I'm hoping she'll tell me first. It's her story to tell."

"It's both your stories. Her accident changed your life too."

"It's not the same."

"Whatever, dude. I'm surprised you both have been able to keep it secret from each other this long."

"You and me both. But it's weird now. I know she's Everly, but Ellie is a different person. When I'm with her, she's no longer Everly. Know what I mean?"

He shakes his head. "It's a jacked-up situation. I'm not sure if anyone would understand." He waves down Ellie for another beer.

Minutes later she's placing two new beers down in front of us. She bumps me with her hip and it takes a lot of self-control not to pull her into my lap and kiss her like I own her so everyone sees.

Instead, she gets a wink and with that she walks away. "You're getting better at that," Cody smirks. I flip him off. He's as good at reading people as I am.

"Stone found something on Casper." His voice lowers, and he leans forward on his elbows. His name isn't Casper, but it's the nickname we use because finding anything on him has been challenging. We've been able to pin point his whole sex-ring organization, but without taking him out, he'll just move on to a new city and start over. Not this time. We're almost certain he's the one who has the judge's daughter. Hopefully we're one step closer to finding her.

I tense when a hand grips my shoulder, hard. "I heard you've been fucking with my girl," the deep voice behind me grits out. Before I have a chance to glance up, Cody's chair scrapes across the floor as he stands tall.

"I suggest you take your hand—" I turn as I'm talking and stop as soon as I catch a glimpse of who's behind me. A sly grin creeps up on his face morphing to a full out smile. I relax my shoulders and stand. "Parks, you want me to hit you, all you have to do is ask," I joke, gripping his hand and pulling him into a hug.

"It's great to see you, Nix," he says, pulling back and looking at me.

"You too, brother. It's been too long. Landry Parks this is Cody, the other guy who was about to teach you a lesson in manners." They both laugh and shake hands. "What the hell you doing here?" I grab a chair from a neighboring table and we all sit. The round bar top was okay for just me and Cody, but you add another large guy, our knees are touching.

"I'm on leave. Was driving through, headed up north to Mom's house so I thought I'd swing by and look at what the hell you've been up to first."

Seeing Parks makes me miss being with my SEAL team. We were in BUD/S together and we've been friends ever since. "How'd you find me here?"

He stares at me with a lift of his brow. "Seriously? I asked one person if they knew who you were. They told me to come here." He slaps me on the shoulder. "You can't hide, you're like a celebrity." My smile fades and I let out a heavy sigh, crossing my arms over my chest. His expression turns serious, and he shakes his head. "You're still blaming yourself, aren't you?" I glance over at Cody and he tilts his head in confusion. Ellie is the only one that knows how I feel about what happened. And the nightmares. "Goddamnit, Nixon. It wasn't your fault. You did nothing wrong. We executed the plan to a fucking T." He pokes his finger against the table as he grinds out the words.

"I don't want to talk about it."

He reaches for my shoulder again, this time his squeeze is light. "We all mourn the loss of our brother and we all carry the guilt he died. But, let that shit go, Kase."

I take a sharp inhale and let it out slowly. I hear him, but I can't figure out how to drop the weight of guilt though. The load has lightened since I've been here, but it's there. I nod at him and down my beer.

"Enough talk about the past, what's been going on with the guys?"

He updates me on our team and what they've been doing. The

more he talks the more I miss it. When Cody gets up to go to the bathroom, he tells me about a mission they completed. I sit back, pissed I wasn't part of it. We've been trying to catch that guy for a year. The dives they've done and the jumps. My blood pressure increases just hearing about them. I'll need to jump out of a plane soon to relieve the pent-up adrenaline I'm getting just from talking about it.

"Can I get y'all anything?"

I peer up at Ellie and smile. I'm about to introduce her to Parks when he cuts me off and says, "You look familiar. Have we met?" Her eyes widen and she stands tall, panic floods her blue dilated eyes. *Fuck!*

"Um… I… uh, don't think so."

"No. I'm sure we've met. I never forget a face." I kick his leg as hard as I can without bringing attention to anyone. He gets the hint and stops talking.

I snap my fingers. "I know where you've seen her. Ellie this is Parks. One of my best friends from the Navy. Remember dude, I told you about her and sent a picture of us."

He nods slowly and points at me. "That's right. Now I remember." He looks over at her. "Nice to meet you, Ellie." The way he says her name, I know he's figured out where he knows her from. And he also knows her name isn't Ellie.

She shakes his hand and manages a smile, but she's rattled. Before turning to walk away, she glances at me so fast, I don't have a chance to do or say anything.

Once she's out of earshot, Parks looks at me. "What the hell is going on? That's Everly."

The problem with being perceptive, we don't forget. Anything. Two years after I joined the military, Parks and I got trashed one night, happy we passed an important test. I spilled my guts about Everly. We formed a plan in our drunken state where Parks would find her when we were on leave to see if she still didn't have her memory. The next morning, my skull felt like it had split in half and I remembered nothing from the night before. But Parks did.

I had saved his ass once, and he felt he needed to repay me, so he went on his own to track her down, unbeknownst to me. When he reported back that she never regained her memories, the hope she'd find me was crushed. It's the day I laid to rest we'd ever be together again.

I lean forward on the table and he does too. "It is. But she still doesn't have her memories." I glance around the room before continuing. Cody nods, confirming I'm in the clear to continue. "It's not until I moved here that I ran into her." I give him the Cliff Notes before Ellie comes back. He eyes me, sitting back in his chair, internally debating what to say. There's not judgement, but there's uncertainty in his expression.

"Brother, you have to tell her."

Cody settles back with a satisfied grin.

"I know I do. But you both just witnessed how she reacted when she thought you recognized her. She wants nothing to do with her past."

"Why?" Parks asks flatly.

"Fuck if I know. She doesn't talk about it."

"Have you ever wondered why?" Hell yeah. It weighs on me as much as the secret I'm keeping. Why doesn't she trust me enough to tell me?

All three of us stop talking when Cody clears his throat and Tori walks up and places the bottles on the table. "Hey guys."

"Well, hello there, beautiful," Parks smiles.

She leans on Cody's chair, smiling back at Parks. "Well, hello back," she beams. "I didn't know we had someone new in the group."

"Tori, this is Parks. He's just passing through town."

"I'm sure there's someone who could convince me to stay a few days." He winks at her.

"Tempting," she replies looking him up and down. "But, I'm taken."

Cody gasps loudly and she swats him on the shoulder. "It's a cold day in hell, baby."

"Oh, you hush. Anyway, it was nice to meet you Parks."

I look up at her, my brows furrowed. "Where's Ellie?"

She blows out a sigh. "She wasn't feeling good, so I told her to go home. It's probably stress from school."

She was fine fifteen minutes ago. *What the hell Ellie?*

"What's Tori's deal?" Parks asks as soon as Tori walks away. Cody tells him about her and Ben. She's scared to settle down, and this is the first time we've ever heard her admit she's with someone. I'll have to let Ben know he's breaking her down. My mind goes back to Ellie as the guys keep talking. What spooked her bad enough that she had to leave?

The rest of the afternoon we spend catching up. I'm talking, but my mind is somewhere else and Parks can tell. "Nix, go talk to your woman. I should get going, I have a long drive home." He stands and I follow suit. We embrace in a hug. "Now would be a great time to tell her everything," he says, pulling back.

"Yeah, yeah. Next time, stay longer."

We all walk out and part ways, heading in different directions. Mine is straight to Ellie.

My knuckles rap against her door. When I hear nothing, I knock again a little louder knowing she's here. I saw her car. She finally answers. She's changed out of her work clothes into a... *bathing suit?* I scratch my head.

"Going swimming?" My words come out slow. I don't wait for her to invite me, rather just walk in and sit on the couch. The scent of coconut oil is intense as I pass her. She mumbles something to herself and shuts the door. An open bottle of Deep Eddy lemonade vodka sits on her counter next to an empty glass. Has she finished or just began?

"What's going on Ellie? I thought you weren't feeling well?"

She thrusts her hands out. "Carpe deem, or however you say it." I bite my lip from laughing. Definitely has already started. "I mean, I have only one life, right? Why spend it worrying about my past?" The struggle to stop her or let her keep going, knots in my stomach. I don't want her to regret her words, regret telling me like this, but maybe this is the way it has to happen.

"Why are you worried?" I ask, sitting forward, resting on my knees.

"Because life sucks sometimes," she slurs. No argument from me there. "I was a different person. I'm not that person anymore. You wouldn't have liked that person." No, I loved that person too. She points at me, wobbling a little. I jump off the couch to catch her, but she balances herself and giggles. "Oops."

"Maybe you should sit down."

"Nope. I'm fine. I'm going swimming. You should come since you loooove the water." She gestures like she's swimming through the air.

"I don't think it'd be a good time to go swimming right now." She pshh's me and rolls her eyes. "Come sit with me and tell me why you're drunk." I pick her up in my arms and walk her back to the couch. I'm an asshole for pushing this.

"Heyyy big guy, I can walk." I can't help but grin at the always in control woman, slurring and over animated words. "I only had a glass."

"Mmm-hmm. Not likely."

She pokes my chest and straddles my legs. "Listen here, hot stuff. I'm the bartender. I know how much I've drunk. I mean drank." She puckers her lips when I laugh. "This is not a laughing matter. In fact, it's cereal."

"Serious," I correct her.

She waves me off and continues. "Your friend was very nice. He's a big guy like you." She closes her eyes for a beat and when she opens them, she flashes a sly smile. "But he's not as hot as you." She tries to waggle her eyebrows, but it ends up looking like she's trying to hypnotize me with her bulging eyes. I'm surprised when I feel the tips of her fingers on my waist. Maybe she was trying to hypnotize me. I angle my head as she pulls up my shirt. "You're like hot, hot," she giggles at herself.

As much as I'd love to flip her on her back right now and have a drink of her, I can't. She pouts as I wrap my hands around hers to stop her from taking my shirt all the way off. "Talk to me, Ellie. Tell me what's wrong."

"Fine," she huffs, letting my shirt free and dropping her hands to her side. "I'm running from my past. Always running. I was a different person. I don't know that person and I don't want it to catch up to me. I left it in the past for a reason, Kase. So there... that's what's wrong. I thought my past had caught up with me and it scared the ever-loving hell out of me. I didn't know how to handle it." Her words fall out of her mouth in one breath.

Tell her. I'm your past.

I'm her future.

I fight with my subconscious. How can I tell her I'm her past with what she admitted? What's important is what we have now and I'll be damned if I ruin that. She's not ready to hear what I'm hiding. She doesn't need to know it's me she's running from.

I pull her into a hug. "We're all running from something, Ellie. Running's usually easier with a partner. I'm just sayin' I'm here if you need me."

She sniffs, her head rests on my shoulder. "Thank you, Cowboy."

CHAPTER NINETEEN

ELLIE

"HEY DAD," I SAY INTO THE PHONE.

I remember a time when that felt foreign to say. It wasn't forced, just not natural. Now, it would be weird calling him by his name.

"Hi sweetie, how's it going?" I love hearing his gruff voice. I don't hear it enough. We talk for a few minutes about school and work. I can always sense the relief in his voice as I chat about my life.

"I met a guy," I say, hesitantly and bite the inside of my cheek waiting for his reaction. I didn't mention Kase last month because we had only been on one date. But it's different now. I like him. A lot. The line stays silent and I wonder if I lost connection. "Dad?"

"I'm here. What's his name?" he asks, his voice curt.

I release an awkward chuckle. "No. I'm not giving you his name. You'll find something on him, even though it's nothing, and make a big deal about it. He's a great guy." Being retired from law enforcement doesn't prevent him from poking and prodding.

"That's what they all say." I shake my head and sigh, knowing he wouldn't be happy. "I worry about you. You've been through so much and have come so far, I just…" He pauses, sighing. " I want the best for you."

"And I love you for that. Okay, here's a little for you. He recently got out of the military and he's working for Max." This will put him at ease. When he found out about Max's team, and how I was friends with them, he acted more relaxed. He'll probably figure out who he is now with just a little digging.

"I should come out and meet him."

We both know that won't happen. "I wish you could, but it's not safe." Having almost died, moving on with my life should have been the easy part. Nothing about my life is easy. But Kase makes me forget and believe there is hope for me yet.

"I understand that better than anyone." His beard scrapes against the receiver as he blows out a breath. "I love you, sweetheart. Be careful. I have to go feed the animals."

"Always. Love you too, Dad."

I hold the phone to my chest. Our once a month chat isn't enough. Someday, it'll be different. Not being able to change the situation, I swallow my emotions and tuck the emergency phone back into my sock drawer. It would be awesome if Kase could meet my dad. They'd get along great. I shake the thought from my head. Don't do this to yourself. It's not a realistic dream. Dating Kase complicates matters, except I can't seem to stop. The other day should have been a wakeup call that I'm not safe anywhere, even if Kase's friend mistakenly thought he knew me. What happens when it's not a mistake? I guess I'll deal with that when and if it comes.

"Time for a trip to the store," I say to myself as I stare into the empty fridge.

Pulling out my list as I push the buggy through the automatic doors, I plan which end I should start at. Ice cream isn't on it so I'll start at the produce side. The bright yellow bananas grab my attention first so I scan for the perfect cluster; not too green or too ripe and no bruising. A cart stops next to mine, so close I'll need to back up to move around them. I look over with an annoyed expression because seriously people, there are things called space.

My scowl turns upward when I meet Kase's eyes. His gorgeous smile makes my knees weak. Desire to step into his arms and have him kiss the ever-loving hell out of me like he did a couple of weeks ago has me blushing. The way butterflies flutter in my belly whenever we talk is unnerving. Is this what love at first sight feels like? Both our schedules have been busy, which is good because I find myself wanting to be around him all the time. Albeit, my drunken night where I almost confessed everything, we've only talked on the phone since then. Surprisingly, he hasn't brought it up. Maybe it was enough of an explanation he won't push further.

"Of all the grocery stores, you had to walk into this one." He winks. "It must be fate."

I can't help the smile on my face. "Considering it's the only one around here, chances were in our favor."

"Shh. Don't ruin my moment." Pinching my lips together, I stifle my laugh. Two women stroll by us, their gaze appraising Kase's body. Yet, his attention never leaves me. Who could blame them, he exudes sex, not even trying. Board shorts hang low on his hips, a white V-neck shirt hugging his thick arms and his hair mussed on top like he ran his hands through wet hair, letting it air dry.

"Did you go for a swim?"

"I did. I would've invited you, but you're afraid of water," he teases.

I swat at him. "I am not."

"Next time, you're coming then."

Yes, please. My dirty mind takes hold and my skin flushes. Gah, I've been hanging around Tori for too long. I glance away from his knowing smirk, my cheeks heat as I try to smother my smile.

"Ellie," he rasps quietly. "You're going to be the death of me."

He discreetly adjusts himself as much as he can. "But I promise to follow through on both accounts."

Now, my whole body is on fire. Thoughts of his skilled tongue and fingers and his promise sends an involuntary shudder through me. Jesus! I spin around and pick up bananas not caring what shape they're in. "These'll work," I squeak, holding them in the air, showing them off for an unknown reason. His eyebrow quirks up. My gaze darts from his amused expression to the bananas and I close my eyes. Could this be any more embarrassing? "To eat," I quickly add. He barks out a laugh as I put them in my cart. If they weren't bruised before, they are now. "Would you scoot out of my way so I can finish my shopping?"

"Do you have a long list?" He eyes the paper in my hand.

I scan it, no longer than twenty things and shake my head. "It's not too long."

"Wanna trade? He pulls out his list and shakes it in the air." I cock my head, confused why he wants to trade lists. He shrugs one shoulder. "There is a lot you can learn about someone by their shopping habits."

I look at it again. "There's no earth shattering thing you'll learn about me on this paper."

"Come on. I bet I can identify at least five things about you based on your shopping list."

My lip twitches. "Okay. Let me add brand names..." I reach into my purse to get a pen, but he snatches the paper out of my hands.

"Nope. It'll be fun guessing." He hands me his list.

"Don't complain when you can't figure it out." I shrug, knowing what's on the list. It'll teach him to want to shop for a woman going in blind. "Just, no generic."

His shoulders drop. "Woman. I got this." He pushes his cart forward. "I'll start at the other end. Don't cheat and check on me. We'll meet after we check out."

My eyes widen. "After?"

He walks away nodding. When he turns a corner, he glances back at me. "See you at the finish line."

Is this a race? My heartbeat picks up and I wonder if I should run the aisles. I push my cart to the end of the aisle looking for him and he's nowhere to be seen. Ugh. I hate not having the rules.

I peek at his list and it's as long as mine with typical things. Soap, deodorant, bacon, sandwich meat. There is no way he'll finish before me. Half the time, men wander around with a dazed expression. I start filling up my cart with his items. When I hit the deodorant area, I stare at the selection. Oh! Choosing one is harder than I thought. I pop open a few scents, trying to find one I recognize. Giving up after smelling ten, I throw one in the cart I like. At least it doesn't smell like the cologne the other night.

With just a couple of things left on the list, I wonder how he's doing. I giggle to myself, he's probably wishing he hadn't started this whole thing. My phone dings from the seat of the cart. I dig through my purse and pull it out.

Kase: Waiting for you at the front ;)

Seriously? I jerk my head up looking down the aisle. An older lady looking at oatmeal must sense me because our eyes lock for a beat. I flash a quick smile. She returns one and continues her perusal. How is he finished? I rush getting the last few things and when I push my cart to check out, I see him sitting on a bench outside the manager's office. He's flashing a sly smile, with his hands folded between his legs. The fullness of the cart catches my eye and I softly gasp. I didn't have that much on my list. I throw my hands out and he shrugs. What in the world did he buy?

"Are you ready ma'am?" the cashier asks, staring at me. I apologize and set Kase's things on the belt.

After checking out, I glide my cart up to his and he stands, slapping my wandering hand away from the bags. I didn't see much, but I catch a glimpse of sticky notes peeking out on a few items. *Where the hell did he get sticky notes?*

"That can't all be mine, my list wasn't that long."

"I might've bought a few extra things."

"A few?"

A fleeting thought that he thinks I didn't buy a lot of groceries because I can't pay for it has me worried.

"Stop over thinking this," he says, pushing his cart out of the store. I follow, still pushing his groceries. When we stop at my car, he pops the trunk and loads the groceries into it. "I'll be over at six for dinner."

My eyes widen in surprise. "What if I have to work tonight? Or I have a date?"

"You don't have to work. Do you have a date?" His smile fades and he steps closer. In an instant, I regret the words, not knowing where they came from, the need to make him wonder if he's the only one when there isn't anyone I want more than him.

"No," I whisper, our eyes lock and he stands close, blocking the sun.

"Good. I would've hated to miss out on a steak dinner."

Understanding what the extra groceries are for now, I release a deep sigh. I scrunch my nose. "I'm sorry I said that. I'm not—"

He holds his finger up to my lips and shakes his head. "I'll be there at six." I smile against his finger, nod and he leaves me with a wink, me appreciating he didn't make a big deal about it.

At home, I take the groceries out of the bags, placing them on the counter. One by one, I search to see if he left a note. He didn't do it on all of them, but I find the ones he did, amusing. 'I ate this when I was ten.' He wrote on the Cap'n Crunch cereal box. I snicker at what his thoughts must have been for one of my guilty pleasures. 'This is interesting', he wrote on the package of hard-boiled eggs. I love hard-boiled eggs, but when I want one, I don't have time to boil it. When I grab a bag full of boxes and pull one out, I double over in laughter. I pull out box after box of tampons. He bought four boxes of different brands, each with their own sticky note. He even numbered them.

Box 1. These seemed to be small, discreet. Figured you might like that.

Box 2. I fit so I know you don't need small. These seem more realistic. Super large.

Box 3. Shit. Maybe they're called normal for a reason.

Box 4. Okay, I give up. You've got me here. You're bound to use one of these right? P.S. I've never been so uncomfortable in my life.

It's hysterical envisioning him standing in the aisle wondering which one to get. Not that I'm keen on him knowing I'm about to start my period, it's funny to see how much he squirmed picking a box. Or four. He can't say I didn't try telling him which one to get.

I put aside the stuff he got for dinner and put the rest away. I follow his instructions on marinating the steak and then glance at the clock on the microwave. Three hours until he'll be here.

I call Tori up and tell her to meet me at the beach. I chuckle to myself, I'll show him I'm not afraid of water.

I'M CHOPPING carrots when there's a knock at the door. Six o'clock sharp. The man is punctual. I stare at the door for a beat, wondering if he waited until the last second to knock. He's always on time, right on the dot, it can't be a coincidence.

When I swing the door open, I ask, "What were you doing a minute before you knocked?" He cocks his head to the side, a confident smile touches his gorgeous blue eyes.

"A minute ago? I was wondering if you've been to the doctor recently?"

"Um... no. Why?"

"Because I think you're lacking some vitamin me." He waggles his eyebrows, pulling me into his arms.

I drop my head into his chest. "Oh my god. You're so cheesy."

"Only with you, Ellie." He kisses me on the head. His hand weaves through my hair and he pulls it back so I have to look up to him. "You make me feel like I'm a teenage boy again who can't deal with his hormones. A minute ago... I was giving myself sixty-seconds to lose the hard-on."

Desire tickles deep within my belly. I step into him, my thigh pressing higher into him. "Did it work?"

He groans, his grip tightening in my hair as his lips slam against mine. The taste of his minty gum cools my tongue. The rest of me is on fire. "We should stop," he rasps.

What? Why? Despite his words, his voice is full of need.

"That's a terrible idea," I mutter. "Cowboy, don't start something you can't finish." I narrow my eyes, daring him.

He grins with a wicked gleam in his eyes. "Ellie, there isn't anything I want more than..." He pauses, looking past me for a moment and then continues. "A sweet ass steak and a baked potato, fully loaded."

I huff and slap him on the chest, pushing back out of his arms and rolling my eyes. His raspy laugh follows me into my apartment. "Woman, there are priorities and I'm starving." I ignore him and return to chopping my carrots. "Aww c'mon, you're not going to fault me for needing to eat so I have energy for later, are you?" His warm breath tickles my ear as he stands behind me, snaking his arms around my waist. I stop chopping, setting the knife on the cutting board and twist in his arms.

"You're like a ball of energy. What did you do today?"

"Besides grocery shopping," he smirks and waggles his brows. "I worked out, went for a swim in the ocean, Hudson and I drove the four wheelers around Max's place, um... oh, and we went to an indoor skydiving place in New Haven. It was wicked fun doing tricks despite it not being the real experience."

I stare at him, dumbfounded, shaking my head. "What?"

Hearing what he did makes me tired. I managed to grocery shop and hit the beach for an hour. It was a productive day for me. I sigh. "No wonder you're starving. You're a busy boy."

He lets out a low grumble. "Boy? I'm a hundred percent man. Do I need to jog your memory?" The counter digs into my back as he pushes me into it, making sure I feel every muscle, every hard place on his body.

I ignore the tingles low in my belly coming back to life from moments ago. He's the one who put the kibosh on us having a pre-dinner workout. Now, he can wait. I slide my hands down his flexed chest, looking up at him from beneath my lashes. "That's a good idea," I purr. When I continue moving past his shorts, my hands brush against his hardened cock, running down the entire length. He inhales sharply and his eyes burn with want. "But... after I feed you." My lips curl into a smile and I shrug one shoulder, saying, "Priorities."

I spin around before he can respond and continue chopping the vegetables for the salad. I internally high five myself for the self-control I exhibited despite the ache between my legs. If only he would step back so I didn't feel all of him on my backside. My will is only so strong. "Shoo, or you'll make me cut myself," I snicker, waving my hand, gesturing to back away.

I sneak a glance back as he walks away, adjusting himself. He catches me and grins as if he won this round. I don't think so buddy. I win.

Hmph, what exactly did I win? I stare at the chopped veggies wondering why I thought this was the better choice. I look back again and see he's leaning against the counter, his arms crossed over his chest as he watches me. Yep, my priorities are mixed up.

"How about I tell you the five things I learned about you today," he says, pulling himself up on the counter, sitting.

"Oh, this will be fun. Let's hear it."

"Number one, you can live off of frozen pizza."

I suck in a breath, slightly offended. "There is nothing wrong with frozen pizza. It has four out of the five food groups and I usually add a banana or apple. Bam! Fully nutritional meal. Number two?"

He fights back a smile. "Okay. Number two, either you're not home often, which I hope is the case, or you don't know how to boil water. To cook boiled eggs."

"You're very judgmental about my food." My mouth twitches at his amused expression.

"I actually love hard boiled eggs, I found your approach somewhat odd."

"Why is that odd? Whether I cook them or whoever does it, what's the difference? It's about convenience. And I know how to boil water." I stick my tongue out before grabbing a bowl for the salad. "Moving on, what's three? And do not go there with my cereal or I'll cut you."

He rears his head back, laughing.

I toss the salad into the bowl with the veggies and mix it, waiting for him to continue. "So, three and four go together and one of them is something I learned about me." He tugs on his shirt as if he's suddenly hot. "Number three... I thought I could handle shopping for tampons, but no. Never again." I think about all his sticky notes and flash an amused smile.

"I tried to make that part easy on you."

"I'm not sure even if I had the brand, it still would've been easy."

I understand, I'm twenty-eight and it's still hard for me to put that box on the conveyor belt right side up.

"And then number four... well that's a given. Someone is visiting or coming to visit soon." He shrugs awkwardly.

I bite my lip, feeling the heat crawl up my cheeks. I'd rather not discuss the impending arrival of my period with him. "Coming to visit. Let's move on to five, shall we?"

"Yes," he quickly says. "Last, but not least you're a slow shopper."

"What?" I say in a clipped tone. I grab the hand towel off the counter and whip it at him. He hops off and runs out of the kitchen with me right on his heels. "I am not. I was too worried about what kind of deodorant you wore or what kind of meat you wanted. Lunch meat was too vague!" I snap him on the ass. "Or protein bars. Do you know how many freaking protein bars there are?" I try to snap him again, but he snatches the towel and yanks it, pulling me to him. I slam into his chest and we're both laughing hard in each other's arms. "And I do not need extra large tampons!"

We fall into the couch and my heart is full. It's in this moment I know, I'm falling in love with him. It's too bad love isn't enough to wipe out my past. I push out the unwanted thoughts and live in the moment. In the arms of a man I hope can forgive me for my secrets when they come out.

CHAPTER TWENTY

ELLIE

"I LIKE YOU IN MY BED. WE SHOULD DO THIS MORE OFTEN," I SAY, angling my head against his bare chest so I'm looking up into his face. Our second time together was better than the first. I can't say I've ever orgasmed three times before having sex.

He flips me like I weigh nothing, hovering over me. "That's supposed to be my line." My heart flutters that he wants this too. "You sure you can handle all this more than every other week?" He waggles his eyebrows and presses his groin against me.

I pretend to be thinking hard. "Hmm. It is a lot to take in." Of course, I meant his ego, but as soon as the words escape my mouth, his lips curl to a confident grin. I'm certain I inflated his ego to a level fit for a god.

"Thanks," he beams. "I take pride in it." I bite my lip, fighting back my laugh. He wasn't hard before, but he is now. With a little grind of his hips, my body is already heating up.

"I wasn't referring to—"

He lies on top of me, bringing his lips to mine to stop me from talking. "Shh," he murmurs against my mouth. "I know it's a lot to take in..." He slides into me and I arch my back, moaning, at the tingling sensation of him inside me again. "But I fit perfectly into that tight pussy of yours." Wrapping my legs around his hips, I hold on while he moves in and out of me in a slow sensual ride. The heat from our bodies is almost too much to bear, beads of sweat pool between our connected chests. We're so close, we move as a unit made for each other. He stares into my eyes, reaching into the depths of my soul, claiming it as his. There isn't any resistance. It's his to take.

The bite of the air conditioner provides relief against our over heated bodies. Half an hour later, we're back in the same position we started from except the pounding of our heartbeats echo in the room. His finger drags across my back in a figure eight, my body relaxes and my limbs grow heavy. "I agree we should do this more often," he murmurs, his voice deep from fatigue. It seems he finally ran out of energy.

Within seconds, his breathing is a slow steady rhythm, his hand resting on my back and I drift off to sleep right beside him.

"Stay with me!"

I'm jolted out of sleep, disoriented. It doesn't take long to figure out what woke me. "Keep talking, just keep talking to me," Kase demands, thrashing and kicking his feet, the sheets flailing around. More murmurs I can't understand slip from his lips before he screams.

I lay my hand on his shoulder. "Kase, wake up. You're okay." Keeping my voice soft and comforting, I repeat the words once more, adding more pressure on my hold as his screams get louder.

His next actions happen so fast, I'm uncertain how we got in this position.

Growls drown out my screams, fingers tighten around my throat and I claw at his arms to stop. "Kase," I try to scream over and over. His eyes are dark, filled with anger. I am the enemy. The panicked rasp in my voice doesn't even sound like me. I do the only thing I can think to stop the pain. Slam my knee up as hard as I can. It connects to his groin area, and the release is instant.

I scoot off the bed as fast as I can, falling to the floor on my ass.

My feet shuffle on their own, scooting me as far away from him as I can. Hitting my back against the wall, I don't take my eyes off Kase. My nightmares come alive. It's not the same. This isn't the same. I repeat those words.

Are you sure? It feels the same, my subconscious replies.

Kase rocks on the bed in a fetal position, holding his groin, muttering curse words. "What the actual fuck?" He growls and looks around the room. With my chest heaving and my hands on my neck, I keep quiet. When his eyes find mine, he freezes for a couple of beats before jumping off the bed and rushing over.

Bringing my knees into my chest and wrapping my arms around them, my body tenses, readying for another hit even though mentally, I know he won't hurt me again. He's awake. He's not like him.

"Ellie, what happened?" He panics, kneeling at my feet. He reaches for me and I involuntarily flinch. Tears burn my eyes, I shake my head. "Tell me what I did." His voice breaks but I can't look at him. The click of the lamp has me opening my eyes. Our eyes meet again and his travel to my neck. "Did I..." He stops, rocking back on his feet when his knees weaken and he drops to the floor. His hands grip his hair in a frenzy. "No. Tell me I didn't do that," he roars.

"You were having a nightmare," I whisper.

"I'm..." The terror in his face shatters something inside me. The shield I'm hiding behind disappears, my fears melt away. This isn't his fault. I should have known better than to touch him. "I'm so sorry," he murmurs, his tone full of regret.

I push forward, my knees dig into the carpet, and I crawl over to his hunched body. "You didn't know what you were doing." It's my turn to hesitate to touch him, but when he can't face me, I crawl into his lap. His arms stay limp at his sides. The intense need to be close to him is overwhelming considering he was choking me mere minutes ago.

I know firsthand what nightmares can do, how hard it is to

refocus your energy. He needs to get out of his head. "Look at me," I softly demand. He lifts his head and the blue of his eyes is cloaked in black. Panic, remorse, and anger reflect back at me. "It. Wasn't. You." I say each word slow so he hears each one. The rise and fall of his chest is the only movement between us. He blinks every few seconds and I wonder if he's trying to communicate with me. As if he's stuck inside his body and can't get out. He needs a push, a shift in the current.

I straddle him, waiting for a response. My therapist wouldn't agree with me right now. She'd tell *me I'm searching for emotional intimacy triggered by an adrenaline induced situation, an escape from the real problem.* The real problem? I would ask her. *He choked you,* she would respond flatly, trying to hide the judgement in her voice. But it's there. *Don't go back down that road. You're better than that.* I yank my shirt off despite her whispers. Maybe she's right. Maybe I'm trying to prove her wrong.

He's not like him.

He's not my past.

He's my future.

I can't stop. I've never needed a man more than now. A simple touch of my lips to his, brings life to his body. In a frenzy of moans and whimpers from his wandering hands, my hips grind down against his hardened cock and his hands wrap in my hair, yanking it back. We gaze into each other's eyes for a moment, his dark with need, mine blazing with acceptance. My rapid heartbeat and heaving chest filled with urgency hurts from the craving.

"Get on your hands and knees," he commands through clenched teeth. His voice is flat, listless, but I don't care. I'll do anything to help him cope with this burden right now.

I submit, turning around, knees and hands on the rough carpet. The sound of a foil packet being ripped open readies me for what is about to happen. Without a word, he snags my panties with his finger, pushing them aside and slams his dick into my wetness. Our grunts and groans fill the room. The slap of our bodies and the tight grip his hands have on my hips spur me on to keep up with his demanding stride. I push back, needing to feel him all the way inside me. I'm not sure if I'm punishing myself for making him hurt me, or offering him all of me as a sacrifice to forget his nightmare. Either way, it's a dangerous position to be in. It's a battlefield of cries from our release and then silence.

He remains silent when he walks into the bathroom to get rid the condom and I wonder what happens next. I wish he would say something. Anything. I crawl into my bed and wait, but the emotional night gets the best of me. My eyes turn heavy and the last thing I remember is him standing in the bathroom doorway, staring at me.

When I wake, the only thing next to me are cold sheets and fear that I might have lost the best thing that ever happened to me.

CHAPTER TWENTY-ONE

ELLIE

"STILL HAVEN'T TALKED TO HIM?" TORI ASKS WHEN I SLAM DOWN A bottle of vodka. I shake my head. It's been five days since he slipped out of my apartment and disappeared without a word.

Tonight, it hurts even worse. The guys are here. I told myself since none of the guys were here they were out of town on a case. Except tonight, that blows that theory out of the water. He's definitely avoiding me.

Tori serves their table so I don't have to play nice with his friends because I'm certain there'd be a few inappropriate comments. It's bad enough I have to act nice to the male population.

The night drags on, not because I'm peering at the door every time it opens, hoping Kase will stroll through it, rather it's the ache building in my heart each time the door opens and it's not him. I knew not to get involved, I don't have time for this. I've known him two months, but I've given him more of my heart than I thought there was to give. And now he's stomping on it like a cigarette butt.

I'm cleaning the back of the bar when I hear someone behind me. "Last call was a half hour ago," I snap over my shoulder.

"Ell, I don't need a drink." I roll my eyes at the sound of Cody's voice. Turning around, I lean against the bar and cross my arms.

"Then why are you here?"

"You're about as snippy as he is." I grit my teeth and glare at him. "Talk to him, Ell."

I throw my rag on the bar. "Don't you think I've tried? Kase won't talk to me."

He pulls in a deep inhale, letting it out harshly. "He's at home right now. There's a lot going on in his head he needs to work through, but I can promise it's not you he has to figure out." Shaking my head, I stare up past him in an unfocused gaze. "Hey, I'm not saying it'll work out. But you two should talk before you decide it's over."

I let out an irritated huff. "I have all the bullshit I can handle in my life, I'm not sure I can add more to it."

His eyes soften and one side of his lip turns up and I'm surprised by a look of understanding. Have they looked into my past? "Maybe you guys can help clean up some of each other's bullshit." He winks and turns, walking away. My mind reels, my past and present colliding and trying to read into what he said all at the same time. I have to breathe through the panic rising inside me.

Tori walks behind the bar, carrying clean bar mats. "Tor, you never mentioned my past to anyone, right?"

"No. I'd never. Why?"

"I got a strange feeling about something Cody said. It's probably nothing. Anyway, he told me to talk to Kase, that he's at home right now."

"What're you going to do?"

I shrug, grabbing the towel and running it under the cold water.

"You should go. It's better to find out now what is going on then let this drag out. You're miserable, but at least you'll have closure."

"Well, that sounds enticing, I'm screwed either way. This is all your fault." Her mouth gapes open as I pull her in for a hug. "Thanks for being here for me, always."

It's not her fault my heart beats wildly for the man.

I POUND on the door a second time, not giving two fucks it's two in the morning. "Kase, open the door. I know you're in there. I'll get louder, then you'll have to deal with me and the police."

The click of the lock makes me stand tall. Readying myself for a bitch fest. The door opens and Kase grips it like it's holding him up. My 'you've messed with the wrong girl' expression morphs into worry. He looks like shit. His hair is tussled, standing on its ends, his face dons at least three days worth of growth and the bags under his eyes tell me he hasn't been sleeping.

His pathetic glance before he turns and walks in, leaving me in the hallway, makes me question everything. I step in, quietly shutting the door behind me. He's sitting on his couch, slumped back against the cushions, his arms behind his head and eyes closed. One would think he's relaxed, except his whole body is tense.

"Hey," I whisper. No response ticks me off a little. He needs to be a part of this conversation. "Kase, don't ghost me."

His eyes lazily open and he lets out a sarcastic laugh. "That's funny. That's what I was trained to do. It's an art I've perfected." I furrow my brows together, not understanding. I awkwardly stand there with my arms hanging, our eyes pinned on each other. Shifting from foot to foot, I wait for him to explain. "You're nervous. Why? Are you afraid of me?"

"No." I still my movements. "I'm nervous because I thought we had a thing, and now I'm not sure where we stand because you won't talk to me."

He runs his hands through his hair. "I'm not good enough for you, Ellie."

He's all wrong. "How do you figure? You're a strong, passionate, loyal man. Not including the last five days, you've treated me with respect. So, please tell me where in that equation is not good enough."

"Respect? Was I respecting you when I was fucking you like any other woman?"

Ouch. The sting of tears threaten, but I blink them back. He sits forward, leaning on his knees, staring up at me like he's waiting for me to react. He's trying to push me away.

"Am I like all those women to you?"

If he says yes, we're done.

His head drops between his shoulders and I release the breath I was holding knowing he can't. "No," he murmurs. "But I have a past that puts you in danger. I hurt you the other night, I can't forget that."

I bite my lip to stifle my laugh at the irony of the situation. If he only knew my past. *Tell him*, my subconscious whispers. *No*, I reply. Turning my attention to Kase instead of the internal conversation I'm having with myself, I say, "Kase, I wouldn't stay with a man who abused me. Ever. But even I can see the difference here."

"This is even worse, I don't realize I'm doing it is the problem which means I can't stop myself. I can't put you at risk. I could have killed you, Ellie."

He's correct but he wouldn't hurt me in his right mind. Clearly, he wasn't himself. Am I a hypocrite if I leave. I'm damaged, and he made me feel the most beautiful I've ever felt when he looked at my scars.

I walk in front of him and kneel so I'm at his feet. "How often do you have dreams?"

"It used to be more frequent, but I've only had two since we met."

Hearing that drums up hope that we are helping each other heal. My nightmares have been few and far between the last two months.

"What do you think prompted it?" He shakes his head and

runs his hand through my hair. I lean into it, reveling in the warmth.

"It doesn't matter. I couldn't live with myself if..." He stops mid sentence. Silence skips between us, the tension in his body creating a barrier around him. "I like you too much to stay."

"I like you too much to walk away," I reply, and kiss his hand. His hand wraps around my head and he pulls me up to him.

Forehead to forehead, he whispers. "Please don't like me." His voice cracks and the pain in his words shoots straight to my heart.

"Too late," I whisper back. I press my lips to his, uncertainty rushing through me, hoping he doesn't push me aside. I ignore the tug-of-war battle in his kiss, nudging closer in between his legs, not losing contact, instead pressing harder against him, determined to go to war with the demon making him think he's not worthy of me. "Please let me in." Oh, the irony. I want to tell him I love him, but I can't bring myself to say it. It feels like it would come out of sympathy. I want to say it when the love is blooming out of greatness and not desperation. Instead, I'll show him.

I lift his shirt and he fists his hands around mine, stopping me. My eyes fly to his, regret etched in his features, I nod tightly demanding he let go. He releases my hands and lifts his arms as I stand, pulling his shirt off. I slip off my sundress, following with my bra and panties. His breath catches as he gazes at my naked body.

"Sit back," I whisper.

He pauses but then leans back into the couch, his hands lax at his side. When I straddle him, I wait for him to touch me. If it weren't for the heat in his eyes, I'd think he didn't want me by his lack of movement. But I can see the desire and need. He wants to, but he's afraid. I scale my fingers down his flexed arms, into his hands, lifting them up to my heavy breasts. His eyes roll back into his head when I place his hands on them, pressing them into me.

"Touch me, Kase."

The knot tightening in my chest loosens when he grips my

breasts, causing me to whimper. My hips grind down against his basketball shorts. The rough mesh rubbing against my bare wetness. I pull his neck forward, bringing his hot mouth to my boob. It sparks a fire within him and his hands are groping and grabbing me in a heated frenzy. I release a tangled cry of desire when his fingers move through my wetness and he sticks two inside me. I rock against his hand begging for my release as he plunges wildly. His thumb circles my swollen clit.

"Show me how bad you want this, babe," he rasps in the curve of my neck. The sound of his deep sexy voice pulls me over the top. I moan out as pleasure ripples through my body. "Fuck," he rasps, withdrawing his fingers and pulling down his shorts underneath me. As soon as his cock springs out, I lower myself onto him, sheathing him entirely, my body shivers uncontrollably. "Ellie, I'm not wearing—"

I make myself gasp as I rise and lower again, taking him as deep as I can. "I don't care." My voice is heavy. "I need to feel you."

He exhales a tight groan and digs his fingers into my hips, stopping me from pushing up again.

Closing his eyes and taking deep breaths, he swallows hard as he searches for the control he craves. But I want it right now. I want all the control. I want him to feel everything I'm giving him: understanding, acceptance and even my love. Our pasts aren't important, it's who we are in this moment despite what we tell ourselves. Two broken people who can find solace in the present without being a prisoner of the past.

"I can't get pregnant, Kase," I remind him, wondering if that's what he's afraid of.

"I don't care about that," he grinds out. His eyes flash open to mine, the raw emotions sending waves of dizzying need inside me. "I want you to be sure."

"I've never been so sure about anything in my life." The ardent words slip out of my mouth without regret. I lean forward and kiss him as I grind my hips so his cock hits every sensitive nerve of my inner walls. In a flash, his hands are all over me and he deepens the kiss as he moves his hips with me, my words bringing him to life.

I hold on for the slow sensual ride. Our gaze never breaks, the silent love between us blooming into a defining moment in our relationship, the point of no return.

We accept each other's hidden scars for what they are; *our past.*

CHAPTER TWENTY-TWO

KASE

"You fuckers make me happy," I slur, stumbling out of the town car.

"Polo, we love you too," Cody yells out the window. I flip him off. My new nickname doesn't sound funny even when I'm drunk. Our job was a success, rescuing the judge's daughter. Tonight is why I chose this job. Seeing the gratitude of her parents in the hospital and the glimmer of hope left in their eyes knowing we found their daughter alive is worth every second sitting in a car for hours watching and waiting for scum to make a mistake.

We completed our mission a day quicker than we planned, so we stopped off at a bar on the way back from the airport to celebrate. I might have had too much to drink. I throw the door open to the stairs and take two at a time.

Ellie, I'm coming for you, baby.

I stare down at the front door handle, a plan forming. I should surprise her. This is the perfect time to see if my lock picking skills are up to par. Slapping my hands together, I blow on my fingers and pull out the pin set Oscar gave me before we left town. Slip it in here. Push here. The simple sound of a click excites me. *Damn, I'm good.*

Slipping inside her house, I close and lock the door. Shit, it's dark in here. I think there's a—

"Oomph." Nope, the kitchen table is right there. *Shhh...* I tell myself, this is supposed to be a covert mission. Rubbing my side, I wonder why the hell I didn't wear my night vision goggles, it would've made this easier. I stretch my neck out, listening for her. Of course, I didn't wake her. *I'm fucking Secret Nixon, the spy of the century.* The only thing I hear is an occasional car drive by. This will be so good. My fingers itch to feel her soft body. Her delicious curves feeding my craving.

"GET THE FUCK OUT!"

"FUCK!" I don't register her screaming at me while I'm being hit in the side with something hard on the shoulder, then my stomach. I cover my head with my arms. "STOP HITTING ME!"

I double over in pain, landing on all fours. The room lights up, blinding me.

"Kase!"

Whatever she was beating me with hits the wood floor. My eyes adjust to the light and I lift my head up to see a bat rolling on the ground. She runs over, wrapping her fingers around my waist.

"I'm so sorry! What in the world are you doing breaking into my apartment?"

I haven't caught my breath, so answering her takes me a few moments. It's a good thing I'm drunk. This'll hurt like a bitch tomorrow. "I thought I would surprise you," I mutter in between my panting, resting my head on the floor.

"You surprised me," she replies in a flat tone.

"You think?" I push up to stand.

She slaps my arm. "I wake up to noises and then hear a man's voice... what the hell did you expect?"

I peer down at her in utter shock. "I was quiet as a mouse," I say, defensively. I try to stand a little taller, but it hurts my head. Instead, I wobble over to her couch and slowly sit down.

"You weren't quiet, by any means. The door jiggling alone,

woke me up. I was reaching for my phone to call the police when I heard somebody had gotten in, stumbling around. So, I grabbed my bat."

That is not at all how it went in my head. I was in stealth mode.

Her brows crease, with a tilt of her head as she studies me. "You're drunk."

"Well, I was." I rub my hip. "But a bat to the body is a buzz kill. You couldn't tell it was me?"

She pops her hip out, crossing her arms. She's not wearing a bra and I can see her nipples through her thin white cotton shirt. It's the first time I take in her body. Her little boy shorts show off her long tanned legs, begging to wrap around my face.

"You're wearing all black. You're supposed to be out of town and you don't have a key to my place. So, I'm sorry I didn't automatically think of you." I know she's talking, but the only thing my senses hone in on is her body. "Kase. My eyes are up here."

I lay back against her couch, stretch my legs out, and link my fingers together behind my head. "Knowing where your eyes are won't stop me from looking at how hot you look right now."

"I don't think I hit you hard enough."

"Baby, I'm definitely hard enough," I say, grabbing my bulge. She rolls her eyes.

"Here I was, worried that I hurt you," she huffs. "Hope that feels good, because it's the only action you're getting tonight." She spins and walks out of the room.

Wait, what? I didn't break in to her place and get clubbed for nothing. I push off the couch, but fall right back into it, the effort to get up not worth the pain jarring my body at the moment. I blow out a heavy breath, my body deciding it's not going anywhere.

"You can at least kiss my boo-boos."

I WAKE to the glorious smell of bacon, inhaling a deep whiff before

I open my eyes. The smell is like pure caffeine in the morning. When I manage to crack my eyes open, I find Ellie standing in front of the stove, in the same thing she was wearing last night. Bacon and legs for days. I might still be dreaming.

She walks to the sink to wash her hands and glances over at me, catching me staring at her. Her full red lips curl up. "And he lives," she jokes.

Chuckling, I sit up, shoving a blanket off me. I wince at the pain in my side. Memories of a bat connecting with it come back. I pull up my shirt to see the damage.

"Oh my god, I did that?" she says, running over and dropping to her knees in front of me. Her fingers graze the gnarly black bruise. I wince again. I'm almost certain I have another one of these on my shoulder.

"Damn, woman. Do you own a gun?"

She looks at me confused. "No? Why?"

"You've maced me. Now you've beaten me with a bat. I'm a little afraid what might come next."

"Let me remind you, you were stalking me and breaking into my place when both things happened." She continues to inspect my bruise, her light touches giving me goosebumps.

I grab her fingers and bring them to my lips. "I'm fine. But I need to go the bathroom and you need to go tend to the bacon before it burns."

"I don't care about the bacon. I'm worried–"

I scoff. "That's like one of the Ten Commandments. Thou shall not burn bacon."

She stands up, shaking her head. "I can't wait to hear your other nine."

After we clean up the kitchen, I slap her on the ass. "We're doing something fun today, go get dressed. Make sure to wear pants." She eyes me warily, walking out of the kitchen. "After you and that bat last night, you'll love this."

"I need to take a shower," she calls out from the bedroom.

"Perfect. So do I after I dirty you up."

———

"WHERE ARE WE?" Her eyes light up when the ginormous white house comes into view. "Who the heck lives here?"

"Max."

She does a double take, straining her neck to get a better look. "This is Max's house? No way."

I nod, remembering my reaction to seeing it for the first time. I never knew Max had money, just knew about his elite team. He's not the type to flaunt his riches. Then again, neither am I.

Watching Ellie's wide-eyed response makes me wonder when it will be a good time to tell her I have money. Hell, I'm keeping bigger secrets than that, I don't know why I'm worried about that little detail.

She points out the stables and the lake, in awe of the property. I need to take her horseback riding. She spent every weekend on a horse growing up. I have some wicked memories of us out in the pastures of Barrow that I'd like to recreate.

I pull behind the guy's cars, lined up on the driveway. We designated today as our team building day. It's a bullshit title for us wanting to blow off steam and have a little fun. After the last two weeks of self-sabotage, the guilt at what I had done to Ellie eating me alive, I realized there would always be parts of my past that would haunt me. She's helping me find ways to deal with it rather than hide behind it. I spoke with a counselor from the women's shelter who gave me some ideas as well. One, which we already gathered, if Ellie wakes me, she has to be across the room. It's still hard to fall asleep when we're together, but I'm told that's a natural reaction to what happened. It has to get better because I'm not giving her up.

Everyone is chilling in the living room when we enter. The

energy is high as the guys load their guns. Stone glares at me while doing his. "You're going down, Nixon."

"Strong words, from a little man."

"It'll be way easier for me to hide."

The guys all howl in laughter. The door opens and Tori and Ben walk in. He's holding two large bags from the store. I tip my head to the side wondering what in the world he bought. Tori bounces in and gives Ellie a hug.

"We're ready," she beams. Ben sits down, emptying the contents on the table and I'm taken back to the nights we were planning our missions out, loading all our armory.

"Ben," Hudson says, holding out his arms. "You only needed two guns, one for each of you. This isn't a mission, it's paintball."

He stops and glances up to everyone, flashing an innocent expression. "I didn't want to come unprepared. Look who I'm up against." His eyes travel around the room.

"We'll take it easy on you," Hudson jokes. "We'll just add you to the list with Stone and the girls."

The uproar from the girls has us all laughing again. Well, except Stone.

"I'm shooting you first," Ellie snaps, giving him a warning glare.

"All right kids." Max stands and everyone shuts up. "There's only one rule, you get tagged, you're out. Winning man—" Tori clears her throat, and he smirks, "or woman, gets the grand prize of a week's vacation of your choice."

Ellie's eyes widen and she bounces on her toes. "We are so winning this."

Max looks at me and shakes his head in disappointment. He's one of few people in here who knows I could take her anywhere in the world in a blink of an eye. And I want to, every day for the rest of her life. And I will, but in due time. I manage to smile at Ellie, despite the guilt Max is throwing my way.

"That's not a prize when we can't do that already," Tori states.

"Honey, if I win, bragging rights alone will be worth millions," Ben says, still filling all his guns with pellets.

"Everyone have a watch? Twenty minutes is all you have to find a place. Then it's free for all." All the guys stand, hollering, ready to get the game started. "Three, two, one!"

I glance at my watch and note the time. The adrenaline is pumping through my body as I grab Ellie's hand and pull her outside.

"Hey, I don't think there are teams," she says, yanking on her hand to stop me. My brow quirks up in amusement. She holds her gun, nose up and pops her hip out. "I'm thinking I'll go this way." She points in the opposite direction.

"Okay, babe." I know she won't last but five minutes with the guys on the loose. But hey, if she wants to go at it alone, I'm all for it. I wink at her. "I promise I won't shoot you."

She runs through the grass and yells over her shoulder, "I can't promise the same thing."

Game on.

I've taken out four of the guys. Although, I haven't seen the girls so I'm not sure if they're out yet. I felt bad for taking out Ben. Max took out Stone so that put a smile on my face. Unfortunately, while I was preoccupied with my excitement, I lost track of Max.

I watch from Max's roof for any movement. I'm in my element. Hit 'em high and quick. After fifteen minutes of zero action, I wonder if I'm the last man standing. I'll give myself five more minutes before I head down.

The sound of a gun going off right behind me makes me duck and roll. But it's too late. I felt the bastard nail me in the ass. Max roars with delight when our eyes meet. I sigh and chuckle at the same time. It figures he'd find me here. Another gun goes off behind him, splat, splat, splat. Two of the three miss Max, but one hits him right in the back. We both look and see Ellie, blowing the pretend smoke off her gun and then jumping up and down.

"I won! I won! Suckas," she yells. She runs over, slapping Max on the shoulder as she passes him, and jumps on top of me. "This was so much fun!" Seeing her excitement was worth it. Also, seeing the look on Max's face when she shot him was priceless too.

"God, I love you." The words slip from my mouth, her body freezes for a second and I wonder if I messed up by saying it.

Her eyes light up and she replies, "I love you, too." I pull her head down to mine and kiss her like she's the only air I have to breathe. She has no idea how happy she made me hearing those words. I could see it in her eyes she did, but hearing it validates everything.

There is nothing stopping us from forever now.

The talk of the game can be heard the rest of the day as we barbecue and swim. Ellie's already been in the pool looking damn hot in her swimsuit. I almost pulled out my paintball gun and shot Hudson for gaping at her. We need more women at these parties if this is going to be a monthly outing. Her words echo in my head and I'm a grinning fool who feels like he won the lottery. I want to say it whenever I get close to her, but I'm afraid I'll scare her off.

I pull my shirt over my head and dive in, blowing bubbles up her body as I stand up in front of her.

"Holy shit, that is not from paintball," Stone says, looking at my bruise on my side and shoulder. "Who fucked you up?"

Ellie ducks her head and raises her hand slowly.

"Someone had batting practice last night," I say, dryly.

"You need to tell them why." She straightens and cocks her hip to the side, showing her feisty side. It's one of my favorite sides. Everyone stares at me, waiting. I open my mouth to explain, but she beats me to it. "He broke into my apartment last night, except he made a shit load of noise, scared the crap out of me."

"Duly noted," Max chimes in from a chaise lounge. "Don't use you when we're doing a stealth mission."

"I was drunk. And I was not making that much noise."

Everyone laughs at my defensive tone. I know Max was joking, but fuck if it doesn't hurt my ego. It already stings he shot me today. I should've heard him behind me. Next time, I'm taking Max out first. And never trust Ellie with a paintball gun.

She was coming after me, Max just happened to be the one still alive.

CHAPTER TWENTY-THREE

ELLIE

Kisses wake me from my dreamless sleep. My smile creeps up when I open my eyes and stare into blue orbs. "You're supposed to be too excited to sleep." The day old stubble across his strong jaw is deliciously sexy, yet the sparkle in his eyes makes him look like a child on Christmas morning.

"Then why are you up so early?" I yawn, glancing at the bedside clock. When I glance at the time, I jerk my head back. "Really, Kase? It's only six o'clock. My graduation doesn't start until noon."

"It's a big day for you." I grin at his excitement as he hops up on all fours, shoving the covers off us. His eyes warm, gazing down at me. The dawn light filters through the blinds and I catch a whiff of mint toothpaste as he kisses me on the nose. "I'm so proud of you."

It's hard to believe we've been together five months already. He has stolen my heart from the secrets that held it captive. He's forced me to learn that love doesn't wait for perfect, it accepts your flaws and molds its own perfect. "Thank you," I whisper.

He leans down and bites me on my nipple, sensations ripple

through my body. I scowl when he hops off the bed. "We have to get moving," he says, walking to the bathroom.

"Cowboy, I'm not ready to get up."

When he turns around, I run my hands over my naked breasts, down to my silk panties. A sexy crooked smile plays on his lips as he watches me glide my palm over my center, already wet from desire. I slip my fingers to the side of my panties, sliding them down my legs, kicking them off in his direction. His gaze follows them, and a flurry of sexual endorphins tingle in the pit of my stomach as he pins his gaze on me.

He lowers his briefs, stepping out of them. There isn't a day I don't gawk at how gorgeous he is. My mouth waters as he takes predatory steps toward me. I sit up, turning on all fours and crawl to the edge of the bed, meeting him. His hard cock bobs in front of me and I lick my lips. He wraps my hair around his fist and I run my tongue down his shaft, back up to the crown before I take all of him into my mouth.

His growl of appreciation spurs me on. I suck around his thickness, sliding back down until he hits the back of my throat. He growls, pulling out of my mouth. I pout my lips when he pulls me up on my knees. "As much as I love my cock in that mouth of yours, I want it in your pussy right now." His fingers snake down my stomach and find their way to my center. I buck against his hand as two fingers slip inside me. "You're dripping wet, beautiful." The bed dips as he climbs on top and he maneuvers us so he's laying down and I'm on top of him. He knows this is one of my favorite positions because he can get deep. "Fuck me, Ellie," he demands.

So, I do. I ride him like I'm a rodeo star. His hands squeeze my breast, holding me as I move up and down his cock. The heat inside me burns, erupting into a gush of hot liquid. I scream out his name and he follows as we ride out our orgasms together.

I fall on top of him, our tangled breaths fill the air. "Are you ready to wake up now?" He teases between his heavy breaths.

"With that wakeup call? I'm ready to make today my bitch."

After Kase makes me waffles for breakfast, I head over to my apartment. I've brought a few things over here the last month as I've been spending more time here, but it's only the essentials. I'm certain Kase grabbed a few things from my place I don't remember taking over, but he acts like he has no clue what I'm talking about.

If it was up to him, I'd be moved in already. My heart tells me to pack my shit and head on over, it's my subconscious reminding me I can't until I tell him everything. The longer we're together, my nightmare seems like it was just a bad dream, one that is easily forgotten.

When I pull out a pair of panties, my heart twists when I catch the shine of the corner of a cell phone sticking out. Shit. Shit. Shit. What's the date? I dig out my phone and sure enough there's a message from my dad. Why can't I remember when he'll call? I listen to the message, and guilt that it's been three months since we talked makes my heart heavy. If he'd stop being a stubborn old fart and answer when I called him back, it'd make me feel better. But his rigid rules of once a month, always a different date, makes it difficult. Of course, when I wasn't dating, I never forgot. I follow his command of texting him I'm okay, followed with the pass-word, daisy, so he recognizes it's from me. Opening the calendar app, I search for next month's date and set a reminder on my normal phone so I won't forget again. I hate he isn't here today to watch me graduate. He'd be so proud of everything I've conquered on my own. It makes not talking to him today even worse.

I tuck the phone back into the drawer and puff my cheeks out, releasing a winded sigh. I'll find a way to go visit him whether he likes it or not. Nothing has happened in years, so a quick trip out to Texas won't kill me. My phone dings atop my dresser. My worries go to the wayside when I see a text from Kase.

Cowboy: Don't wear anything under your gown.

I blush fantasizing about sneaking off with him somewhere in one of the classrooms, but then laugh at my inappropriate thoughts.

Me: Don't hold your breath, dirty boy.

Cowboy: I'd like to dirty you up.

I'm thinking of a witty reply when I notice the bubble pop up showing me he's typing again. I'm guessing what he'll say next. Probably something like 'And then lick you clean.'

Cowboy: And I've been holding my breath since the day I met you, afraid to breathe, afraid I'll wake up from this dream.

Swoon. Definitely not what I was expecting.

Me: You made my panties wet and my heart grow twice its size. You're confusing me.

Cowboy: I've got something growing twice its size too.

"ELLIE KEYES," the announcer calls. A spark of excitement races through me as I walk across the stage. Kase's yelling from the crowd makes my cheeks flush as I shake my head. *Some people's boyfriends.* Can't take them anywhere.

With my diploma in my hand, I rush into Kase's waiting arms. "I did it!" Max's entire team cheers, their deep voices drawing attention, catching the eyes of surrounding girls.

"What're you gonna do, now?" Cody asks.

"I have no freaking clue."

"She's going to help me run the bar." Tori winks at me as Kase growls, pulling me into his arms. He's not a fan of me working there and I promised him it wouldn't be forever. But I have no idea what I'll do now besides continue helping at the women's shelter. Somehow, I'd like to incorporate my photography into a job. I just have to figure out how.

"For now, I'm stealing my woman. I have a surprise for her, so we'll meet you guys at the bar around four."

Tori's closing the bar for the night and we're celebrating.

"Oh, what kind of surprise," I say in a sing-song voice, spinning in his arms.

"One that'll have you screaming my name."

"That is my kind of surprise," Tori beams over her shoulder, walking away with Mr. Silver.

I spend the drive guessing what my surprise could be. "Cowboy, give me a hint," I whine after getting it wrong repeatedly. A smug smile rests on his face as he watches me struggle. "I hate surprises."

"I know. That's why this is so entertaining." I narrow my eyes at him and wish I had something to wash the smug smile off his face. Instead, I sit back and enjoy the ride.

We stop off at a small diner on the way to wherever we're going. I haven't eaten anything since breakfast. Kase probably stopped because the rumble of my stomach was so loud. I tried to mask it by moving around in my seat, but nothing stopped the hunger protest.

"Are you getting me a puppy?" I ask before shoving a fry into my mouth.

His lips twitch and I think I figured it out but then he says, "Nope, but a good guess. If you were to get a puppy, what would you want?"

I tap my finger on my lip thinking. "Hmm... A German Shepherd."

He does a double take. "I figured you'd want a little cute dog."

"Little dogs are cute, but I want a protector."

"What? That's what you have me for."

I smile at his frown, having no doubts he would do anything for me. "Will you shake your leg too when I hit the right spot?" I joke.

His frown turns up, flashing one of his dimples. "You hit the right spot and I'll definitely shake it."

I throw a fry at him. "You and your dirty mind."

"I'd love to discuss how dirty it really is, but we need to get going." He reaches over, grabs a few fries off my plate and stuffs them in his mouth. I slide my plate over and he finishes them in a minute flat. *And I thought I was hungry.*

The drive is quick and I glance over at Kase, brows pulled together, when we drive into an empty parking lot. I lean forward, gazing out the front window at the huge white warehouse building, wondering why we're here. Kase parks and slides out of the Jeep. He walks around the back of the car and stands by me, staring at the nondescript building. I scan it looking for a sign. I spot one on the door.

The Lighthouse.

I've never heard of this place, yet I drive by it when I go to the women's shelter. It's only a few miles down the road. Kase weaves his fingers through mine. "C'mon, let's go take a look."

"What is this place?"

"Your surprise."

My eyes dart back and forth from him to the building. "Should I scream your name now or later?" I tease because I don't know what else to say in my confusion.

He chuckles, poking me in the stomach. "You think you're funny, huh?"

"I have my moments."

He pulls me to the front door and inserts the key to unlock it. When we walk inside, it's a waiting area. The place has recently been renovated, the smell of fresh paint and new couches and chairs fill the space. It's very inviting with colors of grey and orange. I like it. He leads me through another locked door, past the reception desk. The desks, chairs, and computers are all brand new. When we enter the main area, my eyes widen at the massive space. The center of the room has couches, chairs, beanbags, and tables. There are rooms down both sides of the building, at least eight of them.

I feel like I'm supposed to see something that will give away why we're here. When I glance at Kase, his eyes stay pinned on me, watching every reaction I have. I tilt my head and walk around. The first couple of rooms remind me of doctor offices and then the next ones remind me of therapist's offices with comfortable couches. Still not having a clue, I keep walking. There's a dressing room type room filled with women's clothes. I pass more offices and then I stop and gaze into an enormous playroom. A large window allows me to peek inside. Bright colors fill the room with toys and a TV on the wall. I continue my perusal of the place, slowly walking the perimeter of the room.

I freeze when I poke my head into a room. Light from the large window floods the room. There are backdrops hung and professional photography lights. It's a photographer's dream room if they are shooting inside.

Is this my surprise?

I spin around, looking for Kase, but he scares me when he's right behind me. "Oh!" I say, taking a step back. "I didn't know you were right behind me." I point to the room. "Is this my surprise? Did you get me a job?"

He slowly nods. "This whole place is yours."

I stretch my head forward, making sure I heard him correctly. "What did you say?"

"You are officially the owner of The Lighthouse."

"What are you talking about?" My eyes dart around the room. "I don't understand."

"Be the light that leads you," he whispers. "And let that light lead you to The Lighthouse." I think about my tattoo he's quoting and the name of the place.

"Does this have to do with my project?" He nods again, waiting for me to connect the dots. The only problem, I don't have enough information to do it. "And the women's shelter?" I ask, unsure.

"Yes, ma'am."

I go over in my head all the rooms I've seen. It's everything Diane and I wished we could offer at the women's shelter but there just wasn't enough room to provide housing and all that. Is that what this is?

"Is this for real? How is this mine?"

He holds his hand out and grabs mine, dropping the key into my palm. "It is real. This is your dream, babe." He folds my hand around the key and I'm still at a loss of words. "This is your graduation present from me."

"Kase? This is too much. How did you do all this?" I spin around in a circle, taking everything in again. "Did Max help?"

He shrugs a shoulder and grabs me by the waist. "He did, as well as a few others." Realization dawns on me, this is mine. I squeal, jumping into his arms. This is my dream, but it's better than I imagined. I can't believe he did this for me. "Guess that means you like it?"

"I love it! I love you, Cowboy." Squeezing my hands around his neck, he picks me up and spins me.

"You can scream my name now," he teases, wagging his brows.

"I would if I didn't have a million things running through my mind right now. Like where do I start?"

"C'mon, just scream my name."

I wonder why he's being so persistent, but for shits and grins I give in. "Kase! Oh, Kase! Yes, right there," I joke. A second later, I jump in his arms from a rush of people running into the room. My face burns from embarrassment knowing they all heard that. "Oh, my god, I hate you."

His laugh echoes over the excitement in the room. "I didn't tell you to fake an orgasm."

"You also didn't tell me the party was coming here."

This day couldn't get any better. All night long I make plans for this place. Kase already had a list of doctors, therapists, and lawyers who said they'd volunteer here. Diane and I talk about how we'd work together to provide the best for all the women who came into the shelter.

My cheeks hurt from smiling all night. When I spot Kase across the room, our eyes meet and I know in that moment, there is not another man out there for me. He's my forever.

Our love has definitely been molded into perfection.

CHAPTER TWENTY-FOUR

ELLIE

"This is the life," I say up to the sky. The sun's rays blanket me with heat, but the breeze of the moving yacht keeps me from over-heating. Puffed clouds spread across the sky, the outline of one has me amused. "Does that look like a penis to you?" I point to it and roll my head over at Tori.

She props up on her elbows, pulls her sunglasses down her nose to get a better view. "Hmm, if you enjoy the smaller things in life."

Letting out a small laugh, shaking my head I lay back. "You're so..." I pause, trying to find the appropriate word.

"Lucky," Ben finishes my sentence, straddling her. Not really the word I was shooting for. A smile creeps up on her face. "Especially since you enjoy the bigger things in life."

When he lies on top of her, it's my cue to leave. I love them together, Ben keeps her on her toes. He's great at giving her almost everything she wants, enough to keep her coming back. She hasn't been with anyone else for a year, so I don't know what's keeping her from saying yes. She's too independent for her own good.

The wind whips my hair around as I stroll to the back of the yacht. Kase is relaxing in a chair and he watches me wobble back and forth when we hit a few waves. "Whoa!" I say, grasping the side of the boat. "How did you live on a boat?"

He stands and reaches his hand for me to take. Helping me to the chair next to him, he sits back down. "A big boat doesn't feel the waves like this one. Although, I could live on this boat forever." He sighs.

I jerk my head his way, scowling at him through my sunglasses. We've talked about moving in together, and there is no way in hell I'd live out on the water. A day trip is perfect, living on one sounds like a horror movie in the making.

"You'd love it out here," he continues without glancing over at me. "Not having to worry about neighbors." *No, just bad weather.* "Having the most incredible views." *I'm positive it'd get old.* "It'd be an adventure, every day." He peeks over at me and busts out laughing at my gaping mouth.

"It's not funny! Do you want to live on a boat? I'm not sure I could." Panic spins in my voice. I love this man, already had thoughts of being with him forever. And it scares me we're just now having this conversation.

"No, but your reaction was priceless."

I whack him on the chest. "That was a cruel joke."

He stands, leaning on the arms of my chair. "Babe, I know you're not a fan of the water and I'm not living somewhere you wouldn't." He plants a hurried kiss on my lips and stands again. The boat slows to a stop. I glance around, the beach far off in the distance, and wonder why we stopped. Ben yells from the front for us to come up there. Kase shrugs when I peer over at him for answers.

"What's up, Ben?" Kase asks when we reach them.

"Watch," he points out to the water. "There's a whale swimming around."

I smile, remembering back to our first date. I hip bump him. "I've heard that before." He waggles his eyebrows and flashes a cocky grin. It's hard to believe it was six months ago and how hard

I've fallen in love with him. I'm so busy reflecting on our journey I don't notice him taking his flip-flops off. It's not until he's climbing over the railing that I come back to the present.

"Kase! What're you doing?"

"Ellie, it's okay. I'm just going to take a quick dip."

I struggle with what to do, looking at Ben and Tori. They both shrug, so I look back to Kase. "Did you not just hear Ben? There are whales out there, ready to eat you."

"The whales won't bother me."

Ben holds his hands up. "I'm not stopping a SEAL from getting in the water. He knows what lurks down there better than I do."

My mouth opens to plead with him right as he does a perfect dive into the water. I run to the side of the boat, fisting my fingers around the hot metal rail, scouring the calm waters. Relief flows through me when his head pops up. He runs his hands through his hair, his smile bright under the dripping water. "You should come in, it's amazing out here."

"I'm sure it is. I'm good right here though, thanks."

He floats atop the water like he's lying on a solid surface, without a care in the world. My eyes flutter over the water looking for any sign of a whale. Or shark. I blow out the breath I wasn't aware I was holding, relaxing my shoulders and watch the gorgeous man swim instead of freaking out. He knows what he's doing. His board shorts suction around his muscular legs and I try not to stare too long at the outline of his soft cock, knowing it's not even close to its full potential. I'm envious of his relaxed nature. He's the calm to the storm buried deep inside me, making my past a distant memory. The last six months he's shown me there is more to life than waiting for the past to catch up. He's my now. I hope my future.

"One more dip and I'm coming up," he says right before he disappears under the water. Ben comes over, hands me a beer and stares out at the ocean.

"He's a freaking fish."

I chuckle, looking out with him, bringing the cold beer to my lips. "I hope he doesn't forget he's not the biggest fish in the sea."

We both lean against the rail. The salty air, the gentle sway of the boat with the sun low in the sky behind us, makes the tranquil moment envelop me in a place of euphoria. For a hot minute.

I jerk up, straight as a board, scanning the dark blue water. "Why hasn't Kase come up," I snap, gripping Ben's arm. A panicked heartbeat slams against my chest as I move along the side of the boat searching for bubbles, ripples, any sign of him. "Ben!" I scream when he doesn't answer.

"I... I don't know. But don't panic." He holds his hands out as if that will stop me from freaking out.

Too late.

"What's wrong?" Tori asks, coming from the back of the boat.

"Kase went under... and... and he hasn't come up." I point out to the water, every part of my body wanting to jump in and search for him.

It has to have been at least three minutes now.

Still no Kase.

"Where are your life jackets!" I scramble, throwing seat cushions off, searching the storage boxes.

Tori runs to a bench, grabbing one and throws it at me. I haphazardly put it on, snapping it around my chest.

As I'm about to jump overboard, I hear Tori yell, "Wait!"

I can't wait anymore.

I jump in.

The cold water yanks my breath away and it takes a couple of seconds to pull it back. Remember why I'm surrounded by water. What am I supposed to do now? I try to dive deeper, the sting of the salt water on my eyes last only a second but all I see is water. The life jacket fights me reminding me why I'm wearing it-so I don't sink down into the dark waters. When I surface, I jerk around at the sound of his voice. I glance up and our eyes lock from where he's standing on the boat.

"Ellie, I wouldn't have gotten out had I known you were getting in."

I gasp. The joking in his voice makes my blood boil.

"You! I thought you had drowned!" His laugh sends little electric shocks across my skin, zapping me. "Don't. Laugh. Next time, I won't care."

I kick my legs to swim toward the boat, not stopping when his body flies over me, diving into the water.

I hope the whale eats you, jackass.

I squeal as something touches my legs. Even though it's probably Kase... it might not be. I swim faster to the boat but he grabs my ankle, pulling me under water. I know it's him now, but I still fight to free my leg. Adrenaline from panic and irritation churns inside me, my body is in fight mode. When we both surface, I smack him across the face.

"This isn't funny," I snap, wiping the water from my eyes. Hot tears flush out the sea water.

"Hey," he whispers, pulling me by my lifejacket to him. "I'm sorry. I didn't mean..." He pauses, gazing into my watery eyes, his full of apology. "I didn't think you'd jump in after me."

My tears flow freely now from my erratic emotions, I couldn't stop them even if I tried. "What d'you think I'd do? I thought I lost you."

"You didn't. I'm right here."

Thank god.

I blow out an uneasy breath and nod. "Can we get out of the shark tank now?" My body shivers, and I scan the water. "Thanks to you and your grabby hands, I keep thinking something is touching my feet."

"I can guarantee it's not a shark," he says. "But c'mon, I have something for you."

We swim together to the edge of the boat where he pulls down a ladder. Holy shit, my body must have absorbed a ton of water as I pull myself up the ladder. Kase gives me a boost with a push on my ass, taking the opportunity to cop a feel, too. I turn my head to the side and give him a smart ass glare.

He shrugs. "When that fine ass is in my face, you can be damned sure I'll squeeze it. You should be happy that is all I did."

He pops up into the boat after me, with ease. Tori and Ben snuggle on the couch. "Oh, my god. You survived the wild ocean," Tori says, sarcastically.

I flip her off in between unfastening the three buckles on the life jacket. The sun heats my goose bumped body as I search for a towel. After finding a couple, I throw one at Kase and he towels off, barely wiping off the dripping water. He digs in his shorts pocket and pulls something out.

"Look, I found an oyster for you." He holds out an oval shaped oyster. I take the rough shell and turn it over in my hand. I've never seen a whole oyster, only half, ready to eat. Not a fan. The texture of slime and taste of seawater, no, thank you.

"You found this today?" I hold it up. "Is this why you almost drowned?"

He walks over to his bag, searching for something. "I didn't almost drown, woman. Let's open it, maybe there's a pearl in it."

I've looked up the statistics on this and it's like one in twelve thousand. The odds are not on our side.

"I don't want to spoil your fun, but there probably isn't one in here."

He narrows his eyes at me, takes a large step so he's standing right in front of me. "Entertain me," he rasps. The demand in his voice is sexy. If only we didn't have an audience. I'd entertain him and it wouldn't involve opening this oyster. His tongue runs along his bottom lip and he slightly shakes his head. "Such a dirty mind. Later, woman. Now... we're looking inside the oyster."

"Fine," I smile. He exposes a small knife in the palm of his hand and gives it to me, handle first. "You're so prepared." He waggles his eyebrows. Sliding the knife into the already small slit,

I'm surprised at how easy it opens. I gasp and do a double take when the shiny object sparkles inside. What? How?

Kase drops to his knee, taking first the knife out of my frozen fingers and then the oyster. He lifts the ring out and wipes it off on his wet shorts. I would laugh if my heart wasn't squeezing, stealing the air needed to breathe. "Ellie, from the first day I saw you, I knew our worlds were meant to be one. You're the light that leads me, I'd be lost in the dark without you. You're my resolution. My world starts and ends with you." He stares up at me, the depths of his blue eyes shine with love and determination. "There isn't anyone I want to live with except you. Will you marry me?"

CHAPTER TWENTY-FIVE

KASE

No?

I glance at a shocked set of eyes. "Did she say no?" Tori nods. "I fucked up." My body deflates. I didn't plan to be down there that long. We must have drifted farther than I expected. I couldn't locate the damn thing and when I got onboard, she was already jumping in. It was selfish to be excited she loved me enough to jump into the water, I didn't think how it would affect her emotionally.

"Maybe she needs a second to process everything."

I should've waited. Should have let her calm down instead of jumping right into proposing. I figured she was okay, she was making jokes. How was I supposed to know she was still upset? Or maybe she wasn't, and she doesn't want to marry me. I start second guessing everything. It's too soon. She doesn't love me. Self doubt is like the devil pissing on me. The evil thoughts burn.

"Should I go after her?"

She grimaces. "I don't know. She was really upset with you." Her eyes drift behind me for a quick second and her lips twitch up. I spin around, knowing Ellie is there.

She runs at me, flying into my arms with a smile beaming on

her beautiful face. Her legs wrap around me and she says, "Yes, I'll marry you," then slams her lips to mine. I'm slow to react because I'm so confused. I break the kiss, pulling back and make sure I'm not dreaming.

"Are you serious?"

She nods quickly. "Yes."

"But you said no."

"That was payback. Thinking you died is not a joke."

Neither is telling me no when I ask you to marry me.

Instead, I keep my mouth shut. I deserved it. The moment of clarity hits me. She said yes.

She's mine, again.

Forever this time.

CHAPTER TWENTY-SIX

ELLIE

I STARE AT THE DIAMOND ON MY RING FINGER, A LITTLE SAD KASE hasn't met my dad. When I was talking with my dad earlier, I failed to mention the engagement. He'd drop everything and come here once he knows so I need to talk to Kase first. I don't regret saying yes; I regret the secrets I'm keeping. The weight from them, increasing tenfold since Friday. It was easy to forget my past when I was with Kase, but this ring changes everything. Tonight, I'm telling him. I can't move forward after promising to spend the rest of my life with him until he knows the truth.

The oven beeps, reaching the temperature I set. I need to get moving if dinner is going to be ready by the time Kase gets home. After sliding the chicken into the oven, I pull out plates and silverware, setting the table. I smile, giddy that I'm surprising him. He's not the only one who can surprise someone. Cody let me in earlier. There might've been a few threats on his life if he said anything.

At the sound of my phone in my back pocket, I pull it out, biting my lip when I see who it is.

Cowboy: What's my beautiful fiancée doing?

Sneaking around your apartment. I giggle to myself.

Me: Thinking about you.

Cowboy: Are you naked? Are we sexting? I'm sure Stone won't mind if I jack off.

My mouth falls open and I shake my head at the picture he painted.

Me: Kase! No.

Cowboy: Which part? I asked more than one question. :)

Me: All of them! Just keep your dick in your pants.

Cowboy: For now :(

I need to put the phone down to cook the rice, so I send one last quick text.

Me: Call me on your way home.

He should be home in a half an hour. Nerves stir in my belly the closer it gets to him getting home. Will he be able to look at me the same when I tell him everything? Does he love me enough to keep it in the past and move forward? I know he's not a man to take this lightly, so I hope he understands why I kept it from him.

Once I receive a text he's headed this way, I have only fifteen minutes. I take in a deep breath and slowly exhale. Everything looks perfect and smells delicious. One last thing, light the candles. Since I forgot a lighter, I search through his kitchen drawers looking for either a lighter or matches.

"Seriously," I say, frustrated that I've run out of drawers and found nothing to light a freaking candle. I glance at my watch and then around the room. Shit, I have only five minutes left. Dammit! The candles are important.

One last thought to where matches could be, I run to the bathroom and rummage through the drawers. The last one I open, takes my breath away, my knees weaken and I have to grip the counter to catch myself. My brows pinch in confusion as my fingers shake picking up a picture. It weighs nothing in my hands, yet it feels like I'm holding a nuclear bomb, seconds from destroying my world.

CHAPTER TWENTY-SEVEN

KASE

As soon as I open the door, I can feel the change in the air. It's thick and suffocating. The second I see Ellie on the couch, staring down at a picture, I know the air is filled with my lies. It wraps around my neck like a noose, squeezing the life out of me. The life I thought I'd have with her.

Her eyes don't move from the picture of us. When we were younger. *Fuck.*

"I can explain," I say, taking long strides to get to her. She doesn't look up as she drags her finger over our embraced bodies. I sink to my knees, nestling myself in between her legs. "Ellie, look at me."

Her eyes fix on mine and her face twists. One tear escapes. No, don't cry. It's a small lie, an insignificant detail. It doesn't change the love we have for each other. The panic builds each second she doesn't talk and my mind scrambles for what to say. She holds up the picture and opens her mouth to say something, but snaps it shut. Her eyes flitter over the picture again.

"I don't remember this." Her voice is so soft, I barely hear her. "This is us."

I nod. "It is." My words come out slow.

"Why can't I remember you? We had to be around sixteen."

I sit back on my heels and blink. "Of course you can't remember. You can't remember anything from back then because of amnesia."

Her bitter laugh fills the heavy air. "Can't remember? I wish I could forget." She presses me back so she can stand. Her words send a sharp sting to my heart. How does she remember her past, but not recognize me? I am her past.

"Ellie, I don't understand."

"Kase." Her voice breaks as she folds her arms around her waist. "I don't remember you" —she swallows, looking away— "but I'll never forget my stepfather raping and beating me, then dropping me off on a dirt road to die."

My mouth gapes open and I glance around looking for answers. What is happening right now?

"Ellie, you don't have a stepfather," I whisper.

She jerks her head in my direction and her face reddens. "Do you think I'm making this up?" Her voice rises and her eyes turn stormy grey. "That my nightmares about that sick fuck is all a figment of my imagination?"

I squeeze the bridge of my nose. "Let's start over," I say, trying to diffuse the situation. "That picture is us. You were… I mean are the love of my life and always have been. Since we were ten. When we were eighteen, I went away for boot camp and when I came back you had been in a car accident and couldn't remember me. You had amnesia."

Staring intently at me, she lets this all sink in. Her expression shifts to anger. She rushes to the kitchen and reaches for a butcher knife on the counter. "He hired you, didn't he? He found me and sent you to get close? Did you work for him back then?" She points the knife at the picture on the couch and then back at me. "Get out!" she screams and I'm taken back that she's kicking me out of my own place.

"Ellie, what are you talking about? Nobody sent me. Put the knife down."

"No! He won't hurt me again. Leave Kase, or I swear to god, I'll stab you."

I put my hands in the air in defeat. "Ellie, I won't hurt you. Let's calm down and talk–"

I duck just in time for a glass to go whizzing by my head. The sound of shattered glass echoes behind me. Goddamnit woman!

"Okay! I'm leaving. Only so you can calm down, but we still need to talk."

She shakes her head as tears run down her face. My stomach knots knowing I caused this. I hesitate to leave her like this, but I need to find out what she's talking about. When I reach the front door, I turn around before I open it. "I'm sorry Ellie, I never meant to lie to you."

She stands rigid, holding the knife with a vise grip. She stays silent. I drop my head and turn to leave. The lock slides closed as soon as I shut the door. The noise pounds into my heart, sending a sharp pain. What have I done?

I fly down the stairs two at a time and call Tori.

"Hey, Kase, Ell isn't with me."

"I know, I just left her. But she needs you. I can't explain, because I don't have a clue what's going on. I need you to come to my apartment and stay with her. Don't let her leave."

"What the hell Kase? What did you do?"

"I don't have time to explain. Please, Tori. Just know, I love her more than anything and I'd never hurt her." I hang up the phone and slide into my Jeep.

"I NEED YOUR HELP," I say, storming into the frigid room. Stone rolls his head my direction, from his relaxed, feet propped up on the desk, position.

"What's up?"

I pace the office behind him. "Ellie flipped out. She found a picture of us from when we were younger."

"Oh, shit." He pulls his feet down and sits forward.

"I knew when she found out, I'd have a lot to explain, but fuck, Stone. This didn't go at all like I thought it would. She pulled a knife on me, threatening to stab me."

He belts out a laugh and I glare at him. "Sorry. That's just... that's funny."

"The hell it is. She told me she remembers her past. But the past she recalls isn't real, and she didn't remember me." He tilts his head in confusion. "Can you look up her parents? She told me her stepfather abused her, but she doesn't have a stepfather."

"Maybe her mom got remarried after you left."

"That's why I want you to look them up." I run my hand through my hair, trying to rein my agitation in. "But that doesn't make sense because that would've happened after she had amnesia. When I mentioned amnesia to her, she thought I was crazy."

Stone pounds on the keys, I pull up a chair next to him. I tell him her mom's name and the information is in front of us instantaneously. We both look it over. She never remarried. What was Ellie talking about? He continues to run different searches and we look over each site that pops up, giving me nothing I already didn't know.

The last site that pops up are court records. We both stare at the screen, reading the typed documents.

"Did you..." Stone asks me.

I shake my head, surprised by what we're reading. "No."

He types again, digging into parts of the web I wouldn't be able to find my way out of. My head hurts trying to keep up with his lighting fast keystrokes.

Then he gets there. It flashes, clear as day on the screen.

My stomach drops, and my words knot in my throat.

They say love is blind.

I was blinded by an echo and the lights just turned on.

CHAPTER TWENTY-EIGHT

ELLIE

My heart is heavy with so many emotions my chest aches. The picture. That was us. Why can't I remember him? Remember us? We looked happy. Has my mind shut out all the happiness, leaving behind the heartache and pain? Yet, Kase never talked about our past. Did he work for Ray? I fall on my bed, covering my tear-filled eyes with my arms. I'm so confused. What's real? My love for Kase is real and that stings the most. It was all a lie. He has to work for Ray. If he was part of my past, he knows about Ray and that means only one thing.

If he's here now... Ray found me.

Fear trembles through my body, seeping into my bones. Bones that remember breaking and the pain that followed. He can't find me. I push myself off the bed, determined that I have no other choice. I have to leave town.

I snatch clothes out of my closet, yanking them off the hangers, and stuff them into my duffle bag. The same duffle I had when I arrived in Gilley Cove six years ago. I thought I had found a place far enough away and small enough he'd never find me. The shrill of my phone ringing makes me jump. My hand shakes when I pick it up and I blow out a relieved breath when I see Tori's name.

"Hi," my voice trembles.

"Ell, where are you?" she screams into the phone. "Kase called me and told me to get to his apartment, but you're not there."

"I'm at my apartment. Oh Tori, everything was a lie." I swallow my cries. I hate myself for letting my guard down with him. There was something different about him from the beginning. The first night we met, he didn't look at me like he knew me, he did.

"Stay there, I'm on my way." She hangs up before I can tell her not to come.

Minutes later a knock on the door stops me mid zip from closing my bag. Holding the pepper spray, I grabbed out of my bag earlier, I creep to the front door as if the person on the other side can hear me walk. I hesitate looking through the peephole because if it's not Tori I don't want the person on the other side to see the light from the tiny hole disappear. It has to be Tori. My fingers hover over the metal dead bolt when another knock and Tori's familiar voice comes telling me to open the door.

It takes seconds to open the door, pull her in and close it again.

I REACH into the back pocket of my jeans pulling out the picture and handing it to her. Her eyes widen in surprise looking at the two teens in the picture. She waves the picture in the air and looks at me dumbfounded.

"This looks like you and Kase, but much younger."

"That's because it is. I think." Her eyebrow lifts. "I don't remember that. At all." I bury my head in my hands. "I'm so confused. He has to be working for Ray."

"Woah. Ell, he works for Max. If he worked for a guy like Ray, I'm sure Max would know." I step over and snatch the picture out of her hand.

"Then how do you explain this? This wasn't my life. I wasn't this happy. Ever. I didn't have a guy like Kase to look at me like this guy is looking at this girl. They're in love."

"What did Kase say?"

I sigh, regretting my actions. "Before or after I pulled a knife on him?"

"Oh, shit." She walks over, clutches my hand and leads me to the couch. "Start from the beginning?"

I replay the whole event and she stays quiet, listening. Saying the words out loud, I feel stupid for overreacting, but my first instinct was to fight. "He said we've known each other since we were ten and I was in a car accident and had amnesia. He also said I didn't have a stepfather." My hands shake. "But I did, Tori. I'm not making him up."

She gently presses her hand on top of mine, calming me down. "I believe you Ell. I knew you when you first came here. You were scared out of your mind at the drop of a hat. I don't doubt you at all. But something isn't adding up. Maybe that isn't you. Maybe you resemble her so much, he has the wrong person." That has to be it. It's the only thing that makes sense out of all of this. "Let me call Stone. He won't let anything happen to you, so if Kase isn't who he says he is, he'll have a shit storm coming his way." I close my eyes and fall back against the couch. The shit storm is just beginning. Taking a couple cleansing breaths, I try to calm down. Tori's right. That girl isn't me. They say everyone has a doppelganger. This has to be a case of mistaken identity. A flood of new emotions flow through me, reality setting in. He thought he found the love of his life, got me to fall in love with him and now I'm not her. My love for him isn't fake or based on false pretenses, but his is.

Her phone call to Stone is short. When I feel the couch sink, I roll my head in her direction. "He didn't tell me anything specific, but he said you and Kase need to talk. He also said not to be afraid of him."

The different direction my mind is now going, all thoughts of him working for Ray are gone. I nod, salty tears run down my cheeks. Can this day get any worse?

"He loves you, Ell."

"He loves me because he thinks I'm that girl." I blow out my cheeks and brush the tears off them. I guess it's better he finds out now instead of after we got married.

A soft knock comes from the door. "That's him. Stone said he was on his way," Tori whispers. The sound of my heart echoes in the silent room. I stare at the door wondering how I'll tell the man I love I'm not the woman he's been searching for.

"Do you want me to get it?" Tori asks after another knock. Biting the inside my cheek, I shake my head and push off the couch. Every step I take, the tightness in my chest grows. I reach for the doorknob and take a deep breath, exhaling sharply.

"Hi," I say, choking back my tears as soon as our eyes lock.

"Hi." His normal cockiness is gone, and he looks smaller standing there with his hands shoved in his pockets.

Silence hangs between us, heavy from the unknown. "Can I come in?" he murmurs.

"I'm out of here," Tori says from behind me. She squeezes my arm as she passes by and softly smiles at Kase. "Call me if you need me." I watch her disappear into the elevator and glance back at Kase, still planted in his spot. For a fractured instant, I wonder if he loves me for me. But the pained expression written all over his face, I don't think he does.

I gesture for him to enter and close the door slowly. Why rush the end? Our beginning was so perfect, I want to savor it for a few more minutes.

"I'm sorry… about earlier." My voice shakes. He sits down on the couch, leaning forward with his elbows on his knees. He nods in understanding, lifting the side of his lip in a crooked smile.

"You've always been my little hell-cat." I shift my eyes to the kitchen, my heart twists at his words. "Ellie, I love you. Please don't forget that." He darts off the couch, taking a couple of long strides to where I'm standing.

"Kase," I pause, the words getting stuck in my throat. "I'm not her."

His thumb caresses my cheek, wiping the tears. "I know." My brows furrow, and my head cocks to the side. He knows? "It doesn't make a difference—"

"How can you say that," I say, interrupting him. "It makes all the difference."

"I admit, I thought you were her. But when I found out, it didn't change how I felt. You own my heart, Ellie." No, I was borrowing his heart. It belongs to someone else.

"When did you find out?" Inside my cheek is raw from chewing, but it doesn't stop me from continuing as I wait for his answer. Words he's known for months is what I want to hear. Need to hear.

"Today," he sighs.

I drop my head, all hope of things working out, crumbling within me.

"Look at me." His warm hand slides under my chin, lifting my head to meet his eyes. "You're nothing like her. In the beginning, I was stuck on seeing the differences, but as time went on, I fell in love with those differences. They were what made you, you. The way you play with your hair when you get nervous, or the way you tap your foot three times before you cross a street."

My breath catches at my childhood superstition. Tap three times before you walk, all day long have good luck. How did he notice that? "But even with the differences, you still thought it was her. I don't know how I feel about all of this. I love you, Kase. The love I have for you has only been for you, the love you have for me began with the love of another woman. It makes me feel like I'm an imposter." I step back, out of his reach and walk to the window. The ocean has always given me peace, yet right now, it's a blur behind my tears.

"I don't know how to fix this. You're right, you were someone else in my eyes. Would I have fallen in love with you if you didn't look identical to her? I want to say yes, but my heart wasn't looking to fill her spot."

I let out a bitter laugh. "Glad to be second best."

"Fuck! I'm not saying this right." He grabs my arm and whips me around, planting his face close to mine. "Ellie, you are my present. She is my past. You are not second best, right now you are my number one and the only person I want to spend my life with. How we got here is a little screwy, but we're here, and my love for you hasn't changed. Please, don't push me away."

I rest my hands on his taut chest and stare into his pleading eyes. "I need time. It's a lot to take in."

He pulls in a deep breath, releasing it slowly. "There's more and we should talk about it before I leave. I'll take off after that…" His voice trails off.

More? What the hell is he talking about?

"I need you to tell me everything about your past," he softly demands. I tense, my guard goes up. His eyes narrow. "Ellie, you pulled a knife on me thinking I was someone else, and now you tense when I ask you about your past. Is it your stepfather searching for you?"

Having Max's team around me has always made me feel more at ease. I was close enough with the guys, if I ever needed help, they'd be there to help me. Kase is different. I don't want him to know my demons and torment him, they do enough damage. He's been okay with me keeping my past in my past, can't we keep it there?

"Ellie, you're not answering me."

I wince. "I don't think so."

"That's not a good enough answer," he replies with a sharp tone. I roll my eyes as he lifts me off my feet in his arms and carries me to the couch. He plops me down and then settles in next to me.

I twirl my hair and it's not until he stops me do I notice I was doing it. A smug smile plays on his lips. *So, you know my quirks.* I sigh, realizing keeping my past from him is no longer an option.

"When I was four, my dad walked out on me and my mom. We didn't have much, so my mom would work random jobs. I was home a lot by myself. She ended up falling in love with a guy and marrying him when I was twelve. At first, he was nice and tolerated me. But when I turned fifteen, things changed." I can sense Kase's whole body stiffen, but I keep going, staring ahead, not wanting to see his expression. "At first, he would come into my bedroom to say goodnight, being extra feely. His hands would graze my boob when he was rubbing my arm, stuff like that. It continued to progress the next few months. The night I turned sixteen was the first night he raped me."

Kase bolts up out of his seat, running his hands through his hair, making it stand on end. His jaw ticks and I can see the rage swirling in his eyes. "Please tell me this motherfucker is dead," he grates out. "Because he's going to be if he's not."

"Let me finish." I lick my lips, my mouth parched. The last time I told this story, I was in the courthouse, and the devil's eyes were burning a hole in me. He nods once, but stays standing. I knot my fingers together, squeezing them and continue. "When I was seventeen, I finally told my mom what was happening. She didn't believe me. He got a kick out of it so I told him I was going to the police the next day. Gah, I was stupid." I shake my head, remembering the rage that filled his whole body that night, bleed into mine.

Kase drops down in front of me, unwrapping my fingers. He brushes his lips over each fingernail indentation in my palms. "You're not stupid Ellie. You were a teenager trying to get help. It was a defensive tactic. You thought he'd leave you alone if he knew you were going to tell someone."

"It was the exact opposite. He raped me and beat me with anything he could get his hands on. Then he threw me in the car and dropped me off in the woods to die. I remember feeling happy that he couldn't touch me again. I was going to die, and I was at peace with it. I was ready to leave hell."

"Who found you?" he whispers.

"There was a horse on the loose the next morning. The guy who owned the land was out looking for him and found me instead. I had lost consciousness. When I woke up, I was in a hospital bed."

Kase runs his fingers up the scar on my arm, like he's done a million times. This time it's different. I nod my head. They aren't scars to me, they are badges that display the strength and determination that no one can bring me down. I had months of rehabilitation, but I did it. Just to prove to Ray that he couldn't get rid of me that easily. He digs his head into my stomach, wrapping his arms around me.

"He's in jail for life."

"But he's still living," Kase mumbles into my lap.

"Kase," I say, waiting for him to lift his head. "Promise me you won't do anything."

"Why are you scared then? Are you hiding out here?"

My shoulders drop. "He was a high profile pimp, which I later found out he was trying to groom me. He had guys that worked for him and they all knew me because I was his stepdaughter. So, after he went to jail, his guys tried to find me."

"Why didn't you tell me all of this? I would do anything for you, especially keep you safe."

A sarcastic laugh slips from my lips. "Yeah, I guess I could've prevented all this mistaken identity business if I would have."

"It wouldn't have made a difference."

"You keep saying that, but you said it yourself, you weren't open to love."

"I can't go back to what ifs because I don't know. I know that I love you right now and I'll kill anyone that tries to touch you again."

The anger brewing in his eyes scares me.

I won't let him go to jail for killing someone for me. "Please, Kase," I plead with him. His eyes jump back and forth, not focusing on my face, but rather my eyes. With a slight shake to his head, he can't make that promise. Our gazes are locked in a war of will. I don't know why I'm even trying. When he furrows his brow, I ask, "What?"

"You've talked about your dad, but you said he took off when you were four."

"The guy that found me was a retired Texas Ranger. Dalton Keyes. The police wanted me to go into witness protection. Dalton was there for me the entire time. Surgeries, rehabilitation, didn't matter, he stayed by my side. He was all I had, and I clung to him so hard, he couldn't have left even if he wanted to. When he offered to keep me at his place until the trial, I didn't hesitate at all. He became the father I never had."

"He sounds amazing. I can see the love you have for him in your eyes."

I smile softly. "He was my angel."

"I'd love to meet him."

Tears flow down my cheek and I nod. "I'd love that." He runs his knuckles over my cheek, catching the falling tears.

"I'm getting us a couple of beers," he says, standing.

"We're going to need more than a couple."

He nods in agreement and grabs the entire six pack out of the fridge. Once we both have a beer in our hands, I take a long pull, the cool bubbles feel refreshing in my parched mouth.

"Feeling a little better?"

A flurry of emotions swirl in the pit of my stomach as I settle back against the couch. The excitement from this morning, celebrating our six month anniversary, seems like it was days ago. I shrug. "We've talked about so much. Stuff we should've been open about when we first were getting serious."

"I'm sorry. It's my fault," he says, grabbing my hand out of my lap and pulling it over to him.

"I wasn't open with you either. There's one thing that's confusing though." He raises a brow, waiting for me to continue.

"You said we aren't anything alike yet you thought this whole time, I was her. Why?"

"Do you remember the date of when…" He chokes on his words, not able to get them all out.

"August twenty-fifth. It's not like I could ever forget it."

"So bizarre," he mumbles under his breath.

CHAPTER TWENTY-NINE

KASE

"What's bizarre?"

This whole situation.

I focus on her rather than the fury raging inside me. She knows I'm not letting this go. Target practice is happening, and I always shoot dead center. I blow out a heavy breath, clearing my mind because I owe her this much. The truth.

I hesitate to answer because this will rock her world. It shook mine at the core. "Did you know you were adopted?"

She angles her head. "Yes," she says, dragging the word out. "Before I turned eighteen, I asked Dalton if he would adopt me so I could start over with a new last name. That's when I found out. I also found out that my birth mom named me Ellie so I wanted to keep that part. How did you know?"

I take a swig of my beer, set it on the glass table, and rub my hands down my pants. I can't tell if it's condensation from the beer or sweat. "The reason I thought you were Everly was because your DNA matched hers." She tilts her head, pinching her lips together.

"How… could that be?"

"You were born a twin. Everly is your twin sister."

She gasps under her fingers covering her mouth, blinks a

couple of times before releasing a breath. "How?" she squeaks out in a disbelieving tone.

"You were adopted to different parents."

"Who would split up twins?"

I shrug. I hate I don't have all the answers. "We found the documents, but I didn't read them thoroughly. I only know you are part of a twin."

"Twins have the same DNA?" So it seems. She sits forward and covers her face with her hands. I reach for her, but stop halfway, pulling back. I want to comfort her, but I don't know how she'll feel about me touching her. "Oh my god," she snaps, lifting her head. "You love both of us."

"Loved," I blurt out. Her brows knit together. "I loved her. I love you, Ellie." She belts out a bitter laugh. "Everly and Ellie. I can't believe this is happening. I thought worrying about being number two was bad. Knowing you loved my twin sister and thought I was her is so much worse."

She shoves off the couch, grabbing her beer and drains the rest while she paces. She replaces her empty beer bottle with a full one, downing half of that one in one gulp. "It still doesn't make a difference to me," I plead.

"It does to me."

This could be the end of us and there isn't anything I can do because it doesn't change the fact I love two people with the same face. Same DNA. I told her I loved Everly, but that isn't true. I'll always love Everly, she was a big part of my life. It's different with Ellie though. The love I have for her completes me. She gets me and never makes me feel like I have to justify anything I've done.

"Why did you ask what the date was?" She stops walking and stares at me.

"It's the day Everly was in a car accident. They thought she might have passed out because she plowed into another car without even braking."

"Oh my god, oh my god." Her voice escalates. She fans her face as her eyes well up with tears. "He almost killed both of us."

She collapses onto one of the dining room chairs, head down on the table. Her back shakes from her silent cries.

After that, she was done talking, except to tell me I should go. I told her I would leave, but I'd be back to check on her tonight after she had time to think about everything. The salty air hits my face as I walk out of her apartment building. I'm on auto pilot walking through the streets, not caring where I'm headed.

When my feet hit the soft sand, I stare out to the vast ocean. I haven't been out in the deep waters in a few months. Each step closer, I strip off a piece of clothing, only my boxers left by the time I touch the water. This is what I know. I take a few deep breaths before running and diving in. The cool water engulfs me as I slice through it at a high speed. In the shallow waters, my body glides above the sandy bottom, my mind focusing only on my environment, temporarily erasing the last two hours.

A sting-ray glides underneath me in the opposite direction. Those I don't mind, it's the sharks I don't like to play with so I keep a watchful eye. I rise to the top, barely breaking the barrier to the open air and take a quick breath and lower again. The ocean floor drops and the darkness takes me back to many mission dives. Life felt easy then compared to now.

Something falling into the water grabs my attention. I stop swimming and focus on the object covered in bubbles. Craning my neck forward, I see it's a person, swimming toward me so I kick my feet to move me to the surface. The person follows, but the red and white helicopter above our head, tells me who it is. Shit. Hello coast guard.

"Sir, you're going to be okay," he yells. I smirk at the ridiculousness of this. "Put this over your head."

I shake my head and yell, "I'm fine. I'll swim back." Pointing back to the shore, I notice how far I swam. The beach is barely visible, so I think back to how many breaths I took.

"I need you to put this on." The blades of the helicopter swoosh loudly making it hard to hear anything. He's not letting me go, so I grab the harness and put it on quicker than he can do it himself. He stares at me for a moment and mumbles a few things to himself before lifting a thumb to pull me up. The cocky side of me wants to wave at him as we're being hoisted up, but I put it away. They're doing their job and they do a damn good job too. I worked with a team out in California when I was training during BUD/S. I have the highest respect for them for putting their lives on the line to save people.

When we're both pulled into the helicopter, I strip off the harness and all eyes are on me. Pulling my wet boxers away from my junk, I sit and strap in the seat. The crew looks at me confused. I flip my wrist around, showing my bone frog tattoo on my forearm since talking right now without a headset is useless.

"Son of a bitch," I think one says.

They call it in as a false alarm and we breeze through the sky. One guy hands me a helmet. "Where are we dropping you off?" he asks over the headset.

"Just take me back to Base, I'll catch a ride back from there." They've wasted enough resources on me. The New Haven Station is located a few miles away. He smiles and shakes his head. I hold up my hands. "I was just taking a swim."

"We got a call that a guy was trying to kill himself, jumping into the ocean and never surfacing."

"I surfaced. Ten times."

He rolls his eyes, shaking his head. "We'll get you some clothes so you don't make us all look bad." I glance down and remember my clothes are still on the beach. I can picture the scene unfold, what everyone saw. No wonder they called it in.

Half an hour later, I'm dressed in a navy blue coast guard t-shirt and sweats. Thankfully, someone had an extra pair of flip-flops. My hands are in my pockets when the Commander approaches me.

He holds out his hand. "Commander Cooper."

I grasp his hand in a firm shake. "Kase Nixon." He glances at my tattoo and looks back with a smirk.

"Sorry about rescuing you."

I laugh out loud. He knows his guys didn't rescue me. "Next time I take a swim, I'll make an announcement."

"Maybe not look like a desperate guy looking for a way out." I run my hand through my hair, staring down at the flip-flops. The situation with Ellie hadn't crossed my mind for the last couple of hours.

"It's been a shitty day. I needed a release. Sorry for the confusion."

He shrugs. "We all have our days."

A guy I recognize by his tatts from the helicopter, walks up to us. "Your ride is here."

My ride? I turn my attention to the Commander and he shakes his head. "We didn't call anyone other than the local police to follow up on the original call." Hope simmers wondering if it's Ellie.

"I'll make sure to return these," I say, tugging on my shirt.

"That's all right. You can keep them to remind you of the day the coast guard rescued you." The group of people around us laugh. He's a funny guy. "You're welcome to come back here and give my guys a run for their money." I might take him up on his offer.

I shake his hand and the men from the helicopter, thanking them for a job well done. When I walk outside, a bright blue corvette is waiting for me. Cody rolls his window down as I walk up.

"This is fucking epic." Rolling my eyes, I flip him off, pull the door open and slide in. The tires peel out of the parking lot as we speed off. "You know if you needed someone to talk to, I'm always here for you." With the shitty grin on his face, he's far from being sincere. "I mean you didn't have to pretend you were trying to drown yourself to get attention."

I shake my head, letting him get his jokes in.

He puts his hand on my thigh. "I mean, I love you Kase, you're one of the team." I yank his hand off me, shaking my head and cursing through my chuckle. I hope to god none of the guys back on the SWAT team hear about this. This is nothing compared to the shit they'd give me.

"Will you watch the fucking road?" I say, pointing forward. Out of habit, I reach into my pocket to pull my phone out and I remember, it's in the pocket of my shorts I dropped on the beach. "Dammit. My phone's in my shorts on the beach."

"Nah. Officer Sloan picked 'em up for you. As soon as he heard it was you, he grabbed your stuff and called us." We're back in Gilley Cove in no time. We swing by the police station first so I could pick up my stuff. When I hop back into the car, I scroll through my missed calls. Twenty of them. They're all from Ellie and Tori. Fear ripples through me that she's calling me to tell me goodbye. I press play to the first message left. Panic in her voice isn't from her telling me goodbye. Shit. Shit. Shit. Pounding my head against the headrest, I make myself listen to the whole message.

"Kase, where are you? I'm worried sick. They said... they said the coast guard just pulled you out of the water, but no one is telling me where they took you! I love you Kase. Please call me back."

Jesus Christ! This is turning into a nightmare. Each message is the same, except her panic escalates to where she can barely form a sentence. All the messages are within fifteen minutes. Then they stop. I glance over at Cody. "Did you talk to Ellie?"

"Yeah. She called us, hysterical. Damn, that woman frightens me. I tried to tell her you were okay without telling her details." I tilt my head, surprised they didn't take the opportunity to razz me. He shrugs with one shoulder. "We don't give details. Ever," he states matter-of-fact. I slap him on the shoulder and nod. "I told her I was picking you up, and that you were fine."

"Can you drop me off at her apartment?"

I'm thinking positive thoughts when I reach her door. We're getting married. This is only a temporary setback. I tap lightly with my knuckles. The door swings open and Ellie flies into my arms.

"Kase!" I drop my bag and wrap my arms around her waist, digging my face into her neck. Taking in a deep breath of her scent, one I wondered if I'd ever inhale again, my world rights itself despite knowing she's only doing it out of fear. When she finally releases her arms from around my neck, she pulls back and punches me on the arm. "You scared me to death! I thought you had drowned, again! I saw them pull you up and then fly away. Nobody would tell me anything." My lips pull into a smile at her pouty face. "It's not funny." She pushes out of my arms and walks into her apartment. I follow, shutting the door behind me.

"Babe, I promise you, the last way I'll die is from drowning."

She rolls her eyes. "You keep saying that but a shark could have taken a bite."

I laugh at how serious she is. I mean, she's right, a shark could take me out, but the odds are thin. "Ellie, I'm okay."

She lifts her brow as her eyes move up and down my body. "So... doing some on-the-job training," she jokes, pointing to my outfit. "It's kinda hot."

I peek down at my coast guard attire and look back at her, appalled. I yank on my shirt. "You think this is hot?" Her beautiful lips twist and she nods. "You know I'm a SEAL, right? Nothing is hotter than that. Especially not the coast guard." Like I said, I have the utmost respect for those guys, but if my woman is getting hot and bothered over them, it's going down. "I'll show you hot," I murmur as I lift off the shirt and toss it on the floor. She bites her bottom lip, evoking a deep growl from the back of my throat. Her back hits the kitchen counter as I take a couple of long strides toward her. Her sweet gasp as I pick her up and set her on the counter goes straight to my dick.

"I love when you make that noise especially when my dick sinks into you," I murmur into her neck. Her pulse quickens against my lips as I nibble up to her ear and back down her jaw line.

"Then stop talking, Cowboy. I need to feel you inside me."

You don't have to tell me twice. I'm an obedient guy when it comes to sex. She leans back on her arms, arching her back when I suck a nipple through her thin t-shirt. Her ass lifts off the counter a couple of inches, enough room for me to slide her shorts and panties off. I tug my sweats down, not caring to take them completely off. I'm afraid she'll change her mind if I don't hurry. Tell me to leave when she figures out she's doing this for the wrong reason. Fear and passion are a toxic mixture and I'm probably a bastard for taking advantage of it, but I need her to remember what we feel like together. That there's no question how much I love her.

When my cock buries inside her, I close my eyes, relief spiraling around my spine, nothing feels more perfect than this. "I love you," I whisper into her ear. She doesn't say it back, only moans. Just for that, I make sure she's screaming my name by the end.

I pull up my sweats, then lift her off the counter and carry her to the couch. I apologize for scaring her. She tells me about taking a walk on the beach to clear her head. Unfortunately, the timing was bad. When she saw a group of people staring at something in the water, she walked over only to see my clothes sprawled across the beach and me being lifted into the helicopter.

"I was about to kill someone, trying to find answers."

Chuckling, I say, "I heard."

She narrows her eyes. "He could have told me what happened. I was freaking out, and he wasn't much help." I nibble on her fingers. She yanks them back. "Stop. You should put me down as your emergency contact, so they'll call and tell me what's going on."

"That won't make a difference." I push a piece of loose hair behind her ear. "The less you know, the better."

"Well, that sucks."

I nod in understanding, despite knowing it will never change. "Besides that, are we better?" *Say, yes.* Her hand rests on my thigh and I run my fingers in between hers, linking them. I know she loves me.

Although, she was quick to pull a knife on me this morning.

She looks at me with pain in her eyes, I'm afraid of what'll come out of her mouth. "Before we can move past this…" She pauses, inhaling and exhaling sharply. "… I want to meet her."

That is exactly what I was afraid of.

CHAPTER THIRTY

ELLIE

"Welcome to Dallas Ft. Worth," the pilot says over the intercom.

I stare down at the skyscrapers beneath us, lean my head against the window and sigh. My anxiety of coming back to Texas kept me up all night. I should have nothing to worry about, we're far away from El Paso. Layer that with meeting my twin sister, my fiancé's ex who he still has to have feelings for... it's put a lot of weight on my heart. What if he sees her and decides she's the one he wants? *This is why we're here*, I keep reminding myself.

My mind hasn't turned off since we left Gilley Cove. We barely talked on our flight. Kase is letting me figure things out internally and answering questions I've had along the way. It's been a week since I learned I had a twin, but I'm just as confused about everything as I was on day one.

There's one question that keeps popping up in my head though. We have a two-hour drive, so I figured I'd wait to ask when there weren't people around us.

Once we're in the rental car and driving, I tuck my foot under my knee and shift my body toward him, finally asking, "If she was the love of your life, why did you leave her?"

His fingers grip the steering wheel and he expels a pained breath. "I should have brought this up. But I was afraid I'd lose you after what you told me, about your stepfather."

"I don't understand."

He sighs heavily. "You know my mom died from cancer when I was sixteen." I nod and lay my hand on top of his, resting on the gearshift. "Once they diagnosed her, she didn't suffer long. She suffered a lot longer by the hand of my dad. She wasn't strong enough to leave my dad, so she stayed and took it, keeping it away from me. After she died, I was his punching bag until I became powerful enough to defend myself." This breaks my heart, hearing we had similar upbringings. "I tried my best to stay away from him after that. I was usually with…" He stops mid-sentence.

"It's all right. She was your childhood love. You don't need to act like it didn't happen."

"I left right after graduation to go to boot camp. When I came back, I learned Everly had been in a bad car accident. I raced to her house only to discover she didn't remember me. I was wiped from her memory."

"That's… horrible. I can't imagine what that felt like to her and you. If I would have had amnesia, it would've been a blessing. Of course, I didn't have a guy like you to forget."

He manages a small smile.

"So, her memory never returned?"

"I don't know. She never came looking for me." I watch his shoulders tense and he adjusts himself in the seat, sitting taller. His eyes won't meet mine. "After I left her house, I drove back home. My dad was drunk, like normal. He spewed about how no one would ever love me if they couldn't remember me. Shit like that."

"I'm sure it made you furious." Unease rolls off him as he clenches his jaw.

"I couldn't control my anger." He takes in a deep breath, blowing it out through his nose, a bead of sweat falls from his forehead and he wipes it with the back of his hand. "Everly's father was a police officer. He came to my house, searching for me. But it was too late." I cover my mouth, trying to silence the gasp. His face jerks to the side. "I swear, I didn't mean to kill him." My heart squeezes with emotions from his admission. My worst fear is being with a man like my step-father, but Kase isn't like him. He's not like his dad. I can hear the shame, the regret, the unfounded guilt in his voice. I see a teenage boy trapped with an evil father like my stepfather, hurt and angry at life. It's how I spent my teenage years. Life is unfair. I dreamt every night about killing my stepfather, but I could never go through with it. For years I wondered if I fought back hard enough the night he left me for dead, it would've been him laying unconscious on the ground instead of me.

"He was a monster," I say, reassuring him I understand.

"I should've been able to stop. After the years of abuse my mom went through, I was blind to any rationale."

"I'm the last one to judge, Kase. I don't think I would've been able to stop either."

"Jake had to pull me off. He's the reason I left. He didn't like me, didn't think I was good enough for his daughter. So he gave me an ultimatum."

"Leave or go to jail?" I whisper, stunned a grown man would do that, let alone a police officer.

He nods, opens his mouth to say something, but snaps it shut. For a man who demands control at all times, admitting this has to be killing him on the inside. Clearing his throat, he continues. "Nobody liked my dad in town. Jake and my mom were a thing in high school. My dad shows up, a stranger in a small town and my mom took a liking to him. Jake wasn't happy and always had it in for him. I should've stayed and dealt with my mess, but I was a scared teenager given a way out. So, I took it and I haven't been back since." He swallows harshly, sniffs and wipes away his unwanted tears.

We need to turn around. The last thing I want is for him to find himself in trouble for returning. Worry is etched into his sharp features and guilt for making him take me here presses heavy against my chest. If I'd only known everything. "Kase," I finally say. "I can do this by myself. You don't need to go back and risk everything."

He glances in his rearview mirror, flipping on his hazards to move to the shoulder. His lip quirks up and the tension in his shoulders relaxes some. "I'm not worried about that. At all. I'm here for you and I'm not leaving your side. Okay? I just needed you to know."

I nod, turning in and kissing his hand that's cupping my cheek. Not knowing how the next few hours will play out, I hold on to the hope we'll survive this.

CHAPTER THIRTY-ONE

KASE

As soon as I turn onto residential streets, we both quiet and stare at the smaller brick houses lining each side of the road, the anxiety in the space suffocating. Each one that passes by makes my stomach twist more. Why did I agree to this? I understand she wants to meet her sister, but this whole situation has me feeling out of sorts.

When Stone told me the address, it surprised me she doesn't live in Barrow, but a few towns over. He also informed me she recently filed for divorce, and that's where I stopped him. I don't want to know. I'm here for Ellie, I'm not coming here to catch up with Everly. She forgot about me, and as much as that still stings, I've let it go and moved on.

I clear my throat and say, "This next left is her street." Ellie wrings her hands together and leans forward to read the house numbers. I've reminded her every day that no matter what happens, I choose her.

I slow the car and park in front of a pale yellow brick house and glance over at Ellie. She's staring at the house, biting the inside of her cheek. "This is stupid," she says, shifting in her seat toward me, panicking. "Let's go. We can call her and tell her she has a twin."

I grin, having thought that numerous times this week. I wrap my hand around hers and bring it to my lips. "How about I go check if she's home. She won't recognize me, so I'll introduce myself and explain..." I pause, wondering what I should say. "Well, we'll go from there. This isn't something we can plan out."

She exhales loudly. "Okay. Gesture when it's a good time for me to get out."

I lean over, grab her behind the neck and guide her to my mouth. Her lips part and I pour the love I have for her into the kiss. "I love you," I murmur against her lips. She nods when I find her eyes. "It'll be okay."

At least, I hope so.

I hop out of the SUV and shake out my hands, taking a few deep breaths. She won't know you, I repeat in my head. I'm a stranger to her, she'll think I'm a sales person in my khaki shorts and polo. My knuckles rap on the glass part of the door and then I stick them in my pockets. It's afternoon, so she's probably not even here. After a couple minutes of hearing nothing, I spin around and walk down the stairs. I glance at Ellie and shrug. The sound of a door opening stops me in my tracks.

"Kase," a familiar voice says from behind me. Ellie's voice, but with a heavy southern accent. I turn slowly, cocking my head. She didn't just say my name. Did she?

When our eyes meet, my words get stuck in my throat. I always knew Ellie looked like her, but seeing Everly standing there, it's remarkable how similar they are. Those green eyes I fell in love with stare back at me. My brain doesn't seem to be functioning. I told it over and over she wouldn't recognize me, yet she said my name.

"Did you say my name?"

She smiles. "I did." I can see it in her eyes. The recognition. The love. I drop my gaze, focusing on my hands. "Kase, I remember you." She takes a step toward me. I should take a step back, but I can't. My feet are rooted in this spot.

"How? When?" I respond in disbelief.

She turns her attention toward a vehicle coming down the street and her gaze darts down to her watch. She peeks at it again and then back to me. A flicker of panic flashes in her eyes and her shoulders tense. I crane my neck around to see what has her so worried. A truck pulls up, and a boy hops out and rushes up the sidewalk.

"Mom, I got a hundred in PE." He flies by me, holding up a piece of paper.

She runs her hand through his hair, her eyes flickering between the two of us. "Good job. Can you go inside, I'll be in there in a minute." He turns and stares at me. I freeze in disbelief.

"Hi, I'm Reed." He holds out his hand. I focus on his little hand. Long skinny fingers. His eyebrow shoots up when I stand there stupefied, struggling to find my voice.

I slowly lift my hand, wrapping it around his. "Hi Reed, I'm Kase."

"Hmm. That's a cool name." My lips curl up.

"Thanks. I like yours too." His face brightens and I'm staring at myself almost twenty years ago. It's hard to breathe let alone talk when all I want to do is yell. "How old are you Reed?"

"I'm ten. I look younger because I haven't hit my growth spurt yet. It's coming though, isn't that right, Dad." My heart stops. I jerk my head up to Everly, my entire insides twisting in a frenzy. Did he call me dad? Everly's eyes water, her hand covers her mouth, and she shakes her head slightly. What does that mean? He's not mine, or he didn't call me dad? I glance back to Reed but his eyes focus on something behind me. I peer over my shoulder to the man leaning against his truck, his eyes pinned on me.

A flash of rage heats inside me. This isn't happening. He wouldn't do this. He's been my best friend since we were born.

"Kase," Wayne says, pushing off his truck and strolling toward me. "This is a surprise."

My muscles tighten and I draw my head back stiffly. I laugh without humor. You fucking think?

Whipping back around to Everly, I wait for her to tell me what I'm thinking is wrong. When she can't look at me, she confirms my suspicion. I have a son, and my best friend raised him without telling me. I squeeze the bridge of my nose as my body vibrates with anger. There's only been one other time anger flowed through every vein in my body and it didn't end well.

"Reed, please go inside." Everly's voice breaks. Reed looks at each of us.

"Is everything okay?" he asks, peering at me. His question isn't directed at me, but I'm the stranger here. I manage to smile at him and relax my shoulders despite my raging pulse.

"It is. Just go and start your homework. Do it in your bedroom," Everly replies.

His hands flail to the side before they flop down. "What? Why am I being grounded? I didn't do anything this time." Despite my annoyance, I grin at the little guy. He even reminds me of me.

"You're not grounded. I just need you to go in your room, okay?" She lifts his chin so he's looking at her. He nods his head and goes inside. I blow out a ragged breath.

"Kase, I never meant for you–"

I hold a finger up, grinding my teeth. "Stop," I snap. I shift my attention to Wayne. "You son-of-a-bitch." I leap the three feet that separates us, slamming my fist into his face. His fist connects to my side and we both tumble to the ground, throwing punches and kicks.

"Kase! Stop." My back stiffens and I push off Wayne, rolling to my side. Everly gasps and I close my eyes knowing today changes everything.

Ellie.

"What the hell?" Wayne rasps in between heavy breathing and spitting blood.

CHAPTER THIRTY-TWO

ELLIE

I HAVEN'T EVER WATCHED MY LIFE FALL APART, FROM THE OUTSIDE, looking in. These last fifteen minutes in the car, observing has been excruciating. I'd thought about getting out of the car, many times, except each time, something new happened. Something life changing, like watching Kase's name fly out of my twin sister's mouth. Or watching Kase see his son for the first time. My heart broke as soon as I saw the kid's face.

When Kase jumped on the guy, I couldn't wait anymore. What he's capable of and the thunderous expression written across his face; I knew he'd need someone on his side to help him stop.

So, here I stand, three sets of eyes pinned on me. I didn't think this through. The silent street fills with panting and grunts from the two guys. Kase rolls over and pushes up to stand and I rush to his side, struggling to avoid the stares from Everly and the guy.

"This is rich, even for you, Kase. What, you can't have Everly so you found someone who looks just like her?"

"Fuck you, asshole," he rasps, taking a step toward him. I lay my hand on his chest, halting him. He growls, glaring at the guy. "I'm sorry. I need to take a walk." He whips around and stomps off.

"That's right, walk away. You're good at that."

Who the hell is this guy? He's signing his own death warrant and I'm not stopping Kase next time.

"I figured you'd be happy that it was me taking care of Everly and your kid."

Kase's fists squeeze, his knuckles whiten as he remains still and I can see his restraint slipping. Everly must see it too.

"That's enough, Wayne." It's the first time I've heard her talk. I focus on her and I can feel her pain, deep inside my body. I shiver at the trespassing emotion. Our eyes lock and I feel like I'm looking into a mirror. "Wayne, you need to leave," she says without looking away.

"But—"

She shakes her head and finally looks at him. "No, you need to leave."

Wayne's face twists and he pleads with her. "Please don't take away my son. You told me you wouldn't." He wipes his bloody lip with the back of his hand, looking at the blood.

"I can't do this right now."

"I'm so sorry, babe," he says.

She winces and he drops his shoulders in resignation.

"Tell Reed I'll talk to him tomorrow."

When he walks past me, I can see tears falling. It's obvious he loves Everly and Reed. After he drives away, it's down to two.

I shove my hands in my pockets because things just turned awkward. She looks me up and down, her brows creased. She clears her throat. "I don't know what to say."

I let out a muffled laugh. "Hi?"

"Who are you?"

"I'm Ellie. So, it seems we're twins."

Her eyes bulge and her mouth gapes open and I imagine that was exactly my expression when I found out. "We were split up when we were born and adopted to different families." She got the better deal.

She shakes her head fast. "No. That can't be right. You must've received bad information. I'm not adopted."

She stares at me for a few moments and then takes out her phone. Her hands shake as she presses the call button. I hate this for her right now. At least when I found out, I was happy that I didn't belong to my mom. She's about to find out the parents she loves, lied to her.

"Mom, was I adopted?" The words spill out of her mouth with no preempt. "Mom," she snaps. "Just tell me yes or no." She gasps and the phone slips from her hand, landing on the ground. A woman's voice cries out of the phone, calling for Everly. I walk over, pick up the phone and end the call.

"I'm so sorry you had to learn this way." My voice is filled with regret. I hand her the phone when it starts to ring. She takes it and turns it off. I glance down the street to see if Kase is coming back, but he's nowhere to be seen.

"You must think I'm a horrible person right now," she says.

I turn back. "Truthfully, I have no clue what to think right now."

"Do you… want to come inside?"

I understand her hesitancy. It took a few days to let this sink in before I could talk about it. Now, it feels surreal to be standing in front of someone who has your face, your voice. We shared the same space for nine months, we share pain, we share DNA.

We share the same man.

Yet, there is one thing she'll always have that I can't; a child that belongs to Kase. He's been adamant about not wanting kids, but all of that has changed. He has one with her.

"Please," she whispers. "You seem to know more about us, and I'd like to talk."

"I'd like that." I follow her up the steps.

Once inside, shuffling footsteps come down the hallway. Reed walks into the living room and his eyes widen. "Holy shit!" he whoops, looking back and forth between us.

"Reed Williams," Everly warns in a way only mothers can.

"Mom!" He ignores her and walks over to me, looking me up and down. "You got a clone! You said you always wanted one. I didn't know they were real. How much was she? Does she have a turn off button? Can she clean my room?" His questions rattle off his tongue as fast as a freight train. My lips curve into a smile as he continues to observe me. He pokes my arm. "She feels real too."

"Reed," she says, trying not to laugh.

"Mom, this is so cool. How will I know who's who? I don't want to tell her a secret when it's not you." The excitement in his voice is too much. Everly and I both burst out. His eyes brighten and he jumps up and down. "You can even make her laugh when you do!"

"Reed, she's not a clone." Reed gives her an incredulous stare. "She's…" she pauses, wondering how to explain. It might be easier to go along with the clone aspect. "She's my sister."

His smile drops and he jerks his head in my direction and back to her. "You told me you didn't have any brothers or sisters."

"Um… this is a surprise to me too." She struggles with the words to explain. "Can you go outside and play while we talk?"

She manages to get him outside by offering candy. He couldn't care less what's going on when he pops a sucker in his mouth. He runs outside, yelling he'll be at Bennett's. The screen door slams leaving us alone once again.

She walks to her kitchen while I walk around her living room. The soft yellow on the walls match the outside paint and brighten the room. Pictures of Reed are all over one of the walls, black frames surround them in a patterned display. My eyes jump from picture to picture, many with Reed and the guy from outside. My heart hurts for Kase and I wonder how he's dealing with everything. I move along when my subconscious tells me it should be Kase in those pictures with Everly and Reed. My chest hurts thinking that is where he might want to be.

Everly offers me a glass of tea when I'm looking at a picture of her and what I'm assuming is her mom. She's a beautiful brunette. She could pass as our mom. A slight streak of jealousy rears its head. *It's not her fault you were stuck with a rotten mother.* I take a large drink to swallow the feeling and my hand flies to my chest.

"Oh my gosh." I cough and clear my throat of the sugar cube I just drank. "I forget how sweet the tea is here in Texas."

"So… I guess you've been here before? Texas," she clarifies.

"I grew up in El Paso." Twirling my ice around, I glance down to my glass. I can sense she has more questions. "You have a nice home," I say, looking around, avoiding her gaze. I pick up a picture sitting on her TV stand. It's Everly, Reed and the guy from earlier. They seem happy.

"That was taken right before I got my memory back."

"Oh." My eyebrows rise in surprise. Reed isn't much younger in the picture.

"It was taken last year." She's only had her memories back for less than a year? She walks over to the couch and sits.

"Who's the guy?"

"Wayne. Kase's best friend from school." Wow. That explains a lot. No wonder he attacked him. "It's a long story, but until last year, I thought Wayne was Reed's father."

I do a double take. "Did he know Reed wasn't his?" I ask, trying to give the guy the benefit of the doubt. I take a seat on the cushioned chair, opposite the couch.

She takes a deep inhale and blows it out. "Oh yeah. Look at him, he's a tiny version of Kase. Wayne isn't a bad guy, he truly loves me and Reed. We had a great life. He was the perfect husband, the perfect dad. It was all just based on the perfect lie. Until I hit my head from trying to use a skate board. I blacked out and when I woke up, it was the oddest thing. My memories were all there. Old and new. My body was waging a war inside itself. The love I had for Kase was there like it never went away, yet the love I had for Wayne was there too. It was a confusing couple of months," she says, sarcastically.

"Wow," I say, trying my hardest to ignore that she still loves Kase. Her eyes travel down my arm. They stay on my scar for a few moments and then move down to my ring finger. My fingers tingle, and I nervously cross my legs and shove my hand in between them.

"What happened?" She runs her fingers over her arm where my scar is.

How do you tell someone that the bond you share with them is so deep, it's life altering? "I was… someone attacked me." I'm an advocate for the abused. Using my voice and my skills to help women who have been through the same thing I went through is important to me. But in this moment, I've never been more afraid to admit it. Her breath hitches and her fingers touch her parted lips.

"I'm so sorry," she mutters through her fingers.

"It's okay. It's been years since it happened." I wince when I realize my mistake.

"When… did it happen?"

"Um…" I pause, sweat drips down my back and I'm about to excuse myself for the bathroom, but decide it's best to get it out. "When I was eighteen." Her eyes dart around the room. With a slight shake of her head, she's telling herself it can't be possible. But it is. "It was August twenty-fifth."

She pushes off the couch, her breath quivers as she passes me, walking out of the room. I drop my head into my hands. Please don't hate me. I already carry the guilt that this is all my fault. I hear her come back into the room, so I look up. Her eyes are glossed over and she's holding her arms across her chest.

"I just want to make sure I understand this. You were attacked on the same day I was in a car accident where they thought I might have passed out because there was no other explanation." I bite my lip and nod. She clears her throat. "And then you come here… to what? Show me you're getting what I should've had?" Her voice turns to ice and the coldness shoots straight to my heart. I stand up, shaking my head.

"No, that's not it at all. I wanted Kase–"

"Kase was mine. He's not yours. He's only with you because you have my face," she snaps. She throws all my fears at me, each word like heavy bricks, hard and damaging. Coming out of her mouth, they dig deeper inside my heart, leaving a hole that might never heal. I try to hold back my tears, hiding the hold she already has on me. I can't form the words I want to say. They'll all be lost in her hurtful words. She won't hear that I never meant to hurt her. I came here to meet my sister. I came here to see if Kase was over her. I didn't think I was coming to lose him to her.

"Or are you with him for his money?"

I stand up, clutching my arm as my mind races to understand what she's asking.

"You don't know, do you?" She scoffs, glancing down at my ring as if minimizing Kase's and my relationship.

When the first tears fall, I know I need to leave. "I'm sorry I ever came here." Running out of the house, I catch Kase sitting on the swing with Reed, laughing.

The coldness left in my heart from Everly's words, snaps and shatters in a million pieces.

I have the answers I needed.

This is where he belongs.

CHAPTER THIRTY-THREE

KASE

THIS IS MY PUNISHMENT.

I left. I was a coward. Had I stayed and dealt with the consequences of my actions, I would have known I had a son. Taking a walk has only tormented me more thinking about all the what ifs? Each scenario playing in my head, ends with me being a failure as a father. The apple doesn't fall far from the tree. Maybe it played out how it should have.

As Everly's house comes into view, Reed is out front throwing a football in the air. I step aside and lean on a tree to watch him. He grips the football, weaving back and forth, running to the end of the yard. He spikes the football and does a dance. I smile to myself; he gets that from his mom. I stroll toward him, studying his every move.

Our eyes catch when he notices me coming. I can't believe how much he resembles me. "You're with my mom's clone, aren't 'cha?" I smack my head. Shit, I forgot about Ellie. I'm such an asshole for leaving her. I'm not the only one to have my world flipped upside down today. Reed stares at me while I berate myself internally.

"Is she inside?"

"Yeah. They're talking girly stuff," he reports using air quotes.

"If she's my mom's sister, I guess that makes you my uncle?" That fucking hurts.

Running my hand through my hair, I grit my teeth. "Something like that. Can you throw?" I put my hands up, hoping he'll forget this conversation and move on. His eyes light up as he squeezes the ball in his hands.

"Be prepared to be amazed," he boasts, hopping backward farther away from me. I laugh at his overzealous distance. If he can throw that far, I will be amazed. He launches it through the air. It falls a good ten feet short of where I'm standing. Nice try, little dude. I run and pick it up, throwing it back to him so he doesn't have time to feel like he failed. He's a much better catcher than he is a thrower. As he darts around me, I pretend to chase him to the end of the yard. He hoots and hollers, spiking the ball again to signal he made a touchdown.

"Nice catch."

"Thanks. I'm trying out for the football team this year. Mom says I'm too small, but she doesn't see my potential." I follow him up to the porch as he keeps talking. "I could be the next Tom Brady." I try to hide my amusement as he turns toward me. "What? I just didn't want you to have to go running for the ball, so I didn't try very hard." His confidence is twice the size of him.

"I think you should try out for wide receiver. You can catch and run fast. You'd be perfect for it."

"Hmm. Did you play football?" He sits on the swing, so I sit down next to him. The tips of his toes scrape the ground. I spread my fingers across my leg and glance over at his, resting in his lap. I can't stop looking for similarities. This intense, foreign feeling inside me is making me fixate on him.

A passing car is a welcome distraction. I'm going to scare the hell out of him if I keep staring at him and his body parts. "I did. Your—" I stop myself from spilling that his mom didn't like me playing football either. He stares up at me, confused why I stopped. "You're a lot like me when I was a kid. I played wide receiver."

His smile widens and his eyes move up and down my arms. "I have muscles too," he says, flexing his arm up.

I bite back my laughter. Squeezing his tiny muscle, I say, "Heck yeah, you do."

"Why do you have a frog skeleton on your arm?" He points to my tattoo.

"It's called a Bone Frog." I stare at it wondering if I had known about Reed, would I have still gone into the military? I shrug. No matter the answer, I'm still proud as hell to say, "I'm a Navy SEAL."

His lips twist and he peers at me through the corner of his eyes. "I guess you like animals?"

My whole body deflates against the swing. That's not the response I was shooting for. Admiration. Idolization. Worship. Any of those would have been good.

I sit up tall and turn my body toward him. "You've heard of the Navy? Right?"

"Bennett's grandfather was in the Navy."

I nod, even though I don't have a clue who Bennett is. "A SEAL is an elite team from the Navy." My explanation doesn't do it justice, but considering it's better than him thinking I like animals, it'll work for now.

"Oh," he responds, listless. "My dad's a police officer." *A cocksucker, too.* I'm not surprised Wayne's a cop. His father and grandfather were too. I'm sure Everly's dad approves.

"That's cool," I say with a hard smile. "I bet he never jumped out of planes and swam with sharks." I settle back into the swing with a satisfied smirk at the wide-eyed expression. That's the response I was shooting for.

"No way." He jumps up, his arms widen. "You did that?" My heart rate rises the more excited he gets. Yeah, your real dad is a bad-ass. He sits back down, sitting on the edge of the swing. "Tell me more. What else did you do?"

My smile reaches my eyes. His buzz makes me feel like I can conquer the world. I've never wanted to prove myself to anyone more than I do to him, right now.

I halt my words when I hear Ellie cry, "I'm sorry I ever came here." The door flies open and she freezes when she sees me and Reed on the swing. Tears pool in her pained stare. I push off the swing, but she shakes her head and runs to the car. What the hell happened? I glance at Everly, the same face, except anger radiates from her. My heart feels like it's being yanked on. I don't know which direction to go knowing there will be ramifications no matter what I do. The pain in my heart only worsens as the beat begins to pound harder.

I flash Everly a look of regret and turn back to Reed. "Hey big guy, it was great meeting you. Maybe, someday soon, we'll be able to hang out again."

The excitement in his voice from before dulls, but he says, "That'd be cool." He walks over to his mom's side, and she wraps her arm around him. As if to tell me, I'm making a choice by leaving. I guess I am, but I love Ellie. I am choosing her over Everly. Reed is my son though, she can't control that. She will see me again.

When I hop in the car and turn over the engine, Ellie lowers her head into her hands and cries. I don't know what to say, but I need to get her out of here, so I put the car in drive and leave. The ride is silent except for the low radio noise in the background. She won't look at me, just stares out the window.

The hotel parking lot is empty except for a couple cars. I anticipate her move to jump out before I can turn off the car, so I grab her arm as she tries to exit. "Ellie, talk to me." She shakes her head and I watch tears run down her profile. "It's you that owns my heart."

"Then why are you still lying to me?" she cries. I angle my

head not knowing what she's talking about. "Do you have money, Kase?" My belly knots. She won't believe me when I tell her I forgot. But I did. I close my eyes briefly and sigh.

"Yes."

She throws her head back against the seat. "I can't believe this. Did we tell each other anything that was the truth?"

"I love you. That was never a lie."

"How much?"

"More than the water in the oceans."

She gapes at me for a beat and then shakes her head. "No, I mean how much money?"

"Oh." I shrug. "I don't know exactly. Let's just say a lot."

"Why didn't you tell me?"

"In the grand scheme of things, it wasn't important. Money's a necessity to me, not a luxury. I don't care how many zeroes are in my bank account. It's never been part of my life. It's just there."

"It's not important to me either, but it's part of you and we're supposed to be getting married, Kase. I shouldn't have found out by it being thrown in my face." I can't believe Everly brought it up. She drops her gaze and silence surrounds us again. She lifts her head and asks, "Where did your money come from?"

I bite my lip and stare out the windshield. "My great-grandfather was Jerry Barrow." I wait for her reaction, but when she doesn't have one, I roll my head in her direction. She digs in her memory searching for where she knows that name. It shouldn't take her long.

Her mouth falls open and I'm certain she figured it out. "As in Barrow Oil? Barrow gas stations?" I nod. "Holy. Shit. Kase. This isn't a small revelation. Do you own Barrow Oil?"

I shake my head. "It's a publicly traded company. But I do own shares."

She stares at me. "I can't do this right now. I'm sorry."

I reach for her hand to stop her. "None of this matters, Ellie. I love you. Isn't that enough?"

"It does matter." She chokes back her tears. "You don't have the whole story, Kase. It will matter." She yanks her hand out of my grip, leaving me behind wondering what in the hell I missed. Part of me wants to turn around and drive back to Everly, demanding the whole story. What she could say to justify keeping my kid from me, or why she married Wayne?

Drawing in a ragged breath, I push myself out of the car. I grumble when I see a police cruiser in the parking lot that wasn't there five minutes ago. I tense immediately. Come at me, asshole. Wayne and another guy sit in the front seats. He brought his friend. I'd like him to meet a few of mine. He wants me to engage. Earlier was a knee-jerk reaction. It won't happen again. I'll wait for the perfect opportunity and now isn't it. I glare at him until I hit the front doors, not giving him the time of day once I pass through the entrance.

I fucking hate small towns.

CHAPTER THIRTY-FOUR

I'M A PLACEHOLDER.

Thinking I could be anything more to Kase was foolish. I haphazardly stuff my clothes into my duffle bag and quickly grab all my bathroom accessories. Once he comes into the room, he'll challenge my decision to leave and I'm not certain I'm strong enough to fight him. He doesn't know how this story ends.

I do. It's not me who ends up with a happily ever after.

I pull at the zipper, forcing it closed. Snatching my phone off the bedside table, my phone lights up and I search for the Uber app. Not having used it in forever and the fact that my mind is on the verge of breaking down, I can't find the freaking app. My fingers halt at the sound of Kase clearing his throat.

I sigh, not surprised I didn't notice him. "What are you doing?" His voice is raspy laced with anger and hurt. I glance up and he's leaning against the wall, arms crossed and flexed.

"What does it look like?" I respond, dropping my arms to my side. It comes out more snidely than I meant. This situation sucks. For both of us. He found out he's a dad, and he's having to deal with that surprise, but at least he'll have something to look forward to after the dust clears. I'm choking on the dust, only I'll be left standing alone in the end. It's not like I haven't been here before. I've become a pro at picking myself up off a dusty floor and moving on.

"Tell me what happened in there," he demands.

Rolling my lips between my teeth, I close my eyes for a beat and shake my head. "It's not my place to tell. You need to hear it from her." I grab my bag and walk around the bed. "We weren't meant to be," I whisper. The words are like broken glass, shredding my insides as they come out. He stands tall as I pass him and I glance down to avoid his dark eyes. He mutters a curse word under his breath.

His hand grips my arm pulling me back and I shriek as he pins me against the wall. Panic bleeds from his eyes. He doesn't hesitate in taking what he wants. His lips slam down on mine. I resist as his tongue searches for entry. He hoists me up, pushing himself into me. My body warms instantly with him in between my legs. A gasp escapes my lips as he bites down on the bottom one–hard. Using the opportunity of my surprise, his tongue dominates my mouth, showing no signs of mercy, weakening my resolve as he devours my mouth. My bag slips from my fingers, making a loud thump as it hits the carpeted floor. I wrap my legs and arms around him and turn off my mind screaming at me to walk away.

It's in this fractured instant that hope lives where it's only us. He presses more firmly into me and a moan slips from my lips. His hands grip my ass hard enough I'll have bruises later. "You won't walk away from me," he mutters against my lips. "You are mine."

I am, but you're not mine.

The wetness behind my closed eyes escapes. Tasting my salted tears, Kase stops kissing me and leans his forehead against mine. His chest rises and falls as silence hangs between us.

"You're still leaving, aren't you?"

I take in a deep breath and nod. He mutters a few more curse words as he puts me down and walks away. "You were her blinding echo. My eyes might have deceived me, but my heart and soul felt you. I'll admit, in the beginning you were masked by the idea you were someone else, but everything that makes you different, made me want you more. I fell madly in love with Ellie. Can't you see I love you and I chose you. I don't know what else I can say."

"There's nothing you can say right now. I already told you, you need to hear what happened."

"Okay! Stay here and I'll go talk to Everly and then we can figure this out together." He looks down at my ring finger. "Together, like a couple who is getting married."

"Kase," my voice breaks. "You have a son."

"Do you think I don't fucking know that already," he says, getting frustrated. "Is that why you're leaving?"

"No. Yes... no," I finally spit out. "It's part of it, but it's not what you're thinking." I wish he could see I'm giving him a way out. When he finds out the truth, he'll want to make it right with her. He bleeds loyalty, and his loyalty should be with his true love and their son. Not me.

"Fine," he grates. "I'm taking you to the airport." I nod in defeat and he sweeps up my bag. "Ellie, we aren't over. Not by a long shot."

You'll change your mind, Cowboy.

———

"DON'T LET that bitch take your man." Tori's been yelling at me for the last half hour. I'm tired of explaining myself. "She might have the same DNA as you but she's not you, and Kase loves you."

I moan, running my hands through my hair, hiding my face in my arms. My life was complicated before, but this is like a puzzle that took months to put together only to find out there's a missing piece. That piece is Everly.

"And don't even get me started about how pissed I am that she blames you for all of this. Seriously?"

I lift my head, watching Tori walk back and forth in front of me. "I think it was a knee-jerk reaction. In her defense, she had just learned she was adopted, has a twin sister — who was with the love of her life — and by some weird twin thing, she felt when I almost died. It's a lot to take in." I don't blame her even though it hurt my heart.

She rolls her eyes. "I guess we'll give her a pass there. But I'm not budging that Kase belongs with you. Even if you're twins, you're still two different people. She might have been his past, but you're his present."

"You sound like him."

"See. Maybe now, you'll listen to both of us."

I don't want to tell her how inadequate I feel that I can't give him a child. Even though he swore he didn't want kids, his eyes lit up talking to Reed. What if he decides he wants more now? I can't give him a baby, but she can.

She can give him everything.

I fall back against the couch, the tears starting again.

"Why did two hearts have to choose the same one to love?" I cry.

CHAPTER THIRTY-FIVE

KASE

SOMEONE FILLS THE EMPTY SHOT GLASS IN FRONT OF ME TO THE BRIM. I cast my eyes up and nod in appreciation. The older woman smiles. I glance at her name tag. "Thanks, Karen."

"I figured you needed another one. That one's on the house." Need another one? I chuckle to myself. I need the whole fucking bottle. "If you need someone to talk to, I'm your girl." She looks up and down the empty bar. "Got nothin' better to do."

Picking up the amber liquid, I swallow the heat in one gulp. "I'm tired of talking," I murmur, slamming the glass down. Talking didn't keep Ellie here. She left me. I should've gone straight to Everly's house and demanded she tells me everything, so I could leave and fight my way back into Ellie's heart. But a part of me is afraid to hear the truth.

"Hey there, Sheriff," Karen says to someone standing behind me. My head lolls forward and I groan. Can't he give me some fucking space? His eyes burn a hole in my back. Right where the knife is that he put there years ago.

"Hi Karen. This guy causing trouble?"

She looks at me and I roll my eyes, dragging my hand across my cheek.

"Not at all. But if you're here to create some, I'm asking you to leave my bar." She stands tall and stares him down, not the least bit afraid of him. A smile creeps up my cheeks. Wayne's a pussy. He can't even get respect wearing a cop uniform.

I twist my neck, looking back when he doesn't answer. His jaw ticks. "I'm not here to cause problems. We need to talk, Kase."

I return to looking forward and whistle through my teeth. "Not sure anything you say will help me not want to kill you right now."

"You boys better cool your shit. I mean it." Karen looks at me with a side eye, reminding me of my momma when she'd do that to me and Wayne when we were doing something we shouldn't have been. I scratch my jaw, still wondering how my friend screwed me over?

I spin around on the stool. "You're right, we need to talk," I snap, standing and walking to a corner. We both sit and glare at each other, waiting for the other to go first.

"Why?" I finally ask.

"That's a loaded question. I could ask you the same thing."

My eyes widen. "Me? You've raised my son and you're sitting there asking me why?"

"You left us to clean up your mess when you ran," he seethes.

He's right. I was a chicken shit, but he has no idea why.

"I didn't know she was pregnant and I would've never left had I known. But you didn't waste any time taking my place."

His hand slams down. "I did it for you, man."

"Me!" I roar, jerking forward, getting close to his face. He doesn't flinch. Instead, he leans forward an inch so we're almost touching noses.

"You're the one who put a hole in between your dad's eyes," he whispers. I barely register his words. "I covered for you so you wouldn't go to jail because the bastard deserved what he got and if I told you about the baby, you'd come back home. Jake reminded me every fucking day what would happen. What was I supposed to do?"

Listening to the words fall from his mouth, I replay the day my father died. I only used my fist. What is he talking about? He stares at me, waiting for my response.

"I didn't..." I pause when the words *kill my dad* reach my tongue. I did kill my dad. Just not how he thinks. "I didn't shoot him." My voice cracks. Does it matter how I did it though?

Wayne's eyes widen and his back straightens. "Are you kidding me? You'll sit there and lie to me while I'm telling you the shit I went through to save your ass? You're going to turn around and deny it all?"

I drop my head in between my shoulders. "I'm not denying I killed him. You just have it wrong how he died. I didn't shoot him." The silence between us has me looking back up. His face is burning with rage.

"Fuck you, Kase." He stabs his finger toward me. "I saw him lying on the floor with a bullet hole in his forehead. Nightmares invaded my dreams for months seeing him in the shallow grave we buried him in. I. Did. That. For. You."

My elbows dig into the wooden table as I run my hands through my hair. I violently shake my head in disbelief. What is happening here? Why aren't our stories matching up?

"What the hell did you—"

"Stop!" The table shakes as I pound my fist on it. He narrows his eyes at me but stops talking. "I. Didn't. Shoot. My. Dad," I draw out each word. "When I drove home after leaving you, I was still pissed. The girl that meant everything looked at me like I was a stranger. My dad ran his mouth and I couldn't hold my anger back." Memories flood my mind, my heart races as I clench my hands. "I should've stopped when he went down. But I couldn't. All the years of abuse, for my mom, for me, shot out of my fists. Jake pulled me off." I look at Wayne, pain twists my face. "When he told me he was dead, I didn't care. I had lost everything. But I was young and stupid. When he told me to leave and never come back, that he'd take care of it, I did. I didn't want to go to jail." Wayne's brow furrows. "I swear I didn't shoot him. When I left, he didn't have a bullet in his head."

"What are you saying, Kase?" He shrugs a shoulder, giving me a scrutinizing stare. "Someone else put a bullet in your dad after you left? If he was already dead, why?"

Realization dawns on me. I didn't kill my dad. Jake did.

The man who loved my mom, but hated that she chose my dad over him. The man who despised that I was with his daughter because of who my father was. The man who took my life away from me.

I'm going to kill that man.

My foot bounces as anger works itself through my veins. I swallow the rest of the beer, slamming it on the table as I stand up. Wayne struggles to get out of the booth quicker than me, but he's not on a mission.

"He's already dead," he calls out. I stop walking, not needing a reminder that my dad is dead, and I sure as hell don't need a lecture about how nothing I do can change the past. I fist my hand. "Kase. Jake is dead," he corrects. I slowly turn to face him. "He was in an accident four years ago with a drunk driver."

I let out a bitter laugh. "Well ain't karma a bitch?"

He nods slowly, stuffing his hands into his pockets. "That it is." The sadness in his voice tells me there's more to the story. "Please sit back down."

It's hard to look at Wayne in such turmoil. I need to hear what happened, and I'd rather hear it from him than Everly. At least I'll be able to sort my feelings out before I talk to her.

I blow out a heavy breath and slide past him, back into the booth. He sits back down. "Tell me how you ended up with Everly," I say after a couple beats of silence.

He cracks his neck back and forth and I can tell he's nervous. "Jake sent Everly to a hospital in Arizona that specializes in amnesia patients. He told me she was having a hard time. He asked if I would go because we were good friends."

"Oh yeah, you guys were the best of friends."

His eyebrow quirks up. "We were still friends. We fought because we were vying for your time." I shrug at the moot point. "Anyway... I felt bad for her. I tried to call you but you never answered your phone. Hell, I didn't even know if you still had that phone knowing you were on the run."

"I wasn't on the run. I was in the military." Jake knew where I was. I'm positive he made it his business to keep tabs on me.

"Either way, you weren't coming home. Before I left is when he told me about the baby." Wayne lowers his head. I hope this is eating him up inside. "I swear, I wanted to tell you," he says, looking up with glossy eyes. There's nothing to say, so I stay quiet. He didn't tell me. "That's when Jake laid it all out. He said if I ever told you, he'd have you arrested and then your son would still grow up without you and he'd know you were a murderer. I wasn't allowed to tell Everly either."

Jake never liked me, but I wouldn't have thought it ran this deep. He played us like a game of chess, controlling every move until he had us cornered.

"If that's why you didn't contact me, there's a hole in your logic. He died four years ago, Wayne. That would've been a good time to call me."

He takes a pull from his beer, finishing it. His gaze shifts to Karen and he motions he needs another before turning his attention back to me, he lets out a long sigh. "I fell in love with her."

"She wasn't yours to fall in love with. You were my best friend." I lean back against the padded booth and cross my arms. Karen sets two beers down in front of us. The icy stare between us doesn't break while she stands there waiting for acknowledgment, but eventually she lets out a small huff and stomps away.

"I agreed with Jake that it was in the best interest of Reed that you weren't in his life."

My jaw sets with frustration. "That wasn't your decision to make."

"It was! I was there to help her find her way in life again. I fell in love with her and Reed and I promised myself that I would give them the best life I had to offer. For you!"

"You keep saying you did it for me." I throw my arms out wide. "You were with the love of my life and my son! Yet, you think inserting yourself – in what should have been my life – was for my benefit? You're delusional."

"We can argue this until we're blue in the face," his voice lowers. "I fucked up, Kase. I didn't mean to fall in love with her."

"Did she know Reed wasn't yours?"

When he looks away, I nod in understanding. The knife in my back twists, pain shooting straight to my heart. I can understand he wanted to help her. I can even understand him being there for me. But telling her that Reed was his, had nothing to do with me.

His words burn, but I have to endure the pain to know the whole story. They had feelings for each other, so he told her they were together before the accident, that Reed was his. She never questioned it, probably because she didn't care to learn the truth since she couldn't remember anything and she loved Wayne.

This is the truth Ellie was talking about. Everly was lied to. She didn't know about me. She didn't take my son from me. Jake and Wayne did.

I slide across the seat and stand, not able to take anymore. I pull out my wallet and throw a fifty-dollar bill on the table. Wayne stares up at me, gripping his beer bottle in his hands.

"Don't take him from me," he pleads. His brows furrow as panic flashes in his eyes.

I lean across the table, nailing him with a glare. "He's. My. Son." The fucking irony. *Don't take my son*. How about he never should have taken my son in the first place?

Pushing off the table, I storm out of the hotel bar and take the stairs to the third floor. The force from shoving the door open and it slamming against the wall, echoes down the hallway.

The shots and beer wreak havoc in my mind. Whispers echo back and forth.

Everly telling me she loves me.

Ellie telling me she loves me.

I slam my skull into my room door a couple times, hoping I can knock the noise out of it. I love Everly.

I mean Ellie.

Fuck!

CHAPTER THIRTY-SIX

EVERLY

N<small>O MATTER HOW LONG</small> I <small>STARE AT THE DOOR, IT WON'T OPEN ON ITS</small> own. Just knock on the damn door. I will my hand to raise up. Then I halt my trembling fist an inch from touching it. What if he doesn't want to see me? I blow out a breath and lean into the knock. My knuckles hit the red door three times. I think I'm going to throw up.

Wayne picked up Reed this morning, slipping a paper in my palm. No words, just a defeated expression when he walked away. It was Kase's hotel and room number. He left a message on my phone last night telling me they had talked. My heart aches for him. He loves me and would do anything for me and Reed. But I have this deep emotional attachment for Kase that I need to explore.

I jump when the door swings open. Kase's mouth hangs open as if he's about to yell at me. When he recognizes it's me, he snaps it shut. His eyes slowly rake down my body. Goosebumps pebble across my skin and I sheepishly smile when our eyes meet. He looks like he recently woke up. His hair is askew, and he's wearing only basketball shorts. The defined muscles on his entire body tense. I swallow, thinking of dragging my fingers over his stomach muscles. He's not the same boy I knew years ago. He's all man now.

"Everly," he says, greeting me, his voice heavy from sleep.

"So, you can tell us apart," I reply. We're identical and I wondered if he could tell us apart without speaking.

He flashes a half smile, nodding. "Yes." The way he states it makes it seem we look nothing alike.

My smile fades. "Can I come in?"

He opens the door wider and motions for me to enter. Walking into the musty dark room, I see it's a typical hotel room with a queen bed and a desk and chair. I open the curtains to let in some light and pull the chair out to sit. Fidgeting in my seat, I try to find the most attractive position I can. I cross my legs and sit up straight, pushing my breasts together in my V-neck t-shirt. Vying for a man's attention is new to me and I probably look ridiculous. I wait anxiously as he's in the bathroom. I hear a bottle of pills shaking, then the water running. When he walks into the room, he leans against the wall with his arms crossed and a tight smile.

"Are you okay?" I ask, losing some of my courage.

He nods. "Just a headache. It'll go away soon."

"Wayne told me y'all talked yesterday."

He rubs his neck. "We did."

I pick at the frayed seams of my jean shorts. I'm not sure what I expected, but I was hoping for a warmer greeting. "Kase, I didn't know. As soon as I remembered, I left Wayne."

The air conditioner kicks on and I'm thankful for the cool reprieve. The tension between us is making it hot in here. "How long have you had your memories?"

"Ten months."

His breath catches. I wondered how much Wayne told him. "I hit my head and when I came to, all my memories came flooding back."

"Why didn't you try to contact me? I have a son, Everly." His voice breaks and it breaks my already fragile heart.

"I did," I whisper. How can I make him understand that the love I have for him is as strong as it was right before I lost him? He's gained ten years without me, but it's like yesterday to me. "I hired an investigator. He told me you had gotten out of the military and he located you in Gilley's Cove. I flew there right away." His brows furrow as he remembers the day our eyes locked, months ago. I panicked and ran.

"That was you?" I nod. "Why did you run away?"

Because I was afraid of rejection from the man I loved more than anything.

"You were with a beautiful red-headed woman. You looked happy. I… I got scared you wouldn't want me anymore." I stand and walk to the window and scrunch my nose at the overfilled, ugly dumpsters down below. The view is horrible, but I'd still rather focus on it than let Kase see my vulnerability. He's had ten years to forget me.

I flinch as I feel him stand behind me. He wraps his hand around my bicep and squeezes. My pulse races with the pressure of his body against my back. "Pepper was only a friend. I never stopped wanting you," he whispered. "I ran after you. When you disappeared, I chalked it up to me seeing things." I close my eyes, reveling in his touch. "When I saw Ellie, I knew it wasn't a dream, and it was really you. Or so I thought."

Hearing her name is a crux to my soul. I always wondered what it would be like having a sibling. When I first saw her, so many emotions sparked inside me. Confusion. Curiosity. Anger. After they drove away, I felt nothing but loss although I didn't know who it was for. His admission that he thought Ellie was me, incites hope.

I swing around. I'm so close, the heat coming off his body envelops mine. "It was me you were looking for. I'm standing right here, Kase. The real me." I place my hand over his bare chest.

His heart beats heavily against it. I silently beg him to touch me. Love me. Choose me. Anything, as long as it's with me and not her.

The struggle in his features softens as he places his hand on top of mine. I lick my lips in anticipation. He looks down at me through heavy lids and the second his lips touch mine, my eyes close and roll back in my head. I've dreamt about this for months.

His tongue outlines my lips and I willingly open. Our tongues entwine, his demanding possession of my mouth leaves me whimpering but seeking more. I snake my hands up his chest, running them through his short hair. My senses are on overdrive from his familiar taste, yet foreign feel of his body. Images of the last time we were together flash through my mind, the emotions consuming me. This powerful man is a contradiction to the sweet Kase I fell in love with.

A groan emits from deep in his throat as he hoists me up and slams me against the window, his fingers digging into my ass, his hardness pressed firmly against me. I gasp in surprise at the abrupt change in position. I've never been man handled before. Wayne has always treated me like I was made of glass. His touch is gentle, loving, soft. Kase is none of those.

He jerks back. "Fucking hell," he roars making me wince. Sliding me down his body, he takes a couple large steps away from me like I've burned him. My pulse is drumming. "You're not... Ellie." His words knock the breath out of me. Tears burn my eyes as I gasp for air as my fingers touch my swollen lips and I cry out. Damn him for making me think he needed me like I need him. Damn me for imagining we could pick up our lives where we left off.

Mortified, I run past him to the door. "Everly. Wait... I'm sorry. I got caught up in the moment. This all is so confusing."

My hand grips the door handle and my vision blurs from tears. "You don't understand, Kase. Time has mended the tiny breaks in your heart over the years. The breaks in mine are fresh and they're slowly killing me," I say through my tears, keeping the door in my view. "You don't love me anymore."

He sighs loudly. "Everly, I do. I will always love you."

On my way over I imagined him saying those words. My stomach fluttered with a happiness, everything was happening as it should be. Instead, they're tearing up my insides, leaving me bleeding from the inside out.

"But… you love her too," I whisper.

His silent admission is deafening. With every ounce of self preservation I have left, I open the door and walk out.

———

"WHERE ARE YOU GOING?" Wayne asks, walking into my bedroom.

I continue packing my bag. More like pummeling my bag with my clothes as I forcefully stuff everything in. I've had two days to let what happened in the hotel room sink in. I realized it probably has been confusing as hell for Kase. It's confusing for me too.

He might love us both, but she doesn't have what I have. His son. I'm not done fighting. Our love goes deeper than some woman he met that looks like me less than a year ago. I just need to remind him what our love looks like.

Wayne grabs my arm, stopping me. "Everly, where are you going?"

"Reed and I are… going on a trip." His fingers dig into my arm. A part of me wants to punish him for lying all these years, throw it in his face that he's not Reed's father, so he has no right to him.

"You said you wouldn't."

I shrug out of his hold and drop my arms. No matter how mean I want to be, I can't. Wayne gave us a life of love and happiness. He loved my son with all his heart and I can't intentionally hurt him. But I can't stand by and watch Kase walk away without a fight.

"Wayne, Reed will always love you. You've been an amazing dad, but Reed deserves the truth."

His eyes cast down. "He'll hate me."

I've thought long and hard about this. How I would explain this to Reed. Here is where the love I have for Wayne overrides any bitterness I harbor. "I won't tell him you lied to us." He jerks his head up, angling it to the side like he can't believe what he heard. "He knows about my amnesia. I'll tell him I didn't know who his dad was, and we both decided to let you raise him as your own, but when my memory returned, so did the answers of who his father was." It's not too far off from the truth. He might understand our divorce better since he's taken our break up hard.

He blows out a ragged breath and stuffs his hand in his uniform pockets. "Can I tell him with you? I want him to understand I'll always love him no matter who his real dad is."

The raw pain in his voice kills me. I stare at the man who owns part of my heart. No matter how hard I've tried to take it back, I can't. But I also can't forgive him. Not yet. I nod and sigh. "I'm doing it tonight."

"No matter what happens, I'll still be here waiting for you."

"Wayne–"

"No," he holds up a finger. "I've let you have your space to figure out what's going on in your head. I kinda understand. But I need to have my say before you leave." As he takes a step toward me, I wrap my arms around my waist. The barrier I put between us, I'm not sure if I'm doing it to push him away or to keep me from breaking down and running back to him. "I didn't lie to you to make you fall in love with me. I came to you as a friend. We both fell in love. I may have lied about Reed and our relationship after the fact, but I never coerced you into falling in love with me. That was real." Tears escape my eyes watching him plead for our love. "Our love wasn't a ten-year-old crush or high school sweetheart..." He chokes on his emotions. Clearing his throat, he continues, "You've loved me longer than you did him.

How can you throw this away for someone you loved over ten years ago?"

"It's not ten years to me. To my heart." I place my hand on my heart. How else do I explain it? The love I have for Kase, it's alive inside me. It's like my heart was jump-started with the love we shared. The problem was my heart was beating already, filled with Wayne's love. I'm in love with two men and I can't differentiate who it beats for louder. I need to find out.

CHAPTER THIRTY-SEVEN

KASE

SHE WON'T ANSWER MY CALLS. I'VE BEEN HOME TWO DAYS AND IT'S radio silence. Tori told me to give her some time. If I give her too much time, she'll make a decision without including me. I can't prove to her that my soul belongs to her if I can't see her.

Max instructed me to take a few more days off to figure my shit out. I'm not sure a few months is enough time to figure anything out. Being off only gives me more time to wallow in my convoluted life at the moment. I stare at the white ceiling, recalling the last few days. The cushions from the couch are sagging having no reprieve from my heavy body. The phone is within reach on the coffee table. I check it every half hour on the dot and then call her every hour. I've stopped leaving long winded messages. She'll answer when she's ready or tired of me blowing up her phone.

I jump off the couch like I was shocked at a knock at the door. It's a woman's knock. She's here. I'm at the door in three long strides, opening it with such urgency I'm surprised I don't rip the door off the hinges. I freeze at the sight. My eyes see what my heart doesn't. It needs a second to catch up, to understand it's not her.

"Everly, what are you doing here?"

She glances away from my confused expression, extending her arm to the side of the door. Reed steps into my line of sight. He gives me a lopsided grin. Oh, buddy, you're like a beacon in the night. If anything is truth right now, it's you. You are my son. "Hey, big guy."

"Hey, Kase."

I stare at him still amazed I helped create him. Everly clears her throat pulling me out of my trance. "Oh, come in." I widen the door. They walk in and Reed runs to the windows.

"Epic," he exclaims, staring out at the ocean. He whips around. "Can we go to the beach? I've never been!"

I open my mouth to answer yes, but then snap it shut and glance at Everly. "We'll go after a while," she replies. "We should talk first."

Reed walks up and I watch him closely. "I know you're my dad." The earth just shook beneath my feet, knocking me backward against the arm of the couch. He states it matter of fact, no question… just affirmation.

"Way to start a conversation, Reed," Everly says, her voice full of sarcasm.

He shrugs. "Just trying to move this along so we can go to the beach." Everly gives him the look only a mom can give. "What? He already knows, it's not like I told 'em a secret."

He's awesome. Leave out all the bullshit that doesn't matter. He's definitely mine.

"How do you feel about that?" I manage, unclogging the surprise lodged in my throat. He leans his weight from foot to foot, gripping the hem of his shirt.

"It's a little weird. My mom told me you didn't have a clue, so I'm not mad at you." His eyes jump to his mom every few words searching for silent confirmation.

"I didn't. But had I known, I would've been a part of your life. And I'd like to be a part of it now."

His little head nods. "You seem like you'd be a cool dad."

"I'd be the coolest."

Better than Wayne for sure.

Everly blows out a soft sigh, her eyes cast down. She walks over to the windows and gazes out. There are so many things we need to talk about. I grab my phone off the coffee table and call Cody. Having him take Reed to the pool will give Everly and I a chance to talk.

"The pool?" Reed drops his arms in disappointment.

"I'll bring you to the beach this afternoon." I missed all his firsts, I want this one.

Cody shows up a few minutes later and Everly's eyes widen at the huge burley guy with tatts all over. She peeks at me, fear in her eyes. I smirk at her reaction before introducing the two. Cody is a guy I trust with my life, he won't let anything happen to Reed.

"This is crazy shit. You look just like her." Cody studies her, his eyes roam her body.

She plasters a fake smile on her face. "So it seems."

"Sorry." He winces, looking around for Reed, running his hand over his beard. "Hey Reedster, you ready to go?"

After they leave, the awkward silence between us is becoming our norm. The sun casts down on her from the window she's staring out of. We have a son together. It's hard to believe a baby survived the crash.

I finally break the silence. "The whole town would've known Reed was mine, didn't they say anything?"

Without turning, she replies, "I never went back to Barrow. When we left Arizona, my parents bought us a house in Sweetwater. They wanted me to be close, but thought I wouldn't want to deal with everyone recognizing me and me still not remembering them. To be honest, I was happy they did that."

Her dad thought of everything to keep me from them. "Everly, why are you here?" She twists around, leaning against the wall. I chuckle when she clears her throat. "Some things never change."

Her brows furrow in confusion. "You've always cleared your throat when you're nervous."

"You still know me so well."

I shake my head. "No, you've changed. I have too. We're not teenagers in love where life is simple anymore."

"You said you loved me." She steps toward me and I stand still, a sour taste in my mouth as guilt is consuming me for what I'm about to say. I've thought a lot about this in the last forty-eight hours. "I want us to be a family. Reed deserves to have a relationship with you and we deserve to be together after they ripped us apart."

I sigh, rubbing the back of my neck. "You're right. Reed deserves to know me and we deserve to be happy after being lied to for so long." Sweat rolls down my spine, the words heavy in my throat. "But not with each other." I reach for her, but she takes a step backward, shaking her head. Her eyes gloss over and it kills me to see she's hurting. Because of me.

"Did you tell her you kissed me?"

My eyes snap to hers. "Jesus Christ, Everly. No." I pace the room wondering why she's bringing that up. I had a moment of confusion. Who can blame me? But will Ellie understand? I groan in frustration. "She won't speak to me now, so I haven't had a chance."

Her hand stops me as I pass her. "Kase, I'm here. I'm willing to fight for you. Can you say the same for her?"

I let out a sarcastic laugh. "So much for sisterly love."

She releases my arm, cocking her hip out, her expression hardening. "I'm not giving you up for her. We have a son together."

"If everyone would stop throwing that in my face, I'd appreciate it. The guilt of not being there is heavy enough." We're going around in circles and I need liquor to keep going. I offer her a beer and she shakes her head. Is she not drinking because of Reed? Should I not either? Memories of my dad and his constant drunken state flood my mind. "I don't drink a lot," I declare, my voice raising as I put the beer back in the fridge.

"Kase, you're not your dad." Her face softens, and she joins me in the kitchen.

She sighs. "Actually, I would like one."

Taking two beers out, I hand her one and she leans against the opposite counter. Dirty dishes fill the sink where it's usually spotless. My gaze darts around the unkept apartment. Here's to great impressions, I cheer to myself and swallow a gulp of beer.

"Sorry my place is a mess. It's not normally like this. Shit, I'm sorry for a lot of things."

"Me too. I shouldn't have come." She pulls the bottle to her lips and our gazes stay fixed on each other. I wonder if we found each other before I met Ellie if we would've worked. When we were in the hotel, her gasp when I picked her up is what reminded me I wasn't with Ellie. I'm rough around the edges and she's used to sweet. I'm sure Wayne treats her like a princess. "I'm... also sorry about your dad." Her voice breaks. "Wayne explained everything before I left."

I shrug, already having come to terms that he's dead. I huge weight was lifted when I learned it wasn't me. "Thanks. I'm sorry to hear about your dad."

She picks at the label on her beer and laughs without humor. "No, you're not."

"I'm sorry for you. You loved him."

"Had I known what he did, I would've never forgiven him." She takes two steps toward me and puts her hand on mine. I squeeze it, knowing she needs affirmation that I forgive her, though none of this is her fault. The clinking noise of the beer bottle on the counter echoes in the quiet room when I put it down. I pull her into my chest and wrap my arms around her thin frame. Her body shakes as she cries.

The weight of her tears lay heavy on my heart. Regret just adds more weight, suffocating the one organ that keeps me alive. It's hard to breathe. I don't want to hurt her. I tighten my hold, memories replay in my head of the last time she cried in my arms. Her dog escaped and was hit by a car when we were seventeen. He died immediately. I had wished I could take all her pain away so she wouldn't have to bear it. I wish that now I wasn't the one causing it. Instead, I let her have her release. It's goodbye to a teenage love, ripped apart too soon.

She steps out of my hold, sniffs and wipes the tears from her cheeks. "Thank you," she whispers. "We should probably get going."

"Wait." I reach for her. "Can you guys stay awhile? I want to…" How can I say this without sounding like an asshole?

She bites back a smile. "You want Reed to stay. I get it."

"Both of you. I'd like both of you to stay. Unless it's too hard for you." I can't imagine how she feels. Someone breaking your heart one minute, then asking you to stay the next. "I would understand if you want to go."

"I'd like that and I want you to know your son, Kase. He's amazing, and he reminds me of you at that age. Over confident and stubborn," she smirks.

As if on cue, Reed barges through the door, talking to Cody, "Yep, I have a girlfriend. Except she doesn't know it yet."

Everly gives me an I told you so look.

"Reedster, I'm not sure that qualifies as a girlfriend," Cody says, ruffling Reed's wet hair.

"Pshh. We eat together every day and she passes me notes in class. We're unofficially boyfriend and girlfriend."

"Oh, notes, huh?" I joke. "It must be serious."

He shrugs, falling back into the couch. "I kinda like her friend too."

Cody and I bark out laughing. Already playing the field.

I glance at Everly, who's giving Reed the evil eye. "He's not like me. I only had eyes for one girl," I say quietly as I pass her and plop down beside Reed.

CHAPTER THIRTY-EIGHT

EVERLY

H E DOESN'T MEAN TO TWIST THE KNIFE. BUT HIS WORDS CAUSE SO much pain. What's worse, he's only loved two women who are identical, yet his heart belongs to one. And it's not me.

It was a mistake to come here. I hoped I could change his mind because of Reed. Use his guilt against him. God, I was naïve and stupid. I'm not this person. I'm a stay-at-home mom who volunteers on PTA, bakes all day just so I can hand goodies out to everyone the next day. Sweet, loving, everyone's best friend, volunteer of the year... that's me.

Now, I've ruined everything.

Kase and Reed joke around in the living room and I gravitate toward the kitchen. Doing what I do best, baking. Searching the cabinets, I'm surprised to find a lot of the ingredients. I sigh to myself, forgetting that Ellie is probably here a lot. I wonder if she enjoys baking as much as I do? My eyes flicker to Kase's muscular body. At least I know she doesn't bake for him very much if she does.

"Is there a store nearby? I want to get a few things."

Kase glances up at me with a brow cocked. "There's a small market next door. Do you want me to run and get something?"

"No. Stay here and hang out with Reed. I'll be right back."

His quizzical expression stays on his face. He's wondering if I'm coming back. Under the circumstances, running away sounds ideal, but I'd never leave Reed. He's the one stable thing in my life. He's always been. Knowing one thing in a world of unknowns holds a lot of power. He's a part of me. I worked hard to build a solid life for him even though mine was broken.

It'll be hard sharing him with Kase. Another reason I wanted us to be a family. My heart aches when I imagine him around Ellie. It's selfish of me to hope she's decided the situation is too much and breaks up with Kase. I can see the determination in his eyes though. He won't let that happen.

For ten months, I wondered how he had left me so easily after my accident. Piecing together the puzzle when my memory returned, I recall him coming to see me once. And then I never saw him again. It wasn't until Wayne told me what happened—that he thought he killed his dad—and wasn't left with a choice other than to leave, did I understand. I don't blame him. I blame my dad. Hearing what my dad was capable of, the man who would move mountains for me, broke a piece off my heart. My heart has taken a beating lately.

The quaint small beach town is lovely. It's not home, but it's beautiful here. The red brick buildings rich in history, the thick greenery everywhere reminds me of home in spring after we get hit with heavy showers. I've never smelled salt, but the humid air is filled with it. The dark clouds out over the ocean, look turbulent yet fascinating, leaving you wanting to sit and watch the storm unfold.

It's my life.

"Good afternoon, Ellie," the door greeter says as I walk through the automatic doors. I freeze and stare at him. His genuine grin fades. "Are you feeling okay?"

"I... I'm fine." I want to ask if I really look like her, if he can find anything different about me. Kase can tell us apart, why can't everyone else? I'm an intruder. It's like déjà vu when I first lost my memory. I hated it then just as much as I hate it now. Reliving the feeling makes me sick to my stomach. I peek at his badge and say with a polite smile, "Have a good day, George." I avoid eye contact with anyone else in the store.

Two more people greet me—Ellie—before I could get back to the apartment. I've abandoned any thoughts of walking down to the beach to give Kase and Reed some time alone. I can't pretend I'm someone else. It's not worth my sanity.

"That was quick," Kase says, coming into the kitchen, tugging each bag open to peek inside. "Whatcha' making? And do you need any help licking the bowl?"

"Hey! That's my job," Reed exclaims, coming in behind him. He jumps up and down when he sees the ingredients. "Mom! You're making peach cobbler! Kase, wait until you try it, it's so freakin' good."

"Um, watch your mouth, or you're not getting any." He looks down away from my pointed glare but hides a smile.

"Actually... I've had it before. It's still one of my favorites."

I place the vanilla on the table and look up. Why am I doing this to myself? I know it's his favorite dessert, at least it was. If I tell him it's also Reed's, maybe he won't assume I did it on purpose. He doesn't understand the need I have to make him happy.

"It's Reed's, too." I smile.

"No, it's not," Reed barks. I narrow my eyes at him to stop, but he keeps going. "I love your triple chocolate cheesecake."

"Sweetie, I thought you loved my cobbler?" My words grate out between my teeth.

Way to be inconspicuous.

"I do, Mom. I love it," he replies, his voice robotic and slightly scared.

"Great." I turn around, ignoring the strange looks they're both giving me and begin pouring ingredients into a bowl. If I don't acknowledge how stupid I'm being, we can all forget this ever happened. Right? A cloud of flour erupts from the bowl due to tossing it in too fast, followed by laughter as I dust my shirt off. I twist my lips, staring at the cackling duo sitting at the bar. "Y'all think that's funny, huh?" Their heads bob in unison. The spoon clinks the steel bowl as I stir the flour, salt, and sugar together. "Hmm, I have a little too much dry ingredients," I say right before I reach into the bowl and flick some right at their faces.

We break out in laughter when we notice Kase's white cheeks and lips. He puffs the mixture out of his mouth, a wicked smile tugs on his lips.

"It's time to add the wet ingredients."

Pulling the sprayer off the faucet in front of him, he presses down the button and water sprays all over my shirt and then he turns it on Reed. Squeals and laughter ring about the apartment. By the end we're all coated in a flour paste, the place is a mess, our cheeks all hurt from laughing so much and we just made our first family memory.

There might be a chance after all.

Two hours later, the kitchen is spotless, void of any evidence of a flour fight and we're enjoying peach cobbler and ice cream. This day has turned out better than I ever expected.

"Can we go to the beach after we're done?" Reed asks.

"That sounds like a great plan. You coming with us?" He looks at me with a smile.

I nod. *I will go anywhere with you.*

The smile plastered on my face scares me. I'm putting too much stock into a little play time. He was just having fun. It doesn't mean he's choosing me. He's choosing her.

When I walk out of the bedroom, he's answering his phone. He jerks forward off the couch, his shoulders tense and I know the call is about her. The smile I couldn't stop before, drops off my face and disappointment from my unrealistic future sets in, *again.*

CHAPTER THIRTY-NINE

KASE

"SOMETHING'S WRONG."

The panic in Tori's voice makes me shoot up off the couch. "What's wrong," I reply into the phone.

"I... I'm not sure. Ell hasn't called me in a couple days and I understand why she's avoiding you, but there isn't any reason she would avoid me." *Thanks for that reminder.* "I went to her apartment today when she wasn't answering her phone. Everything is in its place."

"Okay." I'm relieved to hear it wasn't in disarray. "Maybe she's at the Lighthouse."

"Kase. Her car is still there. Her luggage is still there. She's not at work. I've gone to all her normal places around here, but no one has seen her either. So, where is she?" she shrills into the phone.

I pull the phone away from my ear. "Calm down, Tori. She's probably out taking pictures somewhere."

"Calm down? What if he found her?"

"Who?"

"What if her stepfather–"

"Why would you think that? He's in jail." Prickles of fear form across my body as I pace the room. Why would she put that in my head? She just needs her space. Right?

"She's always been afraid of him finding her. It's just weird she wouldn't tell me where she was going. She tells me everything, Kase."

"Meet me at her apartment." I end the call and take long strides to my bedroom.

"What's going on?" Everly asks, walking into my bedroom. Her eyes widen as she watches me slip my holstered gun onto my hip.

"I'm not sure if it's anything." I grab my wallet and keys off my dresser and look up at her worried expression. "Ellie's gone missing. I'm sure she needed a break from everything, but her best friend is worried. Just do me a favor and stay here. Don't leave." If by chance, there's any truth to Tori's concern, they could easily take Everly for Ellie.

"This is all my fault. I was a major bitch to her," she says, wrapping her arms around her waist.

I pull her into a hug. "No. If anyone will take the blame, it'll be me."

Her arms wrap around me. I wait for my body to take over and think it's Ellie, but nothing comes. It's about damn time it can tell the difference. I breathe a sigh of relief.

Walking to my bike, I text Cody, asking him to make sure Everly and Reed don't leave the apartment. I relax a little when I receive a thumbs up text. Tori's already waiting in the parking lot when I roll up. I glance around Ellie's car, checking handles to see if it's locked. I make a mental note to get a Slim-Jim from Hudson later to check her trunk. Neither of us wastes any time talking as we head to her apartment. I keep walking when Tori stops for the elevator.

"I'll meet you up there," I say over my shoulder.

"Oh yeah, forgot about your aversion to elevators."

I make it to Ellie's door a few seconds before Tori does. "Is that necessary?" she asks, pointing to the gun on my hip that I have in my grip.

I hold my finger up to my mouth. In a whisper, I reply, "Yes. Did you search her entire apartment when you were here earlier?"

"Um... I mean, I went into the rooms, but I didn't search all the closets," she whispers back.

I nod, holding my hand out for the key. "Stay behind me."

The ingrained instinct of clearing a room takes over. I move from room to room swiftly and efficiently with Tori right behind me. Nothing is out of place, worry setting in more with each step. It's everything Tori told me already, but seeing it for myself confirms what I didn't want to before. Something is wrong.

Tori's eyes follow me as I pace the room. My phone is gripped tightly in my hand while I think of who to call first. Where would she go? Did she see Everly, and that's why she took off? But why didn't she take her car? Questions continue to swarm my head and I'm getting frustrated I can't answer them. I scroll through my contact list and press the Lighthouse's number.

"Is she really there and you're just covering for her?" The question grates out of my clenched jaw.

"No, Kase. She told us she was dealing with something personal, so we thought she was taking off for a few days. Is everything okay?" Diane asks.

"I... I don't know." My head drops. Where are you, Ellie? I pop back up at the sound of a phone ringing. Jerking my head in Tori's direction, she shrugs. "Gotta go, Diana," I snap, hanging up on her. The ringing sound is muted, but it's a phone. We both dash into her bedroom just as it stops ringing. I drop to the floor and look under the bed, but find nothing so I call her phone. It goes straight to voicemail.

"Does Ellie have another phone?"

"She's never mentioned it."

"Go through her drawers," I demand, pointing to her night-stand. "There's a phone in here and we need to find it."

Drawer after drawer we check until my fingers land on some-thing hard in a pile of soft material. "Found it." I hold it up and Tori runs over.

Twenty-five missed calls. Someone's trying to get a hold of her. Staring at the phone, I wonder what else Ellie is hiding. She has an ugly past I just learned about, but did she tell me everything? The black flip phone lights up when I open it.

"Why do you think she has another phone?" Tori asks over my shoulder.

I shake my head. "Not sure. But someone else is trying to find her too. Let's see who it is." It's the only phone number in her contacts and it's a Texas number. I have a hunch it's her dad's number, but why a burner phone. The phone rings twice before a raspy voice answers.

"Well, well, well... my little slut has finally decided to call dear ole daddy." Chills crawl up my spine. Who the hell is this? "I hear you breathing, girly. What's wrong, you think just because you moved away, I wouldn't find you? Well, get ready 'cause Daddy's coming home."

"You fucking try," I roar. "If you touch her, I will hunt you down and tear you apart piece by fucking piece and throw you out for shark food." My chest vibrates with anger, it takes every fiber inside me not to launch the phone against the wall.

This can't be her dad.

His laugh is like a needle scraping inside my veins, making them bleed.

"Seems my little slut has been cheating on me. Do you know her pussy was mine first? It dripped from..." I pull the phone back, slamming it shut. A glass figurine from the shelf shatters into a million pieces as it hits the wall. The slip of anger that worked its way out doesn't help. I need this guy on a fucking gurney and I need to focus to do it.

I'm frozen in place, his voice echoing in my head. A hand touches my bicep and I whip around, drawing my gun.

Tori's hands fly up in the air. "Kase, it's me."

I choke on my breath, lowering my gun. I need to get him out of my head.

Putting my gun back into the holster, my knees give out and I crumble to the ground as I try to catch my breath. "I'm sorry," I whisper, ashamed I lost control.

"It's… okay," she replies, slowly. "Who was that?"

"I'm certain it wasn't her dad." So, whose phone is it? The way he was talking, it sounded like her step-father, but he's in jail.

I push myself off the floor and call Stone with my own phone. He answers, "I hear you have company."

"I don't have time to talk about that. I need you to search the current status of Ray Stevens, stat."

I wait as keys tap on the other end. "Is that…" He pauses. "Kase. We need to get Ell to a safe place."

I growl. "I can't find her! Tell me what you found."

"He escaped from prison three days ago. What the hell do you mean you can't find her?"

"She's missing. No one has seen her the last two days. But he doesn't have her because I just talked to the son of a bitch."

Stone talks to someone else, only when the person replies I realize it's Max. "We're on our way. Stay put." *Easier said than done.*

"I'm at Ellie's. We need to send someone over to Dalton Keyes' house. I'm pretty sure Ray has his phone, which can only mean–"

"On it. See you in fifteen."

Okay, Ellie, where'd you go? I finish going through her drawers, looking for any clues of where she would run to. Finding nothing, I move on to the living room, searching every square inch of her place. Tori sits on the couch, silently crying while she watches me. "You know her better than anyone, Tori. Can you think of where would she go if she wanted to hide?"

"I have no idea," she cries. "I didn't even know about the other phone."

When Stone and Max walk in, they both scan the apartment. "You didn't tell us her apartment had been trashed," Stone says.

"It wasn't. I did it looking for... something to help find her."

Max puts his hand on my shoulder and squeezes. "She's okay."

I do a double take, taking a step back. "What? How the hell do you know?"

"On the way over, I called some friends. She was taken to a safe house."

My head falls back, I say a silent thank you and blow out all the panic twisting inside me.

"Oh, my god, thank you," Tori says, running into Max's arms.

I take a couple long strides to the door, pulling my keys out of my pockets. "Tell me where she is, I want to be there with her." Knowing she's safe calms me a little, but it'd be better if I was there to protect her.

Max's lips twist and he shakes his head. "The FBI isn't sharing that info with me. We have another problem though. Let's go to your place."

My brows crease, but he walks out ignoring my questioning expression. Guess we're going to my place.

"Can I come?" Tori squeaks from behind me. I peek down at her and her eyes plead with me. "Maybe I can help."

Probably not, but Ellie means a lot to her. "Sure. Meet us there."

Not ten minutes later, we're all filing into my apartment. "Ell!" Tori screams, running to Everly and throwing her arms around her. Everly stiffens. "I was so worried about you. I thought you were–"

"Tori," Max cuts her off, shaking his head. She releases Everly and steps back, confused.

"I'm not... Ellie. I'm Everly."

"Oh." Her eyes travel up and down her body. "Wow, you guys look so much alike."

Max shifts to the door when there's a knock, and answers it. He shakes two guys' hands as they walk in. As if there isn't enough commotion, Reed comes out of the bedroom. All talking ceases and eyes flash to me, then him. *I get it people, he's the spitting image of me.*

His eyes widen as he takes in everyone. "I'm thinkin' I need to eat my spinach a little more," he jokes, breaking up the awkward silence.

Stone pats me on the back, leaning over to my ear and says, "He's certainly funnier than you."

I chuckle, nodding my head at the little guy.

I introduce everyone to Everly and Reed. Max takes over, introducing the two guys and I'm not surprised to find out they're FBI. Everly wraps her arms around Reed's chest as she eyes me. I don't want to be the one to tell her they're here for her. I crushed her hopes we could be together and now I'm about to tell her that her life is in danger because of the face she shares with the woman she lost me to. Talk about a double-edged sword.

"What's going on, Kase? Is Ellie in danger?" She looks past me at the guys talking in the kitchen.

I sigh. "No. She's safe." I pause, taking in a deep breath, looking down at Reed. "Tori, can you take Reed into the bedroom."

She hops off the barstool. "Yep. Come on Reed, I've got a deck of cards in my purse, let's see if you can beat me at war."

He glances between me and his mom. She nods, giving him a reassuring smile. "I'll come play in a few minutes." Once they're out of earshot, her smile drops. "Why is the FBI here?"

"They're here for you." Her eyebrows shoot up. "There's someone after Ellie. She's at a safe house so she's safe... but–"

"But, I look like her," she finishes my sentence.

The guys join us and discuss with Everly what'll happen. They waste no time gathering their luggage. She's biting her nails as she watches them take it out the door.

"Come here," I say, pulling her into me. "I'm so sorry this is happening. But if it'll keep you and Reed safe, I'm all for it."

"Where are they taking us?"

"They don't disclose that to anyone. It's better that way. I'd come if I could."

"How long are they going to keep us there?" She pulls back, panic flashes in her eyes. "Kase, we can't just disappear. Reed has school, I have–"

"The guy that's after Ellie broke out of prison. Once he's found, you'll be able to go home."

She spins around and stares out the window. "I can't believe this is happening. One minute I have the perfect life, the next, my brain decides it's a good time to screw it all up. It's been downhill ever since. I wish I never remembered you."

Even though I'm not choosing her, her words hit a sore spot on my heart. I want to tell her I'm sorry, but I'm not. I have a son who should have been in my life from the beginning. This situation sucks all around, but I'll never regret finding out about him. I can't wait to get to know him better and the sooner that bastard is caught, the sooner that can happen.

"It's time to go," one of the FBI agents tells Everly.

"Can I have a moment with Reed?" I ask her, not caring what the FBI agent says. Still staring out the window, she nods.

The typically dark room is bright from the open curtains. Tori and Reed are sitting on the bed playing cards. Tori looks up at me and smirks. "Better watch him, he's a card shark."

"Hey! No, I'm not, you just stink at cards." He laughs. I've never wanted to bottle up a laugh, but damn, I could listen to that over and over and it'd never get old. "Kase, you wanna play?" Yes. *All day, every day.* Tori squeezes my bicep as she walks out of the room.

"I wish I could. There's been a change of plans," I say, sitting next to him on the bed.

"Are we still going to the beach?" He pops up on his knees.

"No. But I promise that's one of the first things we'll do when you come back."

"Come back? Are we leaving already? We just got here."

Everly and I haven't discussed the possibilities of him coming here, but the disappointment in his voice makes me believe it'll happen.

"You remember your mom's twin?" He nods. I run the words through my head first, trying to be sensitive to a ten-year-old's ear, but no matter how I spin it, it's bad. "She's in danger so the FBI is guarding her. Since your mom looks a lot like your aunt, the FBI wants to be diligent in protecting you guys too."

"Are you coming with us?" His big eyes, filled with concern, stare at me. I can't even explain the emotions flowing through me. I've never felt this deep draw toward someone. It's amazing and scary at the same time.

"Not this time, buddy. I'm staying here to help find the bad guy."

His eyes flick to my gun. "Are you a cop like my dad? I mean..." He trails off, looking down, flicking a card against his fingers. As much as it hurts to hear, it's not his fault.

I lift his chin to meet my eyes. "Hey. It's okay. He's still your dad." I swallow the sting. He nods his head in my hand. "But no, I work in security. It's a little like being a cop."

"Do you know how to use a gun?"

"Kase is the best there is at shooting a gun, Reedster," Cody answers, walking into the room.

Reed jumps up on the bed, excited. "My dad taught me how to shoot, he said I was a natural. I must get it from you." I'm not sure if now's the best time to have a proud dad moment, but I am. "Will you take me shooting?"

"Heck yeah. I'd love to see those skills you have." We high five each other and he hops off the bed.

"Kase, they're ready to leave," Cody says.

"All right big guy, do everything they say. We'll have you back as fast as we can." He jerks forward, wrapping his arms around my waist, digging his head into my chest. I take a deep breath, soaking in every millisecond of his touch. When I wrap my arms around him, I melt. Ten years without this. With the hatred I feel for Wayne right now, it's a good thing he's not here.

CHAPTER FORTY

I LOOK UP FROM MY BOOK AT THE SOUND OF THE DOOR OPENING, expecting Agent Clyde to walk in. I'm hoping he'll want to play a card game again because I'm bored out of my mind. This is the fourth book I've read in two days. My eyes widen, and I stand, shocked at who walks through the door. It's surreal looking at yourself across the room.

"Hey, Aunt Ellie," Reed says, bursting into the room like he belongs here. My mouth hangs open. Did he just call me aunt?

"Hi, Reed," I say as he rushes past me out of the living room.

"Don't get into anything," Everly calls out. She turns her attention to me and I flash an uneasy smile, standing and closing my book.

"Hi," she says, raising her hand in a quick wave. It's weird to feel like I'm looking into a mirror, yet the reflection does things I'd never do. She tugs her earlobe before sweeping her hair behind it. When I tilt my head, hers doesn't move, but my mind expects it.

"Hi," I respond. We both jump when Agent Clyde walks in abruptly.

"I'll be outside if you need anything. Make sure to stay in the house," he says to Everly. I've already been debriefed of the rules. She nods, and he walks out leaving us alone again.

"Why are you guys here?"

They are a long way from home. I understand why the FBI is worried about her since she has my face. But why here? Why not in Texas?

"Um…" She swallows, her eyes jumping around the room.

Reed walks in and answers for her. "Kase told us we had to go into hiding because my mom looks like you." He walks over to his mom, and she wraps her arms around his shoulders. I turn away to gather my thoughts, but it freezes on one particular picture. For them to be here, they were all together in Gilley Cove. Like a family.

"Reed, hun, can you give us a minute alone?" she whispers from behind me.

"Geez! Why do I always have to leave the room?" He stomps off.

Tears burn my eyes as I look down at my bare feet on the brown carpeted floor. This is what I wanted for Kase, but to have it thrown in my face is devastating. Thoughts of family pictures, Kase telling her his cheesy pick-up lines, them out in the ocean somewhere makes me nauseous. I swallow the bile rising in my throat. Any hope he would want me instead, crashes and burns.

From the corner of my eye, I see Reed walk into the bedroom. Taking my chances and running away sounds better than staying here.

"Ellie, I'm sorry." Her voice cracks. The heavy emotion in her voice makes me turn. "I went to see Kase, taking Reed with me." She glances to the front door as if looking for someone to interrupt her. "I told Reed about Kase being his dad. I thought…" She stops talking and turns back. Her eyes fill with tears as one falls from mine. Brushing it away, I wait for her to continue. "I didn't want to let go of what we had without knowing for sure."

My stomach knots. I want to ask what happened, but the answer will destroy one of us.

She blows out a long, low sigh, taking a couple of steps into the room and sitting on the chair. Her back straight, butt barely on the chair as she crosses her legs and folds her hands in her lap. It's very formal, yet natural for her. Our upbringing was definitely different.

"He didn't choose me."

My lips part, letting out a quiet puff of air. I'm struggling to speak, to find the right words so I don't hurt her. My heart aches for her. I can sense the pain in her eyes. I was wrong before; no matter the answer, it will destroy both of us. "I'm sorry," I whisper the only words I can muster.

With a humorless laugh, she says, "It's not your fault. None of this is your fault and I'm sorry I ever insinuated it was." She looks down and picks at her jeans. I sit on the couch, tucking my legs under me and clutch a pillow to my chest. Her eyes find mine and she relaxes and scoots back into the chair, the tension in her shoulders releasing. "Are you scared?" When my brows pinch together in confusion she clarifies, "Kase told me about Ray."

"I guess. I've lived in fear since I was eighteen believing he'd catch up with me, eventually. I don't want to say I'm immune to the fear because I'm not, I'm scared. I just wish you and Reed hadn't been thrown into the middle of this. Is Reed okay?"

She shrugs a shoulder, glancing toward the bedroom he disappeared into. "He seems to be handling everything okay. I'm sure he's having feelings he's not telling me."

Agent Clyde walks in again, holding a box. "Figured Reed might like something to do."

I smile and wipe away a couple tears that escaped, thankful he's trying to make the situation better. I hear Reed whoop when he sees what's in the box.

"Mom!" he boasts, running out of the room. "He brought an Xbox. Can I play?"

The shine in his eyes reminds me so much of Kase when he talks about jumping out of planes. I hold a hand over my heart, hoping Kase gets the opportunity to know him. Where do I fit in the picture though? Or do I? He didn't choose Everly, but does that mean he chose me? If he thinks our relationship will sacrifice his relationship with his son, maybe he doesn't want to risk that. I throw my head against the back of the cushion. It's not like I can ask Everly what he said.

"He loves you." I jerk my head up, staring at Everly. "Kase." Her voice trails off.

"You don't need to tell me what happened. I know it hurts."

She takes a deep inhale and exhales quickly. "I know I don't. But I can see the hurt in your eyes too. The faster I accept my reality, the quicker I can move on."

She continues, telling me how Kase thought I had gone missing, the FBI and meeting Max's crew. We move our conversation into the kitchen where we make dinner and our stories morph into stories about our lives. We laugh about how we both have the same likes and dislikes in food. We lose track of time with question after question to see how alike we are. Before we know it, it's dark outside and Reed has passed out on the couch, tired of listening to us. I could do this all night.

It seems Everly can too. After she put Reed to bed, she came back out, and we started up again. Clyde's a good man. He also brought us something. I pour my second glass of red wine and offer the bottle to Everly to fill up her glass. We try to keep our laughter down to a minimum, although the more we drink, the harder it is.

As I'm bringing the glass to my lips, I startle when Reed comes running out of the bedroom. We both stand as Reed runs to his mom, wrapping his arms around her waist tight. "Reed, what's wrong?" Everly asks in a soft voice.

"I heard something outside," he says, his voice shaking. "Something was tapping on the window."

She looks at me, concerned. I walk to the curtain, peeking out and see Agent Clyde in his car. Glancing down the lit street, I notice it's empty. "I'll call Clyde and tell him, but I'm sure it's just a branch. It's a little windy," I say to calm him, despite the fact it's not windy at all. My heartbeat quickens as I call on the cell phone restricted to only call Clyde. "Okay, he'll check it out, but he's pretty sure it's nothing too."

"Can I sleep out here?" he begs, looking up at his mom.

She brushes his hair to the side and nods. "Sure. I'll go get a pillow and a blanket."

Reed runs to the bathroom while we set up a bed on the couch. After dimming the lights, and tucking him in, we move to the dining room. I can't get rid of the uneasy feeling so I down another glass of wine. Clyde called confirming nothing was out there. Everly insists it's just his overactive imagination and the scary situation isn't helping.

THE LIGHT COMING through the drapes shines right on my face. I roll over to escape it. "Dammit," I mutter, rolling right off the side of the bed. Thankfully, we dragged the mattress to the living room floor and slept on it. The old carpet rubs against my arms. I shiver, not wanting to think about who or what has been on this carpet. Lifting myself back up onto the mattress, I can see Everly laughing at me. I glance over at her and wonder if I look that bad. I mean, I probably do, being we have the same face. Her mascara is smeared down her red cheeks, hair is askew and matted on one side. I narrow my eyes at her, I hope she has the same headache.

"I need Advil and the bathroom," I rasp, looking at Reed still sleeping. My throat is sore from talking so much.

"Grab me some too," she moans, laying back. Cheap wine makes for the worst hangovers.

The morning ends up being like last night, minus the wine. We make breakfast and continue our questions. Reed rolls his eyes and escapes to the bedroom, playing the Xbox.

"What's the Lighthouse?"

I pull my head back and stop folding the blanket mid-air, surprised at her question.

"I overheard Kase ask if you were there when your friend called."

Finishing the fold, I lay it on the couch and pick up the sheet to fold. "It's my life. It's everything about me, wrapped up in one place."

I explain how the concept was born, how Kase gave it to me for graduation, how the reason I help these women is because someone was there to help me. I owe my life to my dad. He gave up a life of easy retirement with no concerns, to a life of constant worry.

Something pops into my head I hadn't thought about. Did Kase pay for the Lighthouse himself? He told me he had donors, but that was before I knew he was a millionaire. When I got home, I researched his grandfather and found that he left his entire estate to his grandson. Millions. I still can't imagine Kase being a millionaire, he's the most down-to-earth guy.

I squeeze my eyes shut. He has to be going out of his mind knowing Ray escaped.

At least he knows I'm safe.

I can't say the same for Ray.

CHAPTER FORTY-ONE

KASE

TORI: WHERE ARE YOU?

Me: At the police station. Why?

I wait for her answer, but the text bubble never pops up.

"There was a tip someone saw him in Tennessee, but we haven't been able to confirm it," Max says, pulling my attention away from my phone. I crack my neck, knowing it's not good he's been spotted closer to us. Closer to Ellie.

He's coming for her.

"How's her dad doing?"

"He's alive." The downcast of his eyes tells me he's being too generous with his statement. He continues, confirming my suspicions. "He's lucky the FBI got there when they did. Shot three times and is scheduled for another surgery today." We need to locate this son of a bitch so Ellie can be with her father. She'll never forgive herself if he dies.

"Stone, what'd you find on the guy?" The next fifteen minutes I scribble on the whiteboard as he talks. We have already heard this information, but the task force we set up needs to hear it. The Captain, a couple of local officers, and two FBI agents fill the room alongside our group.

We quiet at the knock on the door and an officer peeks his head in. "Sorry to interrupt, Captain, but there's someone here searching for Kase." All eyes turn to me and I shrug. I'm not expecting anyone. Max walks with me out of the room. Once the lobby comes into sight, I see him before he does me. I set my jaw as my eyes bore into him. He paces the room, gripping his neck. It looks like he hasn't slept for a couple days.

"Wayne." He freezes at the sound of his name. The second our eyes meet, he rushes me, fists ready to hit something. Preferably my face, I'm sure. I duck as he swings, grabbing him at the waist and slamming him against the wall, adding my weight to the force of the hit. He's lucky he wasn't here yesterday, it would've been more than a shoulder.

He grunts, falling forward on his knees. "Where is she?" He looks up, his face beet red. "Why the hell is my son calling me saying he's scared?"

I let out a low growl, my spine stiffening. "He's not your son." An arm halts me from pounding that point into his lying skull. My jaw ticks as I glare at Max.

"Not the time, Nixon." He waits for me to nod and relax my shoulders before putting his arm down. "Did you say you talked to Reed?" Wait, what? When did he call? How did he call?

I close my eyes for a moment, needing to pull my shit together and put away my personal feelings right now. Focus on keeping everyone safe and worry about personal shit later.

Wayne holds his hand out to Max. "Wayne Carroll," he says, shaking his hand.

"Max Shaw."

Wayne's eyes widen, and he jerks his head my direction. "You work for Max Shaw?" he asks surprised, with a hint of envy in his voice. I smirk, crossing my arms. *Yes, I fucking do.* My ego does a tap dance inside my head.

"Wayne, do you mind coming with us into the meeting and telling us what Reed said?"

"Sure," he replies, staring at me with furrowed brows.

We walk in silence into the room. Wayne looks around at everyone, then his eyes zone in on the whiteboard. Max introduces Wayne and explains the situation. I stay quiet knowing this is tearing him up inside. The feeling is mutual.

Wayne shifts in his seat, looking uncomfortable. Finally, he speaks up, "If Everly and Reed are in a safe house, how did Reed call me yesterday?"

"Ellie's burner phone," I reply through gritted teeth, angry with myself that I missed this. "With everything going on, I didn't notice it was gone. I put it on the table when I walked into my apartment yesterday. This morning when I left, I grabbed my phone, but there wasn't another one on the table." Stone looks at me and I nod at his unasked question. If Stone can trace it, so can Ray. That's why he's on his way here. He probably traced it when he talked to me a couple days ago.

"Agent Barsotti, you need to warn your guys," Max instructs one of the FBI agents. He nods and walks out of the room. "Wayne, what did Reed say?"

"He called me last night, upset and said he was really scared. I asked him why and he didn't answer me. When I asked him where he was, he hung up." He glares at me like this is all my fault.

Now I understand why they remove law enforcement for conflict of interest because it's hard as hell to step back and look at this through impartial eyes.

When Agent Barsotti comes back into the room, everyone stops talking. "I informed the agents about the phone. They're waiting on instructions on where to move them." Everyone in this room knows they aren't safe where they are. "They'll report back when they're at the new location."

It's a relief to hear they're safe. But every second they stay in that house, they're sitting ducks. I stand and lean my hands on the table, stainless steel cold against my fingers. "Ray probably tracked them to the house, maybe we can meet him there?" My voice is as cold as the stainless steel.

"We can't disclose that location," Agent Barsotti says.

That's too bad. Fortunately for me, I put a tracker in Reed's shoe before he left.

I glance at Max and his expression is unreadable, but I catch the slight tick of his chin and I know he's thinking the same thing I am.

We're taking a trip.

Everyone discusses the game plan around town, but I tune out. He's not here. My mind is on my game plan. First, head to my apartment and load up my guns. Then, it's hunting season.

I'm on a mission when I walk out of the police station. I'll meet the guys at Max's after I get what I need. Instinctually, I scan the streets, watching for anything that stands out. A hand grasps my shoulder.

"I wanna help." Wayne's voice used to never make me want to kill him. It does now.

I shrug his hand off and walk away. "No," I snap, over my shoulder.

"Kase, whether or not you like it, we share them. And if you think I'll sit back while they're in danger, you're fucking crazy."

Talk about going for the jugular. I whip around and my jaw hurts from clenching it so hard. "The only one crazy here is you. How you thought I'd never find out about him. You took ten years of knowing my son away from me."

"I told you I was sorry. I don't know what else to say. I can't take it back."

A couple people wander by, observing us with hesitant glances. I roll my shoulders and rock back on my heels, letting the heated energy wash off me.

"C'mon Kase, let me in. I'd do anything to keep them safe."

"Fine," I grit out. "You get in the way; I won't hesitate to pull the trigger."

CHAPTER FORTY-TWO

ELLIE

"I was scared," Reed whines to his mom.

"I am not upset at you for being scared." She glares at him and he avoids her stare by playing with his fingers. "You stole someone's phone, Reed."

Clyde left a few minutes ago after reprimanding Reed and confiscating a phone. He didn't look happy. It can't be that bad, it was just one phone call. "No playing the Xbox today."

"What else am I supposed to do in this prison?" His arms flail and he throws himself onto the couch.

"How about we make him do dishes all day, instead." She eyes me as Reed's lips turn up. I shrug. "There isn't anything else for him to do here, let him play," I plead.

"Fine. You better tell your aunt thank you for saving your butt."

That'll never get old. I'm an aunt. He runs over and gives me a quick hug before dashing to the bedroom. "Thanks, Aunt Ell," he calls over his shoulder. My fingers cover my smile as I watch him run off.

"Do you want kids?" Everly asks. My smile fades and I glance down to my stomach.

"I can't have kids, but I'm okay with that. I've accepted it." I manage a small smile before shifting and walking into the kitchen. It was easier to deal with before my sister had a baby with him.

As if sensing my fear, she adds, "Kase never wanted kids. He was adamant he wasn't meant to be a dad."

I spin around. "He'll be a great dad," I say, defending him.

She softly laughs. "Oh, I know. What I'm saying is, it's okay." Is this her way of telling me she's okay with Kase and I being together?

I guess it doesn't matter if there is no us though. I shake the negative thoughts from my head, no need to worry about something I can't get answers to right now.

The day drags on, but we find ways to keep ourselves busy. At least I have a card game partner now. Despite being hidden away in this house, this time with Everly has been worth it. How do you catch up your whole life with someone who wants to know every detail? This time has been invaluable with her. I hope after we leave here, we can maintain our relationship.

"Tell me about Wayne."

Our conversation shifts into the part of our lives we don't want to share. But the inquisitions aren't out of bitterness, just genuine curiosity about each other.

The way her eyes light up, it's obvious she still loves him. "He's a good man who lost control of doing what was right because of love." My lips quirk up in understanding. I get it. "Don't be on his side. He lied to us for ten years." Her voice hardens.

"I'm not." I hold my hands up. "But I can see how love makes people do crazy things. Had he been upfront with you, would you have gone after Kase?"

"I've thought about it. Repeatedly." She pinches her lips together, staring up to the ceiling, lost in thought before she looks at me and shakes her head. "No, I fell in love with Wayne. I wouldn't know Kase from a stranger on the street. I was already confused, having to learn everything again. Wayne was the only thing concrete in my life. I wouldn't have risked that."

"So, do you—"

The front door slams open, hitting the wall, making us both jump off the couches. Panic catches in my throat as the intruder's eyes pin mine. I'm frozen in time. Ten years ago. His eyes, still the bland brown with a few more wrinkles surrounding them and a little more sunken in. When he slams the door shut, I shake out of my stupor.

I glance at the door, hoping Clyde is right behind him. When Ray slams the door shut, I fear the worst. Clyde isn't coming for a reason.

"Honey, I'm home," he grates, taking a couple of steps into the room. His voice is worse than a million spiders crawling on me. I swallow, standing a little taller with my feet wide, readying myself for a fight. "It's been a long time, sweet pea." Shivers run down my back at the nickname he'd call out when he'd rape me.

Don't let him get to you. This is what he wants.

Steadying my breathing, I never break our stare. The sound of shattered glass has both of us turning toward Everly. She holds the stem of the broken wine glass in the air.

"Don't take another step," she hisses.

He does a double take, looking between me and her. Then his cackle echoes through the room. "Well, fuck me, double the trouble, double the fun. If I would've known there were two of you, I would've made it a ménage à trois." My stomach heaves and I have to take a few short breaths so I don't throw up. "If we didn't have to leave sweet pea…" He looks at me and winks and my body shudders in disgust. There is no way I'm leaving with him. "We could've had fun." He pulls out a gun and waves it at me. "Let's go." This isn't happening. Not again.

The floor shakes beneath me and I fight to stay standing when

Reed walks out of the bedroom. "What's going on?" Ray jerks back in surprise, but regains his control quickly.

"Reed, run!" I scream, rushing forward.

It's too late. Ray grabs him and holds the gun to his temple. I freeze in place with my hands up.

"No! Don't hurt him. Take me instead. Let him go," Everly pleads.

"Both of you, shut up."

"Mom," Reed whimpers.

"It's okay, Reed. Shh, it's okay." She tries to calm him, but tears run down his face.

Ray keeps looking down at Reed and then each of us.

"How old are you, kid?"

"T-t-ten."

Ray's eyes widen in surprise before they land on us. I have a moment of clarity and I can't get the words out fast enough. "He's not yours," I spit out. "You made sure I couldn't have kids."

"Of course, you'd say that. Holy shit, am I a dad?" His icy glare pins both of us. "You didn't tell me I was a dad."

Everly cries, "No! He's mine."

"I didn't tell you because he's not mine," I plead.

"I don't believe you. Either of you. Shut up and let me think!" He squeezes his hold around Reed and Everly cries harder. "I don't know which one of you is even Ellie." He keeps glancing at his watch, which makes me think he's in a hurry. Help must be on the way. I just need to keep him here a little longer.

Stepping forward, I admit, "I am. I'm the one you want. Take me, he's not yours. He's my sister's son." I point to Everly.

He narrows his eyes. "And what, your twin gave birth the exact same time you would've had my son?"

He takes a step toward the door and says, "Come on son, we have a lot to catch up on." I scream for him to stop as he drags him toward the door and Everly screams, lunging in his direction. He raises the gun and I know with every fiber in me he'll pull the trigger. He's a psychopath. I jump, shoving her out of the way when the sound of a gun goes off.

I hit the ground and my head dizzies.

Screams ring in my ears.

My vision blurs from the pain.

CHAPTER FORTY-THREE

KASE

"Are they moving them already?" I ask, looking down at the app, watching the dot move away from the safe house. Why is Reed moving?

"I haven't heard."

Max makes a phone call while I stare at my phone. Hudson peers over my shoulder and watches with me. Spikes of unease work up my spine. Something doesn't feel right.

"They haven't moved them, and they can't get a hold of Agent Clyde." Max taps on his earpiece, turning it on. He explains the situation and instructs Stone to head to the house and we'll follow Reed's position. Stone, Wayne, and Cody are in the SUV ahead of us. We split off, heading west.

"Kase," I glance up at Max and he's staring at my jostling foot. I grit my teeth and make my foot stop moving. My racing pulse zipping through me, has my body temperature burning up. "We'll find them."

All my senses are on hyper-alert as I listen for an update from the guys when they get to the house and keep my eyes on my phone, afraid I'll miss something. Squeezing my eyes shut so the burning sensation of not blinking will go away, I take a few deep breaths to calm myself. I won't be any help if I'm not able to take control of my emotions.

"Girls are here," Stone's voice comes into our earpiece. "Ray has Reed." His voice trails off. Or maybe the shock is deafening. Panic laced with confusion runs through me. Why does Ray have Reed? Does he know we're after him and he took him to barter for freedom?

I yank the earpiece out of my ear to stop the ringing in them, but it doesn't stop.

He can't have Reed.

He's mine.

When I look up, I notice we're stopped on the side of the road. "What the hell, Max, we don't have time for this," I growl at Max.

"Get out of the car."

My eyebrows shoot up as Max gets out. We're on the shoulder of the highway, Max walks around the front of the car over to my door. When he opens it, he waits for me to get out. I glance back at Hudson and he shrugs. Jumping out, I stare at Max, standing there with his arms crossed.

"What are we doing Max? I need to find my son." I fist my hands, nails digging into my palms.

"Throw rocks, scream, go run around the damn car. Do something to release some of that anger because I need you focused when the time comes. And the fucking time is coming. But I need to trust that mistakes aren't made because you can't focus."

I growl up to the clouded sky and then glare at Max. "Pick me up down the street."

I take off in a sprint down the highway. Cars zip by me and their speed spurs me to go faster. After two, six-minute, miles, I slow my pace, my legs burn from the intense run. I ignore the couple of honks when I strip my sweat-soaked shirt off me, wiping the sweat from my forehead. My heart is pumping, but my mind is clear.

Max rolls up beside me with the window rolled down. "Let's go find your son."

THE DOT STOPPED MOVING fifteen minutes ago. Ray's taken him to a desolate house in the woods. Branches crunch under our feet in the silent air as we walk through the thick trees.

"It's fifty feet straight ahead," I whisper, pointing in front of me. Max and Hudson nod. When we have the house in sight, we spread out, surrounding the house.

I search around my spot for something to rest my rifle on. A large rock will work. After setting up and making sure it's a stable platform, I focus my scope. The smell of pine wafts through the air and I'm surprised I can smell it in the stillness of the air. I'm thankful for the cooler air although the desert air is what I'm used to in these situations.

A tiny drone fitted with a thermal camera flies over the house and Max reports back they are alone in the house. He says Reed is in the living room, Ray in the kitchen. Looking through my scope, I can see Reed through the front window, but I don't have the kitchen in my line of sight.

Thank god he's alive.

We stay rooted in our spot, waiting for him to come out of the house or into my line of sight for a couple of hours. Hudson's stationed at the back of the house, listening. Right now, Ray doesn't know we're here, so we have the advantage. As soon as the FBI gets wind of where we are, they'll surround this place like bees to honey. And people do stupid things when they panic and feel trapped.

"Come outside," I whisper to myself, my finger itching to pull the trigger.

As the light fades over the trees, the shadow from the old wooden house creeps across the overgrown yard. "Ray's on the phone," whispers Hudson.

The front door opening catches my eye.

Reed darts out.

My heart slams against my chest.

He keeps running away from the house, but I keep my scope pointed at the door.

"Come back here you little shit," Ray screams, chasing him.

I pull the trigger.

One shot to the head.

Ray's body jerks, his lifeless body falls back against the broken stairs of the porch. Reed screams, running into the woods and I jump up and run after him.

"Reed," I yell, following the sound of heavy breathing and cries. "It's Kase. Stop running."

"Kase?" He stops and I catch up to him. He flies into my arms.

He cries on my shoulder, his body shakes from fear. It kills me he had to experience this level of evil at such a young age. I carry him back to the opening where I meet Max and Hudson. Sirens blare in the background and I know this place will be a zoo in a couple of minutes.

"My mom," he cries. "Sh-she... he shot her."

What? I pull back, tilting my head wondering if I heard him correctly. Everly was shot?

I jerk up, meeting Max's gaze. His eyes shut, and he shakes his head. I stand slowly, afraid my knees are about to give out, knowing he's not telling me something.

"Max," I growl.

"We need to go," he replies and Reed cries harder, so I pull him into me. His head digs into my stomach. "Reed, your mom is okay. She wasn't shot."

As his world rights, mine crashes.

If it wasn't one, it was the other.

"Ellie," I choke out, finding it hard to function.

Max nods and my mind flashes to the unimaginable. Her lying

on the floor, surrounded by blood. I stumble back, but Hudson catches me.

"Kase, she's in surgery right now." His words barely register.

Ellie can't die. She can't leave me.

"Kase," Max snaps. "Listen to me. She's still alive." Those words are the electric shock needed to jumpstart my heart. I gasp for air, pulling in deep breaths. "But we need to leave. I've already talked to the FBI. They're on their way and they'll take care of this. Hudson will hang around and wait for them."

Reed's little hand slips into mine and I glance down.

"Let's go," he whispers. "She'll be okay."

I cling to the hope he's right. We walk to the SUV and hop in the back. When he slips right beside me, I wrap my arms around him. Killing Ray, I thought the fight was over.

It happens it was just the beginning.

———

THE SHADOW of fear covers me, filling my head with the worst cases. Everyone tries to reassure me, but I can't hear anything in the heavy fog. I can't look at Everly without the irrational part of my brain spewing anger. This isn't her fault. I want to scream that no one is telling us anything. I want to take another run, but I can't leave.

Needing something to do, I've gotten up at least ten times to get a cup of coffee, only to take a sip and throw it in the trash. It tastes like mud. Every. Time. But I can't stop.

Max taps me on the shoulder and I peer over at him. He juts his chin and I follow the direction. I shove up from my seat as a doctor walks toward us. Running my hand across my rough jaw, I meet him halfway.

"Are you Ellie Keyes' family?"

"Yes, I'm her husband." I lie knowing they won't give out information to non-family members.

"And I'm her sister," Everly says, walking up beside me. She's wearing scrubs, her clothes so soaked with Ellie's blood, she had to change. The smear of blood she missed on her jaw makes me cringe, the ache in my chest intensifying. I squeeze my eyes shut and jerk away, so I can't see it.

He grips his hands and notices me observing him, so he crosses his arms over his torso and settles. He blows out a heavy breath, bracing himself for the aftermath of bad news. "She was in shock by the time she got here caused by internal bleeding, the loss of blood was extensive. The bullet hit her small intestine, so we had to remove a piece. We stopped the bleeding and removed the bullet. The amount of blood she lost and infection is our main concern. Her body is still in shock. She's in ICU and stable for the moment."

I run my hand through my hair, gripping it. 'For the moment' replays in my head. I turn, all eyes on me, waiting for an update. My body breaks out in a cold sweat, my mouth dries like I swallowed sand.

"I'll tell them," Everly whispers as she turns to walk away. Her heavy steps echo in my head.

I spin back around, hoping the doctor didn't leave. His sympathetic eyes meet mine. "Can I see her?"

He nods, flattening his lips. This has to be the worst part of his job. Once a person dies, they're gone. You can't apologize. But the emotions from telling the family has to weigh him down.

"We'll let you know when we have her set up in her room." He places a hand on my shoulder. "She's a fighter, but she needs to keep fighting."

She's the strongest person I know, she's a survivor and she'll be again.

Ellie, fight for you.

For us.

CHAPTER FORTY-FOUR

EVERLY

I KNEW WHAT THE DOCTOR WAS GOING TO SAY BEFORE HE SAID IT. I feel it in my bones. Death. It's like our nervous system is bound by an invisible string. I've felt like this once before. The day of my accident. I thought I had the flu and was on my way to the doctor. Out of nowhere, I was gasping for air and then darkness. When I woke, everything was different. I was different.

It's strange to feel someone else's emotions and not know them. We're bound by something so supernatural, it's surreal. And now I'm going to lose her. Tears spill down my cheeks and I lean forward onto my arms. She found me and the only memory I'll have is her saving me. Wayne leans over and slides his hand into mine, squeezing. "I'm sorry," he mumbles into my back. I shift to his chest and he holds me while I let out the emotions I've been clinging to, hoping I was wrong.

Ellie is dying.

Last night was the longest night of my life. I was in labor for seventeen hours and it still didn't compare to last night. Every time the emergency room doors opened, no matter how close to sleep I was, I would jump up, ready for news. But none came.

No news is good news, I kept telling myself before settling back in, waiting for the next false alarm. But here we are, eight in the morning, Max has brought everyone breakfast and we're all anxiously awaiting an update.

When the doctor comes out telling us she made it through the night, I almost respond with, 'I know' but rather kept that to myself. Wayne walks up to my table with my favorite drink from Starbucks in hand.

I smile, grateful he's here. "Thanks."

He bends over, kissing me on top of my head and returns the smile before walking away. I watch him pass the sliding glass doors, exiting to the outdoors, the tension in his shoulders weighs heavily on my heart. We haven't talked. He has no idea what happened at Kase's before we were whisked away to a hiding place. He's in his own hell trying to keep it together but be supportive at the same time.

I glance at Cody and Reed, who's sitting right next to him. "Hey, I'll be..." I point outside and Cody nods. "Find me if there's any news." Kase went back to sit with Ellie as soon as the doctor let him, so I'm not sure how long he'll be.

The cool air hits my face. It won't be long until winter is here. I shiver at the thought of the winters in this place. This sixty-degree weather is our normal winter. I tighten my jacket around my stomach and scan the area for Wayne. He's sitting on a bench, staring up to the sunny blue sky. When I approach the bench, he rolls his head in my direction.

"Can I sit with you?"

He nods once. The wooden bench squeaks as I sit down. The uncomfortable silence between us is new. It's the first time he's not begging and I'm not fighting back. Is there anything left to argue about?

He thinks he's lost me and I don't feel like fighting.

Where does that leave us?

"Thank you for coming," I murmur, breaking the silence.

He nods again, taking a deep breath. "I would do anything for you and Reed."

I play with the buttons on my jacket. "I know."

"Are you comin' back to Texas?"

I snap my eyes to his. "Why wouldn't I go back? That's my home."

He shrugs half-heartedly. "Kase is here. And so is your sister. What's left in Texas?" The indifference in his voice knots my chest.

"Well... my mom is there." Tears threaten to fall as they pool in my eyes. Is this the end of us? Our final chapter? My gaze darts around, fear ricochets in my head. But I didn't want him last week. Am I only panicking because Kase doesn't want me?

I dig the heels of my palm into my eyes, I'm so tired of being confused. Why do I think I'm making a mistake letting him go? I've been on my own for ten months, what's different now?

"There's also you, Wayne," I whisper. "I told you I wouldn't take Reed away. But Kase will be in his life now, too."

"And what about us? Are we done? Say yes and I'll sign the divorce papers. I can't do this anymore."

"Why do you sound bitter? I did nothing wrong." I sit up taller, irritated by his tone.

He pulls in a deep breath, blowing out his cheeks. "I've lost my wife and I'm losing my boy—"

I clear my throat, wishing he would stop saying I'm taking him away, I'm not.

He pauses for a moment, grimacing, but then continues between clenched teeth, "I have nothing left to be happy about."

His hand wraps around the edge of the bench, and I lay my hand over it. "Reed loves you. And so do I..." He peers over at me with apprehension. "I need time to figure everything out. I'm not saying we're done, but I'm not saying we have a future either. I don't want to go back to you, and we both question whether it was because Kase chose Ellie."

His eyes come back to life at my words. Hope fills his body as he jumps up and then kneels in front of me. "I will wait forever for you, Everly. As long as there's hope, I will fight with everything I have to prove that we belong together."

I grin at the man I've loved for ten years. Admitting out loud that I wouldn't have searched for Kase had I known the truth from the beginning, was eye-opening. Wayne dedicated his life to making mine perfect. And it wasn't a simple task. Standing by a woman who couldn't remember her parents or how to drive and help raise her baby was proof enough he loved me.

"You need to accept that Kase will always be a part of our lives, though."

He shrugs one shoulder, smirking. "I put up with the guy for eighteen years, what's a few more?"

It'll be harder for Kase to accept Wayne. Kase has nothing to lose hating Wayne, unlike Wayne who has everything to lose. I push that aside, not wanting to deal with that at the moment.

"I need to go back inside."

He nods and stands back up. "Are you going to be okay while I run to the store?"

"Yeah. Do you want to take Reed, he'd probably like to get out of here for a little while?"

"Do you have to ask?"

"Thank you, again, for being here." I rub his arm and he moves in to hug me but stops himself and smiles instead.

"Anytime, Jade."

I can't help but smile at the name. When I was terrified, not knowing a soul in this world, Wayne showed up in Arizona to help me. One day, he asked me to pick a new name, said I could be anyone I wanted to be. I wanted to be Jade. No idea why, I just liked the name. It didn't stick, but instead turned into a joke only shared between the two of us. Leave it to Wayne to make me laugh when I needed it the most.

$\cdot \quad \cdot \quad \cdot$

KASE HASN'T LEFT Ellie's side all afternoon. The doctor came out once and gave us an update. She's stabilized, but she's still in ICU due to all the blood loss. I want to see her, but I don't want to take Kase away from her. Cody strolls in with lunch, setting at least twenty bags of Chick-fil-A on the table. My eyes widen wondering if he brought food for the entire waiting room.

"You better grab a bag before they're all gone," he says, leaning over.

My mouth opens to ask why, but then I snap it shut when over-sized muscled men bombard the table, digging in the bags, taking handfuls of sandwiches and fries. Instead, I jump in and grab two and back away with the bags gripped tightly in my fist, eyeing the guys. I'd hate to cook for this crew.

"I'll go see if Kase is hungry."

Nobody is listening, so I slip away easily. The bright hallway is empty, my shoes squeak across the floor so I try to walk lightly, but it doesn't help. It's like eating popcorn in a theater when there is a lull point, you try to chew slower, but you feel stupid thinking everyone is staring at you.

The door to her room is closed and I pause outside her door questioning if I should even be here. I'm not here for Kase, I'm here for Ellie. She's my sister. My twin sister. She's inside me, part of me, of course, I belong here. My knuckles tap against the door and I wait.

Kase opens the door, and in a flash, I'm taken back to when his mom was dying. His blue eyes are dull and his face is tight with worry. I offer a small smile and hold up the bags. "I thought you might be hungry."

His brow lifts and it's the first sign of life I see in his face. "I'm surprised you could grab a bag."

I chuckle. "Your friends are savages. Good thing I'm quick on the draw."

His lips twitch and he nods, stepping back so he can open the door wider. I freeze at the sound of beeping and air being pumped into Ellie's lungs and stare at her body, framed by the blanket and riddled with tubes and wires. My gaze darts to Kase and I squeeze the bags of food to my chest.

"You should sit with her." He motions for me to keep walking. "I'll give you some time together." He squeezes my shoulder as he passes and the door shuts behind me. Wait, I'm not ready. The room's walls close in and I draw in a ragged breath. I'm having an out-of-body experience, looking down at myself, fighting for my life. My steps are heavy as I take a couple toward my motionless body. 'She's not you' my subconscious repeats and I shake out of the dreamlike state.

Sitting beside her, I cover her hand with mine. "Hi, Ellie, it's me. Everly." Tears threaten as our touch sends a flurry of emotions inside me. "I… I hope you can hear me." I wait for a reaction, a squeeze of the hand or an eye twitch. But nothing changes so I close my eyes and rest my head against the cold sheets on the bed. "I just found you. Please don't die."

I take long deep breaths, focusing on our connection. We were once one, maybe being connected again, we can share my energy. She has to feel it. Feel me. When a hand touches my back, I flinch, jumping out of my seat, knocking it backward, the sound of wood hitting the floor rebounds through the room. My heart thumps and I scramble to regain my bearings.

"Hey, it's just me," Kase says, eyes wide open and hands up. He bends down to pick up the chair.

"Sorry. I must have dozed off." I glance at Ellie, hoping to see a change. But she hasn't moved. Disappointment I couldn't help her tugs at my heart. "I can feel her. She's still fighting," I say when he sits down on the opposite side of the bed, weaving his fingers through hers.

"I would question how realistic that twin voodoo really is if I didn't know better."

"Twin voodoo?" I smirk as he nods. "If only I could use some of those special powers we have to help her."

"You being here is helping her."

I blink back my tears. "I hope." Kase's face jerks to Ellie's and I look at her, but she hasn't moved. "What's wrong?"

"Nothing," he beams, standing up and staring at her face. "She squeezed my hand. Ellie, can you hear me?"

CHAPTER FORTY-FIVE

ELLIE

I CAN HEAR MYSELF TALKING TO KASE. I SOUND WEIRD, BUT IT'S my voice.

"Twin voodoo?" I ask.

What is Kase talking about? And how do I hear myself talk, but my mouth isn't moving? Wait, that's not me. Everly is here. Kase's hand slips into mine and I squeeze it, not planning to let it go.

"Ellie, can you hear me?"

I nod, not wanting to open my eyes. My body is heavy and my brain foggy. Voices come and go as I slip back under. Whenever I wake, Kase is always by my side. But my body isn't ready to come alive yet.

Finally, I fight the pull and open my eyes. Swallowing feels like I've eaten a bag full of sharp Doritos. Kase brings a straw to my mouth and I take a sip, praying while I swallow it doesn't kill me. Haven't I been through enough? Balloons and flowers fill the table behind him. He's the only one in the room this time.

"Hey, Cowboy." My voice is so raspy it doesn't sound like me. His smile reaches his eyes, and it's the first time I notice the dark circles under them. "Reed?" I whisper, recalling what happened.

"He's great." He bends down and kisses me on my forehead then sits down. "Ray's dead."

The weight I've kept buried for ten years, crumbles to ash, my body feeling lighter as I imagine a life without fear. Tears fall down my face. "Really? He's gone?" I ask, finding it hard to believe.

He nods, his gaze never leaving mine.

There are moments in your life you'll always remember. This is one. *The feeling of deliverance.*

I'm free.

Kase cups my cheek, wiping my tears away. "You're so beautiful, you made me forget my pick-up lines."

I laugh and then wince from the pain. I slap him on the chest. "Stop making me laugh. You're so cheesy."

"Only with you," he says, scooting his chair closer and then standing, pressing his lips to mine.

When he sits back down, I pull the sheets back and gingerly touch my stomach, my fingers running around the bandage. "He has a thing for that specific spot."

Kase's jaw ticks.

"Too soon?"

He glares at me. *Yep, too soon.*

"Were they able to get the bullet out?"

"Yes. You lost a lot of blood and had internal bleeding."

"Did anyone else get hurt?" His gaze turns down and my heart sinks. My eyes dance around, trying to remember the night. "Was it Clyde?" I'm assuming it was because how else did Ray get passed him? "Kase, tell me."

He pulls in a sharp breath and slowly releases it. "Clyde was found dead in his car. But that's not it. I didn't want to tell you until you were a little more stable." I ready myself for the bad news. *It's not your fault*, I keep telling myself, but the guilt is already hammering down on me, leaving marks. "Your dad was shot, but he's doing great," he quickly adds, as my mouth gapes open. No! No! I cover my face with my hands, my chin trembles as I suck in a breath. All he did for me, he doesn't deserve this.

"He's okay, baby. He's already called to check on you at least ten times." He pulls my hands from my face, making sure I'm listening. "I've talked to him and Max is sending his plane for him as soon as he gets out of the hospital."

Warm tingles spread through my body knowing they've met on the phone. *Oh no.* I never had the chance to tell him about Everly or Kase asking me to marry him.

"What's wrong?"

I wince. "Did you say anything to him about us getting married? Or I mean—"

The door flies open, and I stop talking, thankful for the interruption. We haven't spoken since I left Texas, so I don't know if he still wants to marry me.

"I'm done waiting for my turn," Tori says, strolling into the room. "You'd think someone shot her or something." I giggle at her brash attitude while Kase doesn't seem to appreciate it. "Lighten up, baby-cakes, she's fine." She taps him on the cheek. "Why don't you go get us some chocolate so we can have some girly time."

He glances at me, his jaw tight. "We're not done with that conversation."

Biting my lip, I glance at the wire coming out of my hand, avoiding his intense stare. As soon as he's out the door, Tori jumps in, "Oh, that sounded important, but I recognize that expression and you look like you'd rather go swimming in the ocean."

"A shark eating me sounds pleasant right now."

She snorts and sits on the bed, pushing wires to the side. "I'll just get this out of the way, next time you go missing, send a freaking smoke signal or something! I was going out of my mind worried about you. Also, Everly... holy shit it's weird looking at her and not thinking it's you."

"Just think how it is for me. If I raise my hand, I always expect hers to raise too, thinking she's my reflection. It's a mind fuck, for sure."

She lies down beside me, wrapping her arm through mine. "Don't go jumping in front of any more bullets, mmm'kay?"

"Sounds like a good plan." I can see why Kase has nightmares.

"Now, tell me what conversation you're avoiding?"

I sigh, rolling my head over to her. I haven't been lucid long enough for this conversation, but she won't let me off that easy. "Kase and I. Where we stand. We haven't talked since Texas and the only thing I know is he didn't choose Everly."

She rolls her eyes and gives me an incredulous glare. "That man loves you more than the ocean and you know the weird obsession he has with that." We both giggle. "Don't doubt his love for you. There'll be an adjustment between you and your sister because of Reed, but lover boy isn't going anywhere. If you still want him."

She's right. Us being together might affect Everly and my relationship too. The struggle of wanting to be closer to my sister and being with Kase is real.

I'm enjoying a break of being alone, reflecting on the past week. So much has happened in the small amount of time, it's dizzying. I'm in a wind tunnel, everything rushing past me, surrounding me at a powerful speed. I'm not sure how to come out alive without hurting people.

After a tap on the door, Everly sticks her head in. "Want company?"

Reed's head peeks in under hers and his smile beams. "You definitely want to see me, right?"

I nod and motion for them to come in. Reed always enters a room with a force of energy, there's no denying where he got that from. When Kase enters a room, it's hard to look away.

"Did they let you keep the bullet?" Reed asks while he sits down next to me.

"Reed!" Everly stares at Reed with wide eyes.

He shrugs. "What? It'd be cool to keep something like that. I mean you keep my teeth."

"No, I don't," she retorts. "The tooth fairy keeps them."

His expression is priceless. Hers even more. She learned that her son doesn't believe in the tooth fairy.

"It's okay," I pat her hand, consoling her. "It was bound to happen."

"Are you sure she's not real?"

His smart-ass smirk is identical to Kase's when he gets ready to tell me a cheesy pick-up line. "Mom. As soon as you installed a tooth fairy door, I learned it was you."

My brows pinch together wondering what in the world he's talking about.

"It was so cute though." She smiles wide when she sees my confusion. "It's a little door, with a little door handle and you put it on—" She stops herself and waves her hand. "Never mind. It was cute."

I scratch my face and exchange a knowing look with Reed. His mom is a little too much. "To answer your question Reed, no. They didn't give me the bullet."

His eyes widen. "Do you still have a hole? Can you see through it?"

"No, Reed." Everly shakes her head. "Okay, you said hi, why don't you go back out with the guys."

"Fine. They're cooler than you anyway," he says, strolling out of the room.

"I'm sorry. He doesn't use his filter like he should."

"It's all right. He's a cool little kid."

"So…" She pulls her hair up in a bun, clasps her hands together in between her legs and stares at me for a moment. She sighs. "I don't know if I should thank you or yell at you right now. I've thought a lot about this the last twenty-four hours and I've flipped flopped so many times I'll just do both." She swallows after her word dump. "Thank you for taking a bullet for me." She put a hand up stopping me from talking when I open my mouth. "But why did you do it? If you would've died, I wouldn't have been able to forgive myself."

"Ray wasn't there for you, that bullet was always meant for me. You have a son that needs you, I have..." I turn my head to stare out the window. I've never had a lot of important people in my life. I've always been a loner, always questioning people's motives for wanting to get close so it was easier not to get close.

"Don't you dare say you don't have anyone because the waiting room staff would tell you a different story. I've met so many people who love you that have come to see how you're doing." Her eyes tear up, and she sniffles in between her words. "They told me stories about you and how much you mean to them. And then there's Kase, he would've been destroyed."

I squeeze my eyes shut, the tears falling down the sides of my face from hearing her describe what has been happening.

"Please don't ever think I'm more important than you."

I nod as she holds my hand. Thinking of the people in my life that are important, I surprise myself when the list ends up longer than I had originally thought. I created a family here in Gilley Cove and I was too burdened to notice it. Now that the burden has lifted, I see it.

"And I'm okay if you and Kase get married."

I glance down at my feet and shift in the bed, folding my legs up.

"Ellie." She waits until my eyes meet hers. "I'll be all right. He might have loved me a long time ago, but who doesn't have high school sweethearts they once upon a time loved?"

"This is a little different, Everly."

She takes a deep breath. "Yes. A little. But we can figure it out. You're in my life to stay no matter if you're with Kase or not. You can't take back meeting me."

"What about you? What are you going to do?"

"That's a loaded question. I had my perfect. I just need to see if it's worth finding my way back to it."

"Well, I'm here if you ever want to talk."

"Are you kidding, we'll be talking all the time!"

We both glance to the door when Kase clears his throat. "I don't want to interrupt, but I have chocolate," he smiles, holding up a bag of chocolate covered almonds. *My favorite.*

"Oh, you win. All I brought in here was Reed and he was more interested in the bullet."

———

"What time is it?" I grab Kase's hand and peek down at his watch. My racing heartbeat won't let me sit still. I cross and uncross my leg, fairly certain if I had a skirt on it would've chaffed my inner thighs already from the movement. I glance around the small office, papers askew on the bulletin board and the need to fix them makes me hop up. By the time I'm done, they are straight and lined up. Kase keeps quiet knowing I need something to do while we wait.

The zipping sound of a plane landing outside grabs my attention and I run to the window. "Is that them?" I ask.

"There shouldn't be any other plane landing here," Kase jokes. I narrow my eyes at him and he laughs. "Yes, it's them. Let's go."

I push the door open and rush out, waiting for the plane's engine to turn off. When the plane door lowers, Max is the first one out, followed by the others. I bounce on my tiptoes until I see him. He walks off with aviators on and a scruffy beard, glancing around. When he sees me, a smile spreads across his leathered face.

I jog toward him, still not all the way healed, but Kase would be all up my ass if I full out run. "Dad," I say, wrapping my arms around his neck. I keep it loose knowing he had it rougher than I did since he was shot a few times.

"Hi, sweetheart." His arms tighten around me. "It's so good to see you."

Old Spice fills my nose, a smell I've always found relaxes me. It means he's close. "I'm so glad you're all right."

"Right back at cha'," he says, pulling back, and his eyes move down to my stomach.

"It's healing great. Stop, worrying."

"Never." His eyes shift behind me. "You must be Kase."

Kase steps forward and they shake hands. "Yes, sir. It's great to meet you."

"Call me Dalton. Thanks for sending a private plane. It's better than the commercial planes who cram you in like sardines." His gruff voice makes my heart happy. He's rough around the edges and soft as butter on the inside, but he'd never admit it.

I sit in the back of the Jeep, letting Kase and my dad get acquainted. I knew they'd get along great. It's been a month since Ray shot me and Kase's focus has been razor sharp on one thing, helping me heal. He's pretty much spoiled me to death. The only thing he hasn't done was talk about getting married. Every time I bring it up, he changes the subject saying we have our whole future to plan it, let's focus on healing.

Well, I'm healed.

I figured I'd wait until my dad left to have a serious talk about what we're doing. I haven't worn my ring since I left Texas and Kase hasn't brought it up even though he's made it clear that we're together. Chalking it up to him needing time to deal with his feelings too, I haven't pushed it.

Everly and Reed are coming out next month. She wanted me to heal without distractions and let Kase and I work our stuff out. He told me about the kiss in Texas. It stung to hear, but in the end, I'm glad he did. It helped him realize he wanted me. I talk to Everly almost nightly, but I keep my frustrations about Kase limited to

Tori. I know I won't ever feel comfortable talking about Kase to Everly, but it's a small sacrifice in the grand scheme of things.

Kase carries my dad's bag up the stairs as we take the elevator. "He's a good man," my dad says as we wait for the elevator.

"He's the best. But there's a story, a huge story, behind our relationship." I lean my head on his shoulder, my heart warms, so happy he's here.

"He told me."

I jerk my head up. "He did. And you still think…" I wince, afraid he'll change his mind about him.

"So, it was an unconventional way to meet," he shrugs. "Look at how most the youngsters meet now, online. Talk about being impersonal."

We step into the elevator. "But—"

"No, buts. He's told me how much he loves you and I believe him. He told me about the Lighthouse and the work you've started there. Ell, I'm so proud of you. I really wish I could've been here to see you graduate."

"I know. But thanks to Kase, you can visit anytime you want," I say as we walk down the hallway. Kase is already in the apartment by the time we get there and as soon as I walk in, I freeze. He's down on his knee, holding my ring up. "Kase, what—"

He holds his finger to his lips, stopping me. "I actually never thought I'd have to do this again, but this is the important one. I got approval from your dad this time." I glance at my dad and he's sitting on the chair, watching us, smiling. Kase pulls in a deep breath and I run my hand through his hair. "We're secret-free this time…" He pauses with a lifted brow and I nod. He blows out a quick breath, making me laugh. "Ellie, you were always my destination, even though our starting point was flawed. Your heart is one of a kind and it's mine. I love you with everything I am, and I promise to not make you swim in the ocean."

I cover my burst of laughter with my hand.

"Ellie, will you marry me? For sure this time?"

"Yes," I murmur through my tears. He slips the ring on my finger and the wind tunnel I've been stuck in the last month slows down. Everything suspends in the surrounding air, the quiet moment bringing clarity. My life might be a puzzle, but with Kase by my side, I'll always be able to piece it together.

———

UGH! I groan, staring at Kase walk around the apartment in his board shorts and then plop on the couch. No shirt. Abs on display like a jewelry store case, the one you'd like to have one of everything in. He cannot walk around here half naked. I stomp over and stand right in front of him. He's reading a magazine, so I wait for him to glance up. He lifts his head and flashes a sexy half-smile.

"Ellie?" He cocks his head to the side, probably wondering why I'm irritated.

"So, I know you and your ego barely fit into this room and as much as you think it's so, your dick is not going to kill me."

He belts out a laugh. "I don't want to hurt you."

"You won't. It's been two months and I've been given the green light to do all activities."

"Your doctor doesn't know how big I am," he jokes. I smack my forehead knowing he's being serious despite his playful tone.

"I specifically asked her if I could ride a Cowboy."

His brows pop up. "And what was her response?"

I climb on top of him, straddling his hips.

"'Giddy up, cowgirl.'"

EPILOGUE

ELLIE

A YEAR Later

SERENDIPITOUS.

That's our family, our story unique and puzzling, and explaining it takes longer than I care to, so it's rare I share the story in its entirety. I gaze at the family picture we just took on the camera's screen and the only appropriate response is to laugh. It's been a year and I'm still trying to grasp how we got here.

Everly and I have grown close. She tells me about Kase when he was young, but we don't talk about them as a couple. When we looked at each other as sisters rather than the women Kase loved, the bond forged quickly. Considering she lives close, we spend a lot of time together.

And I wouldn't wish it any other way.

"Would you lay the camera down and come dance with me, woman?" Kase insists, grabbing the camera out of my hands himself.

"I needed to make sure we got a good one."

His brow pops up. "You made us stand there for like ten minutes taking picture after picture. There has to be at least one."

I run my fingers against his rough jaw, humming at the feel of a couple day's growth. He knows how much I love it. "There is. It's perfect."

"It'll be more perfect in a couple of months." His smile touches his eyes, and he lays his large hand across my protruding belly.

Ray took away my chances of having a baby ten years ago, but he also gave it back when he shot me. The doctor didn't realize when he cleaned up old scar tissue that had formed around my fallopian tube close to where the bullet hit me, that he opened it up enough for an egg to squeeze through. We didn't learn this, of course, until I went to the doctor sick as a dog and told I was pregnant. After picking my jaw up off the floor and running to the trashcan to throw up, I cried for our little miracle.

I cover his hand and a little kick bumps against us. She's a fighter already and her daddy is ready to spoil her rotten. He's already started. I glance around the tent, filled with pink and white, twinkling lights, and the high pile of presents. Our friends and family wear smiles, laughing and dancing. Today is our baby shower. Bentley Rose Nixon doesn't know the craziness she's about to be a part of. But it's the only crazy she'll know so it'll be her normal.

At the request of Everly and I, Stone found our birth mom. Her name was Rose, and she was seventeen when she had us. We don't know her story, but we know her ending. She passed away fifteen years ago of a drug overdose. Who knows how she got pregnant, but if not for her, I wouldn't be here today, so I wanted to find a place for her in our family. It was obvious when we found out we were having a girl that was where she belonged. I would honor her by giving my little girl her name.

"Once Little B gets here, I'll have to share you, so I need you to show me a lot of love right now so I don't feel neglected," he says, pulling me to the dance floor, swinging me out and back into his chest. The band sings "In My Daughter's Eyes" by Martina McBride. Their song choices have brought me to tears about ten times. *Make that eleven.* I sniff and pat under my eyes before my tears escape. "Don't cry, beautiful, I'm not that bad of a dancer."

I chuckle as we sway to the music, my belly snug against his. "Cowboy, you're not bad. But you've come a long way from the sprinkler."

He throws his head back in laughter. "Holy shit, I can't believe she told you about that."

"Yeah, I heard about your moves. You might have to show me some."

"Babe, you've seen all my moves." He grinds his hips against me and I wrinkle my nose in amusement when his thigh barely touches the inside of mine. "It's not funny. Little B is already cock-blocking me."

"Dad, what's that mean?"

I peek around Kase, Reed stands there with a shit-eating grin on his face. I can't get over how much he looks like Kase, especially when he smiles like that. Biting my lip, I look at Kase, waiting for his answer. Can't wait to hear him get out of this. Instead of answering, he puts him in a headlock and tickles him.

"What have I told you about eavesdropping?"

Reed squeals as Kase tortures him.

I love seeing them together. Reed decided that he wanted to call him dad. He still calls Wayne dad and sometimes it gets confusing when we're all together, but the guys don't care. Both are happy to be in his life. I think I was the most difficult for him. Did he refer to me as his aunt or his stepmom? He settled on ant-mom, coincidentally after a certain Marvel movie came out.

Ten months ago, Kase bought an acre of oceanfront property and built our house on it. He surprised me last week, taking me to the house. Going there, I thought we were viewing a house to buy, I didn't realize it was ours already. The property and the view are amazing and I can't wait for Bentley to love the ocean as much as her daddy does.

"I'm stealing your wife," my dad says, wrapping one arm around my waist and the other holds my hand in the air. Kase stops tickling Reed long enough to wink and mouth "I love you" and then he pulls him off the floor.

"How you feelin'?" We two step around the floor to a quicker song, one that doesn't have tears running down my face.

"Wonderful. Everyone I love is here, including you."

Kase and I got married the month after we found out I was pregnant. He was adamant there wasn't any reason to wait. I didn't need a big wedding. So, we had the perfect small beach wedding where Tori was my maid-of-honor and Cody was Kase's best man. Max and the team were there alongside our new family. One of the best parts, my dad was there to give me away.

Marrying me and having a son released the remainder of Kase's trust. He wasn't sure if having a son with a different last name counted, but it was a loophole his grandfather didn't plan for. I'm a little bitter that his grandfather made it a requirement for him to have a son, not a daughter, before receiving the rest of his trust. The money wasn't a big deal, I mean Kase already had enough money to last us two lifetimes, but it was the principle. Reed and Bentley, and probably their kids, will be set for life. But I hope they learn from their dad that money doesn't replace hard work, loyalty, and being a good person.

Everly gave Wayne another shot. While I had mixed feelings about it, he loves her, treats her like a queen and she loves him. Kase and Wayne's relationship is strained. They're working on it, but they'll never be best friends again. Everly wanted to be closer to me and Reed closer to Kase, so she made Wayne move a town over from here. I was ecstatic about the move.

I also met Everly's mom who decided I needed a mother figure in my life and she graciously volunteered. Kase thought it was a little awkward at first until I reminded him we lived a town over from his first fiancée, who was my twin. He shut up after that. Things just can't get any more peculiar.

Later that evening, Everly and I sat on the sidelines, watching our worlds collide again. It only took twenty-nine years and one man to bring it all back. The cool spring breeze coming off the ocean fills the tent. It feels fan-freaking-tastic after dancing and being on my feet for hours. So does this white wooden chair. I plop my feet on another one and take a deep breath, reminding myself this isn't a dream. It's my life.

"It's so sweet to watch them," Everly says, eyeing the dance floor. I open my eyes and follow where she's looking. "Who knew that would happen?" I nod in agreement. The grumpy old bastard was never married for a reason. I think he's softened in his old age. We both watch in awe as Everly's mom and my dad dance across the floor, her tight in his arms, both gazing into each other's eyes. They met at my wedding and unbeknownst to us, they continued their little fling back in Texas. They told us a month ago they were moving here, to be close to us. Together.

It's as if we're living the movie, Parent Trap.

"You know, nothing is surprising anymore." I grab her hand, so thankful she's here and part of my life.

I came to Gilley Cove hiding, and alone.

Now it's filled with family and friends.

Not in my wildest dreams could I have imagined this life.

All because I was a blinding echo.

ACKNOWLEDGMENTS

I'll preface this section that this has not been edited. This is me, raw and unedited. And unlike writing a book, I'm allowed to use exclamation points, so I will. I'm crazy excited, so it's warranted.

First and foremost, I want to thank all the readers! I've never met a more loyal group of people. I LOVE Y'ALL! It's because of you that I keep writing. Thank you for hanging with me while it took forever to release this book. And don't worry, I'm working on Twisted Wings. For readers who are new to me, thanks for taking a chance on Blinding Echo. I hope you enjoyed this book as much as I did writing it.

To all the Bloggers who have read, reviewed, and help spread the news about Blinding Echo, THANK YOU! You are an author's *phone a friend* and we couldn't do this without you.

Tiffany, Lori, Traci – you are the solid base to my unsteady author life. Your words and excitement have lifted me up and made me want to keep going. You guys are always there to listen when I need someone and I LOVE you three to death! THANK YOU for being my tribe!

To my husband, who is always there to offer one liners (whether I ask for them or not), I love you! Thank you for letting me follow this crazy dream of mine and being there for me 100% of the time.

My book team who helped package the book, y'all are kickass amazing! Hang, my cover is life. I think I'll keep you forever. You understand where my head is at with just a few words and I love that, because my imagination is larger than my words could ever convey. Ellie, thank you for making my words look like I know what I'm doing. You helped make my story be the best it could be. You and your team are top on my list!

Xoxo,
    Tina

Printed in Great Britain
by Amazon

36541494R00173